VAMPIRES

OF

MANHATTAN

The New Blue Bloods Coven

Melissa de la Cruz

hachette **BOOKS**

NEW YORK   BOSTON

Copyright © 2014 by Melissa de la Cruz
All rights reserved. In accordance with the U.S. Copyright Act of 1976, the scanning, uploading, and electronic sharing of any part of this book without the permission of the publisher constitutes unlawful piracy and theft of the author's intellectual property. If you would like to use material from the book (other than for review purposes), prior written permission must be obtained by contacting the publisher at permissions@hbgusa.com. Thank you for your support of the author's rights.

Hachette Books
Hachette Book Group
1290 Avenue of the Americas
New York, NY 10104

www.HachetteBookGroup.com

Printed in the United States of America

RRD-C

Originally published in hardcover by Hachette Book Group, Inc.
First Hachette Books trade edition: July 2015
10 9 8 7 6 5 4 3 2 1

Hachette Books is a division of Hachette Book Group, Inc.
The Hachette Books name and logo are trademarks of Hachette Book Group, Inc.

The publisher is not responsible for websites (or their content) that are not owned by the publisher.

The Hachette Speakers Bureau provides a wide range of authors for speaking events. To find out more, go to www.hachettespeakersbureau.com or call (866) 376-6591.

Library of Congress Control Number: 2015935912

ISBN 978-0-316-25718-3 (pbk.)

VAMPIRES

~ OF ~

MANHATTAN

For Margie Stohl
A friend in need is a friend indeed—
Thank you, my friend.

VAMPIRES

~ OF ~

MANHATTAN

Hell's Bells

THE PRESENT

SUNDAY TO FRIDAY

. . . Never send to know for whom the bell tolls;
It tolls for thee.

—JOHN DONNE

1 | OMENS

*T*HE ALARM WENT OFF like an air-raid siren at midnight, and the hand that shot out of the bed slammed the snooze button so hard the side table shook. Half an hour later, Araminta Scott jumped out from underneath the blankets, kicking off the covers and cursing loudly. She'd dreamed she was late for work again and she was right—that wasn't the snooze button she'd hit. She scrambled into her clothes, putting on a worn black sweater over her thin black tank top, grabbing a pair of black jeans from the pile on the floor, and pulling them up over her skinny hips. She ran to the sink, splashed water on her face, finger combed her platinum bangs, and smoothed the soft, shorn hair at the back of her neck as she met her dark, baleful eyes in the mirror.

Ara wiped her hands and face on her lone, grungy, gray towel and took a rueful glance at the squalor that was her home—the nest of sheets, half-empty Chinese food containers on the kitchen counter, dust balls that seemed to be growing out of the walls like a cozy gray fungus. She should really clean this place once in a while. Or take a shower. She smelled pretty ripe, but there was nothing she could do about that now. If she was lucky and the L train was running without delays, she might just make it in time without catching heat from the chief, which she really didn't need right now. He wasn't exactly a fan of hers lately. Besides, she liked the way she smelled, like sweat and hard work, after spending the last seventy-two hours sitting on her suspect.

Policy mandated that anyone who didn't read as mortal and wasn't registered with the Coven had to be checked out. These days, that was all it took to rouse suspicion from the brass, who were still twitchy after last month's raid. Things had been relatively peaceful for the last decade since the War had ended, except for a renegade vampire or a demon popping up every now and then. Lately, though, the Nephilim, those half-demon, half-human abominations, had started showing up in the city again in greater numbers, and just a few weeks ago the Venators had found their hive and destroyed it.

Ara had followed her guy for three days straight as he wandered around the city. So far he hadn't done anything more malicious than fail to tip the barista at a trendy coffee shop, but she'd noted his visits to a few interesting locations, secret places that were known only to their kind: the burned-out building that used to house the Repository of History; the church of St. John the Divine, where a significant battle had taken place; the old Van Alen place on Riverside Drive, the childhood home of the girl who had saved all their skins and had slain the Coven's nemesis, father of the Nephilim, Lucifer, the Morningstar, the Fallen Prince of Heaven. Schuyler Van Alen had thrust the archangel Michael's sword straight through his black heart. Rest in peace, motherfucker.

But Ara lost the trail somewhere on the Upper West Side, so she'd called it a day and slept for fourteen hours straight. Not that it was any excuse for being late. Chief was a hard-ass about stuff like that. He was old-school and liked to remind the new recruits that he'd been battling dark angels in Hell when they were just getting their fangs.

She burst out of her apartment, boots clomping down the stairs, then abruptly turned around and ran right back up again. She must really be out of it to have forgotten these, she thought, as she stuffed her weapons—two crescent blades as beautiful as they were deadly—into their sheaths in her back pockets and checked to make sure her gun (outfitted with silver bullets they called demon-killers for that very reason) was secure in its holster.

It was a moonless night in September, chilly, and the sidewalks were teeming with young people congregating in front of restaurants and bars even on a Sunday night: girls with glasses that were too big for their faces wearing awkward-length skirts and ugly shoes, texting furiously on their smartphones as they headed to the next watering hole; boys in suspenders wheeling old-fashioned six-speeds home, twee bow ties around their necks, who looked like they spent their days editing copy with red pencils instead of on screens until their faces were as pale and bluish as the light from their computers.

This had been quite the ghetto neighborhood once, but the tornado of gentrification that swept through broad swaths of the city during the last decade shook up Williamsburg until it was almost unrecognizable. The dirty urban landscape of bleak tenements that had once been home to junkies and starving artists was now filthy with money, was hipster central, counting bankable artists, boutique owners, artisanal chefs, and earnest young bearded men who made small-batch chocolate among its residents. She entered one of the last remnants of the former neighborhood, her favorite bodega, a shabby storefront where candy bars were kept behind bulletproof glass, and nodded to Bahir, who had her cup of coffee at the ready.

At least some things never changed.

Ara walked toward the Bedford Avenue station sipping her coffee and occasionally blowing on it through the lid to cool it down. The subway platform was filled with Manhattanites heading home, the new bridge-and-tunnel crowd, she mused, remembering that old insult, when Upper East Siders like her used to sneer at the outerborough weekend crowd. In her old moneyed life, she never even took the subway—maybe once in a while, just for kicks, to slum it with her fellow Merryvale girls. But that was as far as she went underground. She never even touched the subway turnstile with her hands if she could help it; she would push it with her hip.

For the first thirteen years of her life Ara had lived on Eighty-Third and Park Avenue and had worn the same thing every day: a white button-down shirt, a green plaid skirt, and a blue blazer with the gold school crest. She was a Blue Blood in every sense of the word; her family used to summer in the Hamptons and Bermuda and winter in Palm Beach. She'd had long glossy hair that fell past her shoulders, and her friends were rich and popular. Ten years later, the silly, spoiled girl she had been back then, back when she was still called "Minty," was a distant memory. But some things remained the same—she still wore a uniform, she thought, looking down at her all-black outfit. Preferred it even since it was one less thing she had to worry about. Besides, black blended in with the shadows. Fading into black was the opposite of drawing attention, and attention was the one thing Ara couldn't afford. Not in her particular line of work.

How far Minty had come since Merryvale. Good riddance. Ara missed nothing about her own life, not really. Well, maybe the manicures, she thought, examining her nails.

The train clacked into the station and screeched to a halt. She pushed in with the rest of the revelers calling it a night, finding a place to stand without having to touch anyone else too closely. It was amazing how polite New Yorkers were, how they allowed each other a certain degree of personal space even when shoved up next to someone's armpit. No one made eye contact. It was only the perverts and the weirdos who stared directly at you; everyone else kept their eyes trained above at the Dr. Zit posters or below at the grimy floor.

Ara leaned against the doors and savored her coffee, zoning out with the rest of the passengers. She got off at Fourteenth Street and caught the N downtown. It was almost one in the morning and the subway car was empty now, rattling passengers like bones in a cage. Not a lot of people headed to the financial district in the wee hours. Ara wasn't worried and for good reason. She was probably the most dangerous thing in there.

Her destination was the newly christened Orpheus Tower, the headquarters of the new Coven. Once upon a time the building had housed one of the most powerful investment banks in the world, but the bank had crumbled in one day, disappearing with most of the world's wealth. The Coven had snatched the building up for a song. As Ara walked through the glass-and-chrome lobby, she never failed to marvel at just how much things had changed. Vampires no longer hid in their corescrapers, buildings that tunneled deep into the ground, as the *new* Regent—and he was still relatively new at ten years in, given their former leader had led the vampires for centuries—decided they had as much right to the sky as the rest of the world. She pressed the button for the top floor—SECURITY— and pricked her finger on the blood key. The elevator whisked her up and opened to a bank of surveillance screens surrounding a massive desk in front of an imposing steel door.

"Chief wants you," the night clerk told her with raised eyebrows. Ara sighed as the clerk buzzed her through.

Since she was already in trouble, she decided to pick up her files first. That suspect she was trailing had an unrecognizable aura; he was definitely immortal, but he wasn't one of them. Chief might be interested to know the list of vampire hot spots he'd visited.

Her office was one of the corner ones with a floor-to-ceiling window and a panoramic view of the Brooklyn Bridge and the bright lights of the city. But as far as Ara was concerned the most impressive thing about it was the plaque on her door. The one that read:

ARAMINTA SCOTT
VERITAS VENATOR

It never failed to give her chills. Most nights she couldn't believe she actually made it through training and was now part of this elite squad, the most prestigious and exclusive police force in the world. She was a card-carrying badass. A truth seeker. A hunter. A killer. _Veritas Venator._ Venators had the ability to read and destroy minds, enter and manipulate dreams. They brought death and destruction in the name of truth and justice.

The old Minty would have been terrified of what she had become, whereas the new Ara couldn't have been prouder.

"Where've you been? Chief's looking for you," Ben Denham said slyly as he walked by her office. Denham was a new recruit, a new Venator—a _noov,_ still in his first year of training and overly excited about everything. Baby cops were the worst.

"Tell me something I don't know," she said crossly as she looked through the stack of case files on her desk. Her office was as disorderly as her apartment, and every folder and piece of paper was stained with coffee rings.

"Hear what the day shift found?" Ben asked eagerly.

"You gonna tell me or do I have to guess?" she snapped, annoyed she couldn't find her file. She swore she'd just left it on top of her desk before she left yesterday.

"Another pentagram," said Ben.

"Yeah? Where?"

"Sewers below Canal, and bloody this time."

"Bloody?" she asked, looking up at him.

"Juicy," he said, nodding.

"Like mortal blood, you mean?"

"Yeah." He grinned, flashing his fangs. "Tasty."

Pentagrams were popping up all over the city lately. Chalk-drawn ones against brick walls in Soho, neon spray-painted ones on billboards in Chelsea, tiny little ones scratched on the glass windows of taxicabs. A bloody pentagram? Mortal blood? In the sewers below Canal? What was that all about? Was he serious or just pulling her leg?

"Really?" she asked, looking directly at him. "This isn't just some noov bullshit you've gotten all scrambled in your soft little head?"

"Might've caught a body, too. They don't know yet. Chief wants you."

She nodded, her heart starting to pound in her chest. There hadn't been all that much action around here until she and her former partner had busted the Nephs—and Ara still felt a flush of pride when she remembered that night, when she'd empathically proven she was worthy of her badge and title. Orders from on high were to meet each threat, however small or trivial, with vigorous force and finality, and that was exactly what she did. No trial, no courtrooms—justice was meted out by the Venators' blades, by bullets from their fancy new guns. The Regent of the Coven didn't mess around.

Ara gave up looking for the file and walked down the hall and straight into the chief's office without knocking, a habit she'd been trying to break. But she'd stormed in before she remembered she wasn't all that welcome in there anymore. Sam Lennox looked pointedly toward his watch.

"What about the fifteen-minute grace period?" she protested.

"What happened, you hit the wrong button?" he asked. Chief knew her too well, and she tried not to blush.

"Sorry, Chief—they said you, uh, wanted me," she blurted, then bit her tongue.

"I did," he said. "I mean, I do," he quickly added, which made the awkwardness between them even more palpable. Sam had the world-weary air of a longtime security enforcer, a melancholy sadness underneath his gruff demeanor. He was stocky, and his hair had streaks of gray.

Her blush deepened and she looked away. The chief hadn't been too happy with the way she'd figured out where the nest was hidden. She'd taken a Death Walk and invaded a captured demon's mind, entering its psychotic subconscious, risking her own immortal life and sanity in the process. She still shuddered when she thought about the things she'd seen there, when she remembered what it felt like being immersed in that much darkness and evil, but it was worth it. She got what she needed. When the chief found out, though, he was furious. "Death Walks are too dangerous," he'd yelled. The dangers of jobs like theirs weren't limited to death by stray silver bullets, and that little trick of hers could have gotten her killed. But what was the point of being a Venator if you couldn't stretch your muscles? Use your powers? Besides, he'd trained her well, and the Neph hadn't gotten the better of her. No Neph would ever get the better of her. "So what's up?" she asked. "This about the pentagram?"

"What penta—Damn noovs talk too much. Yeah, but you can deal with that later. Called you in 'cause we got you a new partner," he said. "Starts today."

Ara frowned. She still missed her old partner, Rowena Bailey, who had recently moved up in the food chain. Ara had been offered an opportunity to move up as well but preferred to remain right where she was. She didn't want to shuffle papers and fall asleep at conclave meetings. She wanted to be in the center of the action. She liked the street. She liked the energy and the adrenaline. She also liked not having to look bullshit in the face every day and act as if she didn't see it.

"Yeah, who's the lucky asshole?" Ara couldn't get the edge out of her voice, not that she was trying that hard.

Sam motioned toward the doorway in his office. It was cracked open to the adjoining room.

Ara jerked her head and blanched. "No way."

The guy slouched against the wall was her suspect. The one she'd been trailing for three days.

"You've got to be kidding me," she said and noticed the file she was looking for was right on the chief's desk.

"What can I say? If you had taken the time to report your findings to your superior officers like you were supposed to, you wouldn't have wasted your time or mine," he scolded.

"What do you mean? I was too busy doing my job. He's

unregistered. He's immortal. He's lucky I didn't shoot him on sight. He has a *demon's* aura."

"Yeah, but that can't be helped considering where he's from," chief agreed. "Come on, it's time you met him."

Ara frowned as she followed the chief into the conference room.

"Ara Scott, meet Edon Marrok."

Edon Marrok?

Had she heard that right?

How could she not have known?

She supposed it was because the scruffy, dirty guy in the faded flannel shirt and beaten army jacket who was standing in front of her wasn't quite what she pictured when she thought of Edon Marrok, the legendary golden wolf, one of the heroes from the final battle. The wolves were skinchangers, keepers of the Passages of Time, creatures of the underworld, and bred in Hell, which accounted for his shady aura. They were also beautiful and powerful, and without their help the vampires would have lost the War to Lucifer and his legions.

Edon sure wouldn't win any beauty contests right now. His hair was dry and brittle, and his eyes were red and bloodshot. His beauty was all but destroyed, a ghostly memory in the lines of his haggard face. No longer the golden wolf of legend but a dirty yellow mongrel. He looked like he crawled out of the alleys of Nevada, not Las Vegas, but its outskirts—Henderson, those little desert towns. Nowhere towns. Although she couldn't help but admit there was still something magnetic and compelling about him, from the sexy stubble on his jaw to his hungry, hooded topaz-colored eyes.

She looked away, trying not to stare. Trying not to let on that she was impressed, that she cared anything at all about what he'd done or where he'd come from.

Still.

The wolves had taken up their historical positions as guardians of Time, so what was Edon doing in New York? Plus, the wolves had an uneasy alliance with the Fallen; they were no fans of the vampires.

She glanced back at him, just in time to catch him shooting her a yellow grin, and for a moment it looked as if his incisors were as sharp as points.

She inhaled sharply.

"Hey, angel," he growled, rolling his vowels like he had all the time in the world. "Looks like you've drawn the short straw."

"Chief? A word?" she asked.

Sam nodded. "Help yourself," he told Edon, motioning to the pink box of doughnuts on the table.

Ara followed the chief back into his office and shut the door. "What the hell?"

Sam shrugged his shoulders. "He's been helping out Venator squads all over the world, specializing in Nephilim activity. Thought you'd be best for him since you've been following him around anyway." He grinned, clearly enjoying himself.

"So why'd he spend three days sniffing around taking the vampire history tour, then?" she asked, annoyed.

"Ask him. Nostalgia? Curiosity? I fought next to him in the War. He's a good guy. I trust him. You'll learn to." Sam attempted a real smile this time. "C'mon, Scott, be a team player for once."

"Fine," she said, gritting her teeth.

Ara stomped back into the room where Edon was finishing his breakfast. "Let's go, wolf, but if you call me angel again, I'll strap a collar around your neck so fast you won't have time to beg for a dog biscuit," she said.

"Woof, angel. What'd I ever do to you?" he asked, feigning hurt.

She considered punching him in the face but stopped short.

He stood up, wiping crumbs from his mouth with a napkin. "Come on, Scott, let's start over," he said and offered his hand to shake.

She took it warily. She could already tell he was going to be just another pain in the ass.

As the chief liked to say, *New Coven, same old shit.* She was a Venator and there was work to be done. Nephilim were back in New York, and now there was a bloody pentagram in the sewers below Canal Street.

Ara felt invigorated, her heart pumping, her fingers itching, ready for whatever monster their investigation would turn up. She would hunt them. She would find them. And, if necessary, she would kill them, even if she had to walk that dog along with her to do it. She would uncover the secrets of the darkness and bring the truth to light.

2 | KING OF NEW YORK

*O*NE HUNDRED LAPS and he wasn't even tired. Oliver Hazard-Perry pushed off the shallow end one more time and took a deep breath, one that took him across the seventy-foot-long Olympic-sized pool without having to take another. He burst up at the other side and sent a spray of water splashing against the glass windows. Pulling himself out in one smooth motion, he grabbed one of the extra-long Turkish cotton towels that were rolled and stacked pyramid-style on a nearby bench. He dried off and wrapped the soft cloth around his waist, shaking water from his hair. The pool water was warm and salty on his tongue, but easy on his eyes—no harsh chemicals here, only pure, filtered saline. Better than the ocean, an *improvement* on the ocean, its designer might argue.

The water wasn't the only thing easy on the eyes.

Oliver walked over to the windows, which boasted a rarefied view of Central Park and the city skyline. From where he stood the rambling park looked like a delicate bonsai arrangement, a lush green square bordered by a vase made of skyscrapers, while the Empire State Building loomed in the background, a grand and stately dowager. It was a view only available to the residents of what the tabloids dubbed the "Power Tower": 13 Central Park West. Home to the richest and most connected people in the world, where lavish apartments sold on the market in the high eight-figure range, although the latest sale to a Russian oligarch was rumored to cross into the nine-figure threshold to the tune of a cool one hundred million. The building was also home to the Regent of the Coven, the head of the vampire community, one Oliver Hazard-Perry. *Nice guys finish first*, Oliver thought, savoring the view. People who said that thirteen was an unlucky number had no idea what they were talking about, either. As far as Oliver was concerned, this tower proved thirteen was the luckiest number in the lot.

It was a little after dawn on Monday morning, and he had the fitness center, a veritable fitness mecca—with its gleaming and brand-new exercise equipment (the latest in stationary cycles, treadmills, and elliptical machines), hot yoga and pilates studios—all to himself. The bankers had already left, getting their workouts in before catching the London markets; trophy wives and trainers wouldn't fill in till after ten, rock stars appearing around noon. So for now he savored the quiet stillness. Oliver walked away from the windows and caught a glimpse of his reflection in the mirror. He'd been a skinny human teenager, but he was almost thirty years old now, and to put it bluntly, he was *ripped*. He used to slouch, but now he stood tall and proud. His chestnut-brown hair was cut short to the scalp in a Caesar cut, and his warm hazel eyes had taken on a steely glint. The immortal blood running through his veins took his senses to a whole new level—he still couldn't believe how much he could see, how much he could hear: The flutter of a hummingbird's wings looked slow to him, he could hear whispered conversations down hallways through locked doors as if he were in the same room. It was overwhelming sometimes.

Sometimes, Oliver also wondered how much he had lost when he gained his immortality. His sense of humor, for one; he hadn't laughed in a long time. He never used to take anything seriously—money and position least of all. But now he was Regent of the Coven, and he had no time for childish games, and there was little trace of the sarcastic teenager he had been. He missed that kid sometimes, mourned him even. He had grown up to be someone else, someone he never quite expected to be.

But this morning, all he could think was how much he loved his new life. He padded out of the room and took a private elevator up to his penthouse. The doors opened right into the grand foyer, where his valet stood waiting, holding up a pristine white bathrobe. Peakes was so thoughtful, with a sixth sense of what his master would require. A skill that had been honed over many years of impeccable service. "Thank you," Oliver said, as the old gentleman helped him into the lush robe.

"Would you care for anything else, sir?"

Oliver shook his head and dismissed his man. He cinched the belt and, as was his daily ritual, took a minute to appreciate the sculptures and paintings, true masterpieces, that hung on the walls in his living room and lined the staircase. Old masters next to impressionists, midcentury modernists Diebenkorn, Rothko, and Warhol alongside contemporary powerhouses Koons and Hirst. *Old masters for a new master*, he thought, with some satisfaction.

He had assumed he was inured to the trappings of wealth, that there was very little that could impress him. After all, he had grown up across town, when the Upper East Side was the priciest neighborhood in the city. But the breadth and depth of the wealth at his command was staggering. While detractors would argue that Oliver had assumed the position of Regent through luck, it was all hard work on his part. There were few survivors of the War, and even fewer who did not take the Almighty's offer of salvation to ascend to Paradise. When Oliver took over as Regent he had assumed that after the near destruction of the Coven, the coffers would be bankrupt, or close to it, as the vampires had scattered or left. He assumed he would have to rebuild from scratch. How wrong he was.

The Coven funds were liquid, healthy, and almost embarrassingly robust. The finance committee had made some very sound investments in the technological sector before the end, hence the ability to purchase this apartment—not just this apartment, but the building downtown that housed their headquarters—as well as fund Venator squads across the globe. So many problems could be solved with money, Oliver mused. So many things money could buy. Peace. Safety. Stability.

Most of the art he was looking at now was actually from the Coven's private collection, from the hidden Repository archives, where it had been stored for safekeeping for decades and most likely forgotten. Oliver had unearthed these gems and had them restored, and now they were proudly displayed in museums and galleries around the world. He'd had the decency to keep only *some* of the best ones for his own enjoyment. It was hard to let go of Vermeer's *The Concert*, and he had no idea how it came to be in the Coven's possession, but the Isabella Stewart Gardner Museum was so grateful to have it back, he knew he'd done the right thing.

He had brought the Coven ten years of peace and prosperity, and now it was time to party. Time to bring back a grand old tradition that he had coveted as a human Conduit with his nose pressed against the glass. The Four Hundred Ball, the annual celebration that feted the vampire community and all its glory. Known as the Patrician Ball during the nineteenth century and once held in Caroline Astor's ballroom, it was traditionally a vampire-only event, and Oliver intended that its return after a long hiatus would mark the reestablishment of the community, to commemorate their victory over darkness, to show the world and themselves that they had not only survived, but were thriving in its aftermath.

That they had something left to celebrate at all.

There had not been a Four Hundred Ball since before the War, and the tenth anniversary of their victory over Lucifer felt like the right time to bring back the party as well as finally perform the ritual for his investiture. The leader of the Coven was traditionally called the Regis, the king of the vampires; his word was law, his every action infallible. But when Oliver had taken office, he had taken the lower title of Regent—he was not yet a king, but a mere steward. That would change on the night of the ball, when the heart of the Coven would be bound to his immortal blood. *L'état, c'est moi.*

By the end of the week, Oliver would have everything he had worked so hard for. Yes, everything he touched, everything he owned, everything in his orbit was rare, beautiful, and expensive, but none more so than the treasure in his own bedroom, the most exquisite jewel in his kingdom. Oliver felt his fangs sharpen in anticipation at the thought. He walked up the circular stairs that led to his chamber and opened its massive steel doors, the same ones as were installed in the Venator offices—one could never be too careful, after all. The curtains and blackout shades were drawn, and the dark room was as cool as a tomb, a proper vampire lair. As a boy he'd liked to feel the sun on his face to tickle him awake, but not anymore. He'd discovered far better ways to be awakened now. There she was, lying in the middle of his custom-made California king-sized bed, buried underneath the covers, the long, tangled locks of her sunflower-blonde hair the brightest thing in the room. Seraphina Chase.

Finn.

His human familiar.

His mortal beloved.

Oliver shrugged off his robe and trunks and slid into bed under the blankets, wrapping his arms around her waist and nuzzling her neck.

"Mmm," Finn murmured, her voice still heavy with sleep, her face turned to the pillow. "You're dripping on me."

His hair was still wet from the pool, and tendrils were brushing against her soft skin. A decade since they'd first met and he was still in awe of her beauty, of the shining pure goodness that was her soul.

"No, I'm not. You're still dreaming."

He moved on top of her and she moved with him. "Mmm," she murmured. "Nice dream." She began to turn her body toward him, but he stopped her. "Stay like this," he said, as he put his hands on her arms and pinned them to her side.

"Kinky," she murmured.

"Not my fault you have kinky dreams," Oliver said as he pulled the sheets and they fell away from her body.

"Don't be so sure," she purred. She was wearing the tiniest slip, a swathe of silk from Paris that cost more than most people's entire wardrobes, and he impatiently tugged it down, undressing her so that they were skin to skin. This was his favorite way to start his day, when she was half-asleep, when she pretended not to know what was going on, even though she was so ready for him.

She arched her back as if she knew what was coming.

Because she did.

He couldn't wait any longer, and as he pushed her hands deeper into the bed, he rammed into her body and plunged his fangs into her neck at the same time, all his senses alive and tingling with pleasure as he performed the Sacred Kiss, rocking against her as he drank deeply of her blood. He knew everything about her—every memory, every emotion, every desire, every disappointment. It came out in the blood bond, when he drank her very essence. What he felt for her was beyond love, beyond feeling—they were one soul in two bodies. He was hers and she was his. They had no secrets between them.

She sighed, trembled, groaned, and when he was done he fell away from her in satisfaction. The sheets that wound between them

were red with blood, like a crime scene. Thank goodness for dili-
gent housekeepers who never asked questions. Thank goodness for
so many things, he thought, closing his eyes.

"Brown sugar on your oatmeal?" Finn asked an hour later, when
they were properly dressed and eating breakfast in the wraparound
terrace overlooking the park.

Oliver could still imagine her naked body beneath the silk and
linen, and he wondered if she was thinking the same of him. "Yes,
thanks," he said, marveling once again at her classic, restrained
beauty, from her long, slim neck to her elegant hands. She wore her
hair long and loose, and the two bite marks near her delicate collarbone were barely noticeable, with little scarring. He loved those
little bite marks and what they symbolized, that she was his, his
very own human familiar. He had been a vampire's familiar once,
too, when he had been mortal, and he knew the pull of the blood
bond—the all-consuming hunger for one's vampire mate, the intox-
icating agony and delirium.

Sometimes he wasn't sure it had been the right thing to do to
Finn, but it was too late now. He marveled over the twist of fate
that brought them together. He had been helping his best friend,
Schuyler Van Alen or Sky—he called her Sky; he was the only one
who called her that—unravel the mystery of her mortal father's
family, which led the two of them to Finn, Sky's half sister. He still
remembered how radiant Finn had looked when they met, a carefree college student with no idea about her link to the Coven. How
cheerful, happy, and innocent she had been. She had wanted to be
an artist like her father. She had different dreams for her life, but
she had fallen in love with him, and he had convinced her to help
him rebuild the Coven, to work for the vampires, to *serve* him, to
realize his dreams and give up hers. She had been willing and eager
back then, had wanted him as much as he wanted her. But still, he
felt a twinge of guilt, mixed with the pride, every time he saw those
tiny scars.

He knew the doubts she harbored, her secret fears, and he did as
much as he could to assuage them, especially as she had been quiet
and withdrawn lately. She was probably worried about the party.
As the unofficial First Lady of the Coven, the logistics of the Four
Hundred Ball were her responsibility, and for months now Finn

had been stressing over every invitation, every menu item, every last detail. He wanted to tell her not to worry—the party would be the most wonderful night of their lives. He understood the pressure she felt was intense. Finn held the highest position in the Coven that a mortal had ever achieved—which some members still found unsettling. Historically, human Conduits were seen as little more than servants, worker bees who devoted their lives to the care of their vampires, and human familiars who gave their blood had no voice or influence in the Coven. Finn was both Conduit and familiar, but as Oliver kept telling the ruling conclave, times had changed, and the vampires would have to change along with them.

"So, you got in really late last night?" Oliver asked, filling his bowl with oatmeal from the silver tureen in the middle of the table.

Finn frowned. "I know...I know. I was dealing with some party stuff."

"Till midnight?" he asked. "You're working too hard."

"Oh...well, when I got home I went for a walk. I couldn't sleep," she said, coloring a little. "Don't worry. I didn't go far, just around the block."

He nodded. He knew how stressed she was over the party; he hated to see her so anxious, though. He made a mental note to see about getting his assistant to help her more as he sprinkled his oatmeal with a spoonful of brown sugar and took a bite. He chewed, grimaced, and put his spoon down.

"Not hungry?" Finn asked, raising an eyebrow.

"No." He shook his head.

"Wonder why," she teased. "You're probably full *of me*."

"Ha," he said, pushing the bowl away with a smile. His oatmeal tasted like sand, gravelly and gritty, with very little trace of the sugar he had just heaped on it. While his senses had become heightened, his ability to enjoy food had waned lately. He wondered if it meant there had been something wrong with his transition, as he remembered his vampire friends eating and drinking like mortals, except they never gained weight and they never got drunk. Maybe he'd ask one of the Repository clerks about this phenomenon, though he hated giving anyone a reminder that he wasn't like them. He wasn't born a Blue Blood; he was the only living mortal on earth who had been made into one, gifted with immortality by the Almighty at the end of the final battle.

He was, as he had always been, the exception. And now he was going to be Regis. As if they didn't already have reason enough to resent him.

"Sir?"

Oliver turned to see Peakes holding his cell phone on a silver tray.

"Pardon for interrupting, but you have a call from the Venator chief; he said it was important and insisted I get you on the telephone as soon as possible."

"Perry here," he said after taking it with a nod. He listened for a few minutes and frowned. "When? Why didn't you call me as soon as the day shift checked in? Okay. Next time, keep me updated as soon as you know. Right. Let me know what else they find," he said sharply.

He slipped the phone into his jacket pocket.

"What's wrong?" Finn asked, concerned. "Those pentagrams again?"

Oliver nodded. Damn pentagrams. What did it mean? He was still wishing it would prove to be nothing—that it was the work of a random graffiti artist or some Bansky prank. Of course this disturbance would appear now, with plans for the Four Hundred Ball well under way.

The chief had just told him the latest pentagram was made from human blood. Which meant there was a victim, a body. There had been no bloodshed since the War; the only victims were their enemies, like those damn Nephilim the team recently busted. This latest development didn't bode well.

Oliver sighed. Nephilim attacks, pentagrams, and now human blood on the eve of the biggest moment of his life. He couldn't shake a sudden sense of foreboding. Oliver believed in omens. And this wasn't, couldn't be good.

3 | HAPPILY NEVER AFTER

*T*HE MYTH OF PERSEPHONE was such bullshit. The goddess's daughter gets kidnapped by the lord of the underworld and has to live six months on earth and six months in Hell, and the whiny little bitch acted as if it was a punishment.

At least Persephone got six months on earth every year.

Mimi Martin took a sip from her glass of white wine and rolled it on her tongue, savoring every drop. The buttery richness of the white Burgundy did a lot to liven her mood, just as it always did, but somehow today even that wasn't enough. "Happy anniversary to me," she said to the empty seat across from her. She was having lunch by herself that Monday, had stolen away from work with the intention of indulging in a long and luxurious meal to forget about the train wreck that was her marriage.

So why did she just feel irritated and alone?

It was ten years since the final battle and Lucifer's defeat. Seven years since their wedding, and her husband was nowhere to be found. Kingsley had chosen to remain in the underworld while Mimi was up here, back in New York, alone. It was only supposed to be a trial separation; Kingsley had even joked that it was their "Persephone clause." But she had been away for only a month, and it was already hard to imagine going back anytime soon. Not even if she missed him so much she cried herself to sleep most nights, hoping he would change his mind, forsake the underworld, and decide to join her.

Damn him. Damn him to Hell, she thought, aware of the irony.

The waiter brought her a bread basket and she tore into the baguette ravenously, slathering butter over a piece of the airy, crusty bread before taking a huge bite. She missed her husband so much she couldn't forgive herself for what she was doing—what she had *done*. She had *left* him. She had actually left Kingsley Martin. The love of her life, her soul mate, her husband, the man for whom she had sacrificed so much. Mimi had been certain that if anything, it would be Kingsley who would prove to be unfaithful, that he would be the one to leave, to go back to his wild ways, bored by the monotony of monogamy, and that she would be the one left bereft, heartbroken, and alone.

Instead it was she who had said adios. She who had told him she just couldn't take it anymore. Not another day in the underworld. It wasn't him. She loved him, she still loved him, deeply, desperately, but she couldn't do it anymore. She couldn't live *there*. Mimi twirled the silver ring on the fourth finger of her left hand, remembering the day Kingsley had put it on. She had been such a happy bride; she had never been happier in her entire life. And for a while, they had been happy, ecstatic, even though they lived in Hell. They were so hot for each other, to make an awful pun. She had promised him forever, had promised him the rest of her immortal life. But how was she to know forever meant...*forever*? That it meant never eating a great meal in New York again, never shopping on Madison Avenue, never visiting the Met, never seeing the leaves change, never having a glass of champagne ever again.

Of course she shouldn't have been surprised that he had chosen his lofty position over their marriage. Kingsley Martin, the Angel Araquiel, was lord of the underworld, Duke of Hell, and every creature and soul behind its gates was a subject in his unearthly kingdom. One thing about Kingsley, he took his responsibilities seriously. She knew that, and yet she had still demanded that he choose her over everything.

Mimi sighed and startled at a sudden sound. There it was again— a faint ringing in her ears. An annoying noise that came and went, a high-pitched trilling; it could turn anyone mad. She shook her head impatiently, trying to make it go away.

"Have you decided, madam?" the waiter asked, returning with his notepad and holding the pencil expectantly.

Madam?

Was he talking to her? She could barely hear him over that horrid ringing in her ears, but yes, he had called her madam. The nerve!

Okay, so she was no longer the slim-hipped, dewy-skinned sixteen-year-old who rampaged through New York's best nightclubs. She was an old, married—even worse, *separated*—lady now. But she was still beautiful, wasn't she? The long, thick blond mane was as lustrous as ever, the catlike green eyes just as smoldering, and come on, she could still fit into her superskinny jeans! And this dress she was wearing was practically skintight. But it was so unfair to discover since she had left the underworld that she had actually *aged*. Although in her defense, living in the underworld was, um, *hell* on the skin.

Mimi decided to forgive the waiter. She liked this place, a darling little French bistro in the far West Village. On weekdays during lunch hours it was filled with models, artists, and the occasional celebrity. It was a cosmopolitan, attractive crowd: tall, eye-catching women in swathes of colorful scarves and battered leather jackets, bearded men in horn-rims reading *Le Figaro*, groups of young editors and photographers huddling over iPads, discussing their latest shoots. She frequently ordered the same thing. Oysters on the half shell, the chicken paillard, and a glass of white wine. She liked that the waiters wore proper neckties and aprons just like in Paris, and took down your order instead of memorizing it, an irritating gimmick she was sure originated with bored actor slash servers in Los Angeles.

"Yes, I will start with the onion soup and the *assiette de saumon fumé*, then the steak frites with béarnaise and a side of the *légumes verts.*"

"Very good," he said, expertly whisking away the menu.

She sipped her wine and looked around. This was what she had missed all those years living in the underworld—*life, color, vibrancy*— the sound of conversation all around her, tinkling glassware, the scraping of chairs across the floor, the sun shining brightly through the glass windows, so unlike that strange netherworld where the sun never rose or set and the sky was orange from the glow of hell-fire. Kingsley had had this idea that he was going to remake the underworld anew, bring life to the barren lands. When the War ended, after the demons had been locked back in their cages, he had grown more interested in fertilizer than fighting. For years she had worked by his side, tending their small green patch until it had grown so large that flowers bloomed in Helheim once more. She remembered Kingsley kneeling in the garden, humming happily to himself as he weeded.

For a while she had been content—that dreadful word—because she had everything she wanted. She had *him*, after all. They were supposed to live happily ever after. So why did she fuck it up?

Because she missed home, she missed New York so much it was like a toothache that never went away, a real physical pain that throbbed, much like the ringing in her ears. *What was that?* There it went again, that annoying noise. She tried to ignore it. In any event, she couldn't spend the rest of her immortality *gardening*. She wasn't cut out for it, no matter how much she tried to change, tried to muster enthusiasm for her husband's small successes. When she met Kingsley he was sex on legs; he was the head of the Venators, a cocky, mouthy, devilishly handsome alpha, whose life was as big as his heart and as busy as his outsize personality. Now he was a stodgy farmer. She hated to admit it, but she missed the guy he had been. She just wasn't cut out for life in the suburbs. When she was growing up in Manhattan she used to joke she'd rather move to Hell than Brooklyn, even though the outer boroughs were so chic now.

The waiter presented her with a crock of French onion soup, the Gruyère cheese crusted to a golden brown and oozing over the sides. Mimi dug in eagerly, letting the gloppy richness of the cheese and the perfectly cooked, slippery onions ease the pain of being alone at thirty. They called it comfort food for a reason.

She'd been so bored in Hell she would have killed herself if only she could. Her last few days at home had been tense; they had argued a lot, with Kingsley accusing her of being overdramatic, selfish, and spoiled as usual, while she had called him complacent, stubborn, and docile. She never thought it would happen to them—the long good-bye, the drifting apart, the slow fade that ended so many marriages, so many unions. She had thought they were special, and it was a bitter disappointment to discover they were just like everybody else. Struggling to make it work. It was so ordinary—and Mimi had never been ordinary (ever) in her entire life—that it made her want to scream. And so she had. Screamed at him until he finally surrendered and agreed to the "trial separation."

Of course, she had expected him to leave with her. That was the thing, the unspoken argument between them—she couldn't believe that after everything they had been through together, he had just let her go. She had made him choose. Hell or me. And he had chosen wrong. Had let her walk out of his life, just like that. He didn't even beg her to stay. He had just watched her walk away from him, and so she hadn't looked back, not even to wave good-bye.

Mimi had returned to the city with little fanfare. She avoided her old friends, especially Oliver, as she didn't want to explain why she had left Kingsley and didn't want to answer any uncomfortable questions or see the pity in their eyes. Manhattan was a small island, and the Coven an even smaller community, but so far she had escaped notice. One of the things she'd learned as a former Venator, after all, was how to disappear. She promptly settled into an apartment in one of the fabulous new buildings by the water in west Chelsea— once upon a time her father had been the richest man in the city, and she herself had briefly been Regent of the Coven—so though she was so happy to be back in New York City she could live in a box, a six-bedroom penthouse overlooking the Hudson River was so much better. She found work in a small art gallery because she needed something to do, and it turned out answering phones and making jokes with the artists and buttering up the clients was something she was good at.

It was a nice enough life, although one she never thought would be hers. She had no idea what she had thought her future would bring exactly, but certainly living this bohemian life downtown was not what she had in mind when she was the reigning queen of the Upper East Side. For one thing, she never thought she would hold a job. She was going to be one of those people who ran the world from behind the shadows. Instead she was a simple clerk, someone who did as instructed and worked to make things comfortable for other people.

The rest of her meal arrived, and she cleared her plates quickly but lingered over coffee. She was still feeling melancholy and unsure of what happened now, where her life would go from here. She had no desire to date, but she didn't want to be alone, either. She was still married, even though her husband was nowhere to be found.

Truth was, she didn't want anyone else but him, but they couldn't be together, so that was that.

She paid and walked out of the restaurant, her high-heeled boots clicking over the cobblestones.

The gallery was buzzing when she arrived as her boss, a high-strung man named Murray Anthony, was haranguing his hapless young assistant. They were loaning a few of their paintings at the last minute for some fancy party at the Modern next week, but nothing had been wrapped or shipped yet. The museum had called wondering where the paintings were, and now Murray was having a meltdown.

"Here, let me help," she said, getting up to lend a hand as the two of them packed the crate.

"Mimi, thank goodness you're here. I got off the phone with the museum to find Donovan about to *roll* the work! Can you imagine? They'd be ruined!" Murray said, glaring at the guilty party. "They have to arrive flat, flat, flat! He was going to send it in two FedEx poster tubes taped together! The lady who's throwing the party doesn't mess around." His eyes continued to throw daggers at his assistant. "Donovan said she was practically screaming at him the other day, but can you blame her?" He sighed.

"What's the party for anyway?" she asked.

"A shindig they're calling the Four Hundred Ball, a party for some secret society," Murray said, sounding totally bored. "Another group of self-important New Yorkers, no doubt. Apparently, they want this series of paintings because it's all red and the party will feature an exhibit called *Red Blood*. Go figure."

Mimi stared at him, not quite believing what she'd just heard. So the Coven was throwing a Four Hundred Ball again, were they? She felt a little wistful, remembering one of the very last ones they had before the War had taken over. She had made her debut at the event, claiming her rightful legacy as Azrael, Angel of Death. As much as she had tried to avoid returning to the past, somehow her subconscious, or the universe, had pushed her to this place. Everything happened for a reason, as Kingsley liked to say.

So the Four Hundred Ball was to include an exhibit called *Red Blood*—a nice little vampire inside joke, since Red Blood was what Blue Bloods called their mortal kin. The paintings the museum had requested from the gallery were large-scale canvases painted all over in a deep, rich scarlet color. The work was textured, visceral, and somewhat gory, so dark it looked almost like blood, which was the point. The artist, Ivy Druiz, a rather pretentious young woman, explained that they were representations of women's fear—red being the color of menarche, of childbirth, of pain. Mimi tended to roll her eyes at such easy political, pseudofeminist assertions of "art," and while it wasn't quite to her taste, she understood the appeal of a simple statement, not to mention their clients paid a lot of money for the pieces.

"Let me do that," she said, as she picked up the crate with ease and set it on a rolling board.

"Who are you, Superwoman?" Murray asked, lifting his circular, gold-rimmed eyeglasses that made him look like a grown-up Harry Potter to admire her strength.

"Something like that." She smiled. "I'll call the museum and tell them they'll have it this afternoon." She knelt down and helped Donovan carefully pack the rest of the pieces. "Don't let him get to you. He just gets a bit neurotic right before openings," she told him, speaking like a pro even though she had started working there only a week earlier than he did.

"Thanks." Donovan smiled. "He's much easier to deal with now that you're here. But I've got this—looks like you've got a client."

She stood up, brushing lint from her knees and smoothing her hair. Murray was standing at the front of the gallery, talking to a tall, dark-haired stranger who was staring intensely at a sculpture nailed to the wall. He was wearing a black coat, black jeans, and black boots. Mimi felt her heart thump. She knew that set of broad shoulders and that shock of jet-black hair anywhere.

"Mimi," her boss said with a beaming smile. "You never told me your husband was so cute!"

Kingsley Martin turned around. He looked skinny and hot, like a rock star who'd just stepped offstage, and he was wearing his Venator gear again. Her heart skipped a painful beat, and her breath caught in her throat. God, she'd missed him.

"Hello, darling," he drawled, cool as ever, even as his eyes were filled with sadness and pain. "Happy anniversary."

4 | LEFT BEHIND

*I*T WAS THE HOLY MOTHER of pentagrams, Ara thought, as she and Edon walked toward it—seven feet in height and diameter and made of blood. Painted crudely on a wall in the tunnels underneath Canal Street, most of it had crusted and dried by Monday afternoon when they arrived. They would have gotten there hours earlier, except there was a delay on the paperwork to get Edon outfitted with the proper blades and ammo, and the chief wouldn't let them leave with him unarmed. By the time they were ready to roll, it was lunchtime, and her new partner didn't take kindly to missing a meal.

The Venator team who had found the pentagram the day before looked impatient for relief. One of them, Ara was rattled to find, was Deming Chen, the beautiful Chinese Venator who had lost her identical twin during the final battle. Venators who knew her before then whispered that the loss had hardened her, and she hadn't been all that cuddly to begin with. Deming narrowed her almond-shaped eyes at them, but to Ara's surprise, the usually aloof commander greeted Edon with an affectionate punch on the shoulder. "Well, well, look what the cat dragged in! What're you doing here in our timeline, wolf boy?" she asked.

"Slumming, obviously," he replied with a slow grin. "Good to see you, too, angel."

Deming gave Edon a bear hug, and he shot Ara a victorious look as if to say, *She doesn't mind being called angel.*

"So what's going on?" he asked.

"Not much. Nephilim raising their ugly heads again. Now we've got this nonsense to deal with, and the Regent's freaking out because the Four Hundred Ball's on Saturday," Deming said, motioning to the pentagram. "I thought you were working with Bozeman's crew?"

"Yeah, we tracked down a Neph cell in Morocco, took care of it." He shrugged. "The brass sent me here when they heard about those pentagrams, see if I could be of any help."

"Well, we need all the help we can get. How're the boys?" she asked him.

"Good, good, you know, the same. Rowdy."

Deming smiled. "You been working undercover or something? You look like...well, you know what you look like. Take better care of yourself, will you?" she said to Edon in the tone of a scolding older sister.

He grinned. "Yeah, something like that. It's good to know you still care, D."

"Shut up, it was just battle sex." Deming laughed her throaty laugh, incongruous with her small frame, and which made her look even sexier than she already was. Deming always managed to look as though her Venator uniform was cut by a designer couturier, and for all Ara knew, it probably was.

"Is that what it was? Didn't feel like it at the time, angel," Edon teased.

"We were all just happy to be alive," Deming said with a serene smile on her face.

Ara tried not to feel too left out, but it was difficult to compete with the instant bonding that veterans shared. The chief had mentioned he'd fought side by side with Edon during the War, and as Deming was yet another hero of that long-ago conflict, of course she knew him, too. And apparently she'd slept with him. Didn't seem to regret it too much, either. Well, Edon wasn't as wrecked and destroyed looking back then, and he was clearly charming enough for Deming.

"Is the reunion over?" Deming's partner, a crusty, white-haired Venator named Gavin Acker, asked grumpily. "Or are you two gonna get a room?"

At least someone felt the same as she did. There was work to do, and the sooner they did it, the sooner they could get out of this dark, abandoned tunnel.

"We took a few scrapes for the lab," Deming said, turning serious. "Acker set up a dampening zone, in case there was any dark magic in it. Should be neutralized now."

"Did you run a blood test?" asked Ara.

Deming shook her head. "It's dead. There's nothing to be found from it. It won't call up any memories."

"But you didn't try?" Ara insisted. Working with blood was what Venators did; they used their senses to unlock the memories, truth, and history hidden in its makeup, and she couldn't hide her surprise that the senior Venator hadn't even attempted it.

Deming frowned, obviously annoyed at being questioned. "No. Like I told you, it's useless."

"And you haven't found the body yet?" Ara asked. Chief was sure there was bound to be a body somewhere underground, not too far away—a body that had been drained of its blood to make the pentagram. He had pressed upon them the urgent need to find it before the regular police did. The Venators didn't usually concern themselves with the murders of mortals, but the pentagram was a magical instrument and fell under their jurisdiction. If it had just been a smear of blood on the wall or even a regular dead body, the chief would have kicked it over to his Conduit at the NYPD. What the chief didn't say, didn't need to say, was that there had not been a death related to the Coven in a decade. The Venators were supposed to keep everyone associated with the Coven safe, vampire and human alike, and for ten years, they had succeeded.

"We've searched every inch of the tunnels underneath from Battery Park to Harlem. Perhaps you'll find something we missed, but I doubt it," Deming said coldly. "Come on, Acker. Let them take it from here. Maybe they'll find something we didn't," she said, in a tone that indicated she didn't believe they would.

When they were out of sight and hearing, Edon gave a low whistle. "What did you do to her? When I knew Ming she was pretty chill."

"It's complicated," Ara said with a shrug. She didn't want to get into it, and she bristled at being admonished. What happened wasn't her fault really, although she should have known better, and she couldn't help it if Deming was a cold bitch.

He nodded and didn't press for more, which was a relief. They studied the bloody marker in front of them.

"I thought pentagrams were a witch thing, you know, drawn with chalk," said Ara. "But you know about them, huh? I thought wolves didn't mess with magic."

"We know some," Edon allowed. "They're often used to call up power or magnify your own. That's what the witches do with them, if they're practicing white magic."

"And if not?"

"Then it's illegal. Their Council doesn't allow it, nor does yours," he said, as Ara leaned in for a closer look.

Edon took out his phone and took a few pictures. "Hey—" he said, making a face as Ara scraped some blood off the stone with her fingernail and licked it. "That's disgusting."

She didn't answer and instead concentrated on the blood on her tongue, closing her eyes and letting it disintegrate until it was part of her, so that she could try to access the memories hidden in its makeup. Edon was right—it was disgusting and probably as useless as Deming had insisted; it was too cold, the blood trail was dead. But sometimes you could catch a feeling—a faint echo of the living soul that had given the blood. Ara pushed her senses as hard as she could, but there was nothing. It was cold, dead, useless, gray; wait a minute—there was something—she was in a dark tunnel, like this, but it was narrower, smaller, and suddenly Ara was overwhelmed by terror, by a fright that chilled her to her soul. Her hands began to shake and she was suffocating, drowning in blood, and there was a familiar smell she couldn't place—she knew that smell—but before she could figure out what it was, it was over, and she jolted back to reality with the sensation of her blood being drained from her body.

"You all right?" Edon asked. "What did you see?"

Ara nodded, trying to shake off the fear and panic that she had tasted in the blood; her throat hitched and her heart was pumping fast—just like the girl's, right before her death. "A girl. I read her death in the blood. Come on—she's down here somewhere."

"Not much of a first date, is it?" Edon joked, as he and Ara circled their way through the dark, abandoned tunnels one more time. "Me, I like a little wine, candles to set the mood, maybe one of those violinists or two—or better yet, those dudes who come by with all those roses in a basket—you know? They force you to buy one or you'll look cheap in front of your lady?"

"Like you ever would," Ara said absently.

"Feel cheap?" He grinned. "Nah."

"Hush," Ara said, tired of his endless chatter. Their footsteps echoed across the cavernous space as they scoped every inch of the tunnel slowly and methodically. So far they had found nothing aside from the remains of a few homeless camps, but there was no sign of the people who lived there.

Ara led the way, not caring if she was splashing through grime or walking through cesspools. Neither of them needed flashlights, as vampires and wolves could see in the dark. Edon was breathing hard beside her, sniffing, coughing, wiping his nose.

"What's wrong? Smell getting to you?" she snapped.

"Relax, I just have allergies...mold. I used to live in Hell, so this don't bother me none," he said, and she could sense his sideways grin in the dark.

She could also sense that he spoke like that, in the rough slang of the street, just to rile her up. Prove to her how unlike him—and his world—she really was.

He didn't know her at all.

"Sure you're from Hell and not the hood?" she scoffed.

"What's a little Merryvale girl like you know about the hood?" he bantered back.

"You did some research on me?"

"Had to know who was on my ass now, didn't I?" Edon sighed, and she could hear his bones crack as he stretched his neck.

"Why don't you go?" she offered. "I can finish up here. There's a stairway not too far back from where we ran into that homeless camp."

"Are you kidding me? And let you take all the credit?" he asked, but his tone was joking.

"Fine," she said, as they passed a large wet puddle filled with something Ara did not want to think too long about. They kept walking in the dark until she stopped short and Edon bumped against her back.

"Whoops, sorry."

She held up a palm to quiet him. There was something—she could feel it, sense it, something hidden that she couldn't see—a feeling of menace and foreboding lingering in the air, and the trace blood memory from the pentagram awakened in her brain. Ara walked toward a deep fissure in the wall and pressed her hand against it, then almost fell into unexpected air.

Edon caught her before she stumbled. His hands were strong and firm as he helped tip her back to regain her balance. "Thanks," she said. "See that?"

"Yeah." He nodded. There was a hole in the wall, but one they couldn't see until they were standing right in front of it. Ara would never have known it was there if it wasn't for the blood memory. She tried not to feel too victorious, but she knew she would enjoy seeing Deming's face when she discovered they had indeed found something her team had missed.

Ara stepped into the hole, which opened up into another tunnel, a smaller one. Beside her, Edon drew his gun and held it away from his body, pointing it forward. She did the same. They walked a few feet away from each other, in order to provide cover.

"Stronger this way," she said, as the tunnel veered sharply to the right, and the walls became much narrower, closing in on them. She walked into it until the walls were so tight there was hardly any space for her to walk through. The space was only as wide as her shoulders, and Edon had to walk sideways.

"She's here," he whispered.

"No shit," she said, trying to keep her breathing even. Something black and fast and disgusting ran past her face and she screamed. Bats—or rats—what was it? *Bats*, she thought thankfully, since they could fly—she had felt their leathery wings flapping against her cheeks.

"You all right?" asked Edon, his voice shaky.

She felt better knowing he wasn't pretending that it didn't bother him. And she was glad at that moment that she had a partner again, even if it was a total hound like Edon. "Yeah."

"Come on." He nodded and pushed forward.

They kept walking through the tiny, narrow tunnel, which suddenly opened up again, and for a moment Ara was worried they were back where they started or that this was some kind of trap— until Edon put his nose in the air. "Smell that?"

"No, what is it?"

"She's right here," he said. "Death, rot, I can smell it—"

But the tunnel was empty. There was nothing except crumbling brick walls, the empty aqueduct, pools of murky water. They began scanning the wall, putting their hands on the stone, to see if there was another offshoot, another hidden wing. There was a similar dark crevice, and Ara put her hands tentatively on the wall, expecting to find nothingness again, air, but instead she hit something solid, something that was not made of stone, something fleshy and cold—something or someone—that had once been alive. "Here," she said. "She's here, Edon."

The dead girl had been folded into a crevice. Stuffed, like trash, into a hole, Ara thought. As if she were garbage. As if she didn't matter. Ara knelt down and touched the dead girl's skin. She was covered in her own blood, and her left arm ended in a bloody stump. Whoever killed her had used her own hand to draw the pentagram.

Edon shook his head.

Ara felt a deep, welling rage and helpless sadness at the sight. The girl looked young—early twenties—not much younger than Ara herself.

"Look," Edon said, kneeling down to examine her neck, where the blood was darkest, thickest. He wiped the blood to reveal two deep and ugly puncture wounds. Bite marks. "Call it in."

Chief was right. Her killer was a vampire. The Venators had failed.

5 | THE LATEST CONSPIRACY

*A*STATELY DOORMAN HELD open the lobby door, and as Oliver walked through, he spotted his driver holding the door open to the town car that was parked nearby. Such was his life now: servants at the ready, everything he wanted at his fingertips. He flipped his aviators over his face even though it wasn't terribly sunny, but as he'd grown older he found his eyes had become sensitive to light. He blinked at a small smudge of dirt on the glass doors that the doorman held open. Were his eyes deceiving him—or was that a pentagram?

"Arthur," he said. "What is that?"

The doorman peered at it. "Looks like some dirt. We'll take care of it, sir."

"Please do," Oliver said, concerned his mind was playing tricks on him.

He made his way to his car as the pack of reporters who were idling by the falafel cart jumped to attention upon sight of him. He frowned, bracing himself for another round of this nonsense. He had hoped that by ducking into the office after midday the reporters who congregated in front of his building every morning would have dispersed. No such luck.

"Mr. Hazard-Perry! A few questions—"

"Care to comment on the upcoming exhibit?"'

"Sorry, sorry," he said, wading through and brushing them off like pesky flies. He had almost made it to the car door when one question stood out from the rest.

"Is it true that your company condones the deaths of young women in the name of art?" The reporter was an angry-looking young woman, probably from one of the louder tabloids. The *Daily Post* had been milking this "controversy" for all it was worth since the exhibit had been announced in the press.

"Excuse me?" he asked, stopping in his tracks.

The angry reporter shot him a smarmy smile. "One of the artists who is part of the exhibit is said to have used his dead wife's blood in the paintings."

The Overland Trust was the finance arm of the Coven, and the Overland Foundation was its nonprofit charity organization. One that funded concerns that were of interest to their kind: blood banks, blood-borne disease elimination (just because they were immortal didn't mean they couldn't get sick), DNA research, and the occasional cultural grant, including the upcoming *Red Blood* exhibit for the Four Hundred Ball.

The reporter pressed forward, so that Oliver could almost smell her gum-scented breath. "If the rumors are true about the paintings, you have blood on your hands," she hissed.

"Is that right?" said Oliver mildly, nodding to his driver and handing him his briefcase.

"Yes. The paint used in the works contains the blood of a girl who has been missing for over a decade now!" the reporter barked. "Missing and presumed dead!"

Well, he wouldn't call Allegra Van Alen a *girl*, really. Even when she had fallen into a vegetative state and had been kept alive for years in a room at NewYork-Presbyterian, Allegra wasn't a girl. She was a vampire, an angel, and for sure, she was gone. But she wasn't *dead*. When the vampires had been offered salvation after their victory in the final battle, the majority of the Coven accepted it and returned to their home in Paradise, including Allegra. But try explaining that to this scandalmonger.

The whole event was turning into quite a headache. He'd only agreed to sponsor the exhibit as a favor to Finn, since one of the most prominently featured artists in it was her father—Stephen Chase, Allegra Van Alen's husband and human familiar. Finn was his daughter with a mortal woman, conceived before he married

Allegra. Oliver agreed that Stephen deserved more recognition for his work when Finn had campaigned for this splashy exhibit.

Besides, the reporters got it all wrong. While Stephen's paintings of Allegra did contain blood, it wasn't hers—all the blood in the paintings was his own. Oliver rubbed his temples in annoyance. He should never have given in to this exhibit, the path to Hell being strewn with you know what.

He held up his hands and grimaced as flashes popped and microphones and smartphones were thrust in front of his face. "Ladies and gentlemen, there is no truth to these despicable rumors. The Overland Foundation is a patron of the arts. These are important pieces of work by an artist who has been overlooked by the culture at large and who has made important contributions to the history of art. We are very proud of our participation in this groundbreaking exhibit. And now if you'll excuse me, I'm late for a meeting."

Oliver gave them his most charming smile, even though it was the complete opposite of what he was feeling, and settled into the backseat of the plush vehicle at his disposal. Even if he wanted to, it was much too late to call the whole thing off. He was starting to believe that the sooner this party happened, and the sooner this exhibit opened and closed, the better. Showcasing Stephen's controversial paintings was a bad idea. Some things were better off left in the past.

It was the future Oliver cared about, and the future of the Coven was foremost in his mind as he toured the gleaming rows of books in the Repository of History when he finally arrived at work. The secret Coven library filled with all the important books on vampire lore had burned down during the War, and Oliver considered its reestablishment inside the Orpheus Tower one of his greatest successes.

"What's all the hubbub?" he asked, noticing a group of excited human Conduits and young vampires gathered around a tall and austere middle-aged woman, asking her for autographs. "Isn't that Genevieve Belrose?"

"Indeed," Fletcher Heller, his assistant, told him with a twitchy smile.

"What's she doing here?"

"She's on tour for her latest book."

"Another?"

Fletcher, a sharp young man with a supercilious way about him, gave him a knowing look. "Conspiracy work, of course."

"Of course," said Oliver. The Conspiracy was one of the great secrets of the Coven. The vampires disseminated false information about their kind in the mortal population—popular falsehoods included the notion that they were hideous creatures of the night who were to be feared and that a vampire's bite could turn a mortal into one. What a laugh. Genevieve's breathless and best-selling vampire romance series was the latest contribution to the canon— mortals couldn't get enough of her troubled and eternally hunky vampire hero, Alden Cummerbund. Sometimes Oliver wondered if the Conspiracy was having *too* much fun.

"You can't say she's not doing good work, considering she's somehow convinced the public that all we do is woo young women whose blood smells good to us," Fletcher said, wrinkling his nose. "Who even *likes* the smell of blood? Gross."

Oliver agreed he had a point. He was about to congratulate Genevieve personally, when from the corner of his eye he spotted Sam Lennox making his way toward him.

The Venator chief looked rumpled and worse for wear. Regents and Venator chiefs never agreed on much, with the Venators demanding more freedom to cross boundaries in order to keep the Coven safe, while Regents were careful not to allow them too much opportunity to use the dark arts against their own people. For instance, permission to look into dreams? Without the vampire's knowledge? Yeah, no. But while the two of them had battled in the past, they had a good working relationship.

He looked forward to his interactions with Sam; the two of them shared the same paranoia concerning anything demon related. Oliver was relieved when the Venators had found and destroyed that Nephilim nest out in Brooklyn, stomping out the cockroaches, so to speak.

"What's up, Chief?" Oliver asked.

"They found the body."

Oliver's shoulders sagged. "And?" This was not a prank. This was not a drill. There was a body count now, a victim. In his mind's eye, Oliver saw the peace of the Coven shattered like glass against a dark wall, and somewhere in the background, a demon was smiling.

"Young girl. Puncture marks on her throat," Sam said, flipping through the file he carried. "Bled to death."

Oliver cursed.

"Blood signature is murky. Can't find a match with Coven records, anyway. Unregistered. Looks like the work of a renegade."

"What about that Nephilim hive we shut down? One of them got away maybe? Did this?" he asked.

"Maybe," the chief acknowledged, although Oliver knew he was insulted. The Venators had cleared that hive with holy water, and nothing could've survived that raid. "I don't know. Bunch of strange vampires in town for the ball..."

Oliver nodded and pressed the tips of his fingers to his lips before speaking. "All right. Let's put all the teams on high alert. I want you to scour this fucking city and find her killer."

Sam Lennox nodded. "We won't rest till we do."

"Whoever did this is going to burn," Oliver promised. The Code of the Vampires protected mortal as well as immortal life now; it was one of the first changes he had made as Regent. Vampires who ran afoul of this law were in danger of losing their immortal lives.

There were no more second chances, not in his Coven.

6 | TAINTED LOVE

IMI FOLLOWED KINGSLEY OUTSIDE the gallery to the side-walk, where he popped his collar and pulled a cigarette out of his pocket, lit it, and took a deep, satisfying inhale. He blew a smoke ring and watched it drift. He was back to his old habits, she thought, and something told her he hadn't come straight from the underworld. He had an earthly sheen on him; he wasn't sallow-faced and pale like she had been when she first arrived. How long had he been back? she wondered.

"So how'd you find me?" she asked, crossing her arms. "I made sure to put a cloaking spell on my aura so that the Coven wouldn't bother me."

Kingsley's smile was smug and the darkness in his eyes faded a little. "And who taught you how to do that?"

Of course he knew all the tricks. He was the one who invented them. Plus, she had to admit she had been waiting for him to show up and beg her to come back ever since she had arrived in New York. She hadn't been hiding so much as playing hard to get. "I'm not going back with you," she said suddenly. "I can't." And the moment she said it, she knew it was true. Part of her wanted to throw her arms around him and beg him for forgiveness, as seeing him only reminded her of how much she had missed him. But she couldn't go back to the underworld.

"Sweetheart, I'm not here to ask you back."

Those terrible words they had said to each other before they had parted hung in the air between them, but Mimi still recoiled as if she had been slapped in the face. It had never occurred to her that he would be here for any other reason. Okay, so it wasn't like he had begged for her to stay, and he had pretty much let her go without even putting up a fight, but this was Kingsley Martin she was talking about here. He was mad for her, he always had been, up to the night before she left. He could pretend he wasn't interested, but she knew otherwise. She decided to rile him up a little; she was good at that. "So why are you here, then?" she asked haughtily. "Heard a new nightclub opened up?"

He didn't take the bait. "Take a walk with me."

"I can't, I'm working."

"Right," he said, not even trying to hide his amusement.

It was her turn to feel indignant, and unlike Kingsley, she showed it. "I'm not completely useless," she said defensively.

"I never said that," Kingsley said mildly. "And you never were."

"Murray says I have a good eye. I might even pick an artist or two to represent."

He nodded, looking weary of the conversation. "All right, then. What time do you get off?"

She told him and he nodded, all business. Aside from the fact that he had remembered it was their anniversary, Kingsley gave no indication that he had given a minute's thought to the demise of their relationship. It was as if even after all their years together, they were right back to square one again, and everything each had endured and sacrificed for the other didn't matter in the least. He *had* to be bluffing. That was the only explanation. He could never resist her in the past, and so now she fell back to the usual feminine devices, the ones that had never disappointed her before, the ones he had been so susceptible to when they had first fallen in love. "Is it a date?" she asked, her eyelashes fluttering.

"No," he said, and flicked the cigarette to the ground and stubbed it with his toe.

It was hard to concentrate on work, but she did. The museum was glad to hear that the paintings were finally on their way but asked if the gallery could help them get in touch with their artist. Mimi left a message for Ivy Druiz, creator of the "period pieces," as she and

Donovan had dubbed them behind her back. Oh, they were so very clever.

"Hi, Ivy, it's Mimi Martin from Murray Anthony Fine Art. The curator at the Modern wants to ask you a few questions for the program. Can you give him a call when you can? They've tried you all week, apparently. Thank you."

Mimi shot off an e-mail and a text message, as well. Artists were so irresponsible, she thought. Was it so difficult to return a call? She had heard Ivy was fond of pulling disappearing-into-the-desert-to-get-in-touch-with-my-inner-child acts. It drove Murray up the wall.

"Hey, Murray, have you heard from Ivy lately?" she asked, when her boss wandered to the front to look up a price from the catalog.

"I saw her two weeks ago at the Whitney gala," he said. "Why?"

"She's not answering her phone, and the museum has to ask her a few questions so they can write the copy for the pieces."

"Well, that sounds exactly like Ivy not to call them back. I told you about her."

"Yeah, her whole 'My work speaks for itself,'" Mimi said, making air quotes. "They also wanted to confirm her attendance for the patrons' dinner on Thursday night." The Coven was certainly back to its swanky heyday, she noted.

She dialed Ivy again. Even if the artist was a bit childish and irresponsible, Mimi thought it was a bit odd she hadn't bothered to return the curator's call. Ivy was incredibly ambitious and would've bitten off her hand for this opening—the biggest of her career.

Mimi decided she would pay Ivy a visit at her apartment tomorrow if she didn't hear back. Although when she saw Kingsley waiting for her after the gallery closed, she knew she was just worrying about Ivy in order to take her mind off the fact that her husband was finally back in New York City. Or was it ex-husband? He was certainly acting like an ex.

"Let's grab a drink," he said.

"I thought we were going to take a walk."

"Changed my mind."

They repaired to a bar not far from the storefront, where off-duty artists and gallery workers liked to converge. The place was all white and chrome, as minimalist and stylish as its patrons. She nodded to the bartender as they walked in and led Kingsley to her favorite table in the corner. The waitress came around and they ordered, a dirty martini for her and a Scotch double neat for him. A few minutes later, drink in hand, she took a long sip and appraised her husband over the rim of her glass. "So if you're not here to ask me to come back, why are you here?"

He tapped the end of his cigarette against the table and stuck it in his lip.

"That's not allowed inside anymore," she told him. "And it wasn't even when we were still in New York."

Kingsley sighed, tossed the cigarette on the table, and downed his drink in one shot. "I need your help," he said finally.

"Okay," she said, curious. "What's going on?"

"Hear that?" he asked, drumming his fists on the table, which he did when he was anxious. She had a vision of him doing the same thing on their kitchen table not so long ago, and she felt a sudden sadness that she had broken up their happy-enough home.

But she kept her thoughts and feelings to herself. If he wasn't going to talk about their relationship, then neither would she. "What?" She looked around the bar. "You mean that terrible cover of 'Don't Stop Believing'?"

He smirked. "No—the ringing," he said, leaning over. It was the closest they had been all day, and Mimi felt a familiar spark at their proximity, and fought an urge to put her hand on his arm and pull him in, to stop pretending that they didn't want what they wanted. Maybe this separation had been good for their relationship—she hadn't felt more attracted to him than she did at the moment. She had forgotten how sexy she'd found his indifference. But then, she'd always responded to rejection.

She studied his face, fighting a rising heat as he stared right back. Finally she replied, "Ringing?"

"In your ears—don't you hear it? You must," he said, continuing to slap the table.

Her face fell. "Oh, that."

"Yeah, that."

"You hear it, too?" she asked, plucking an olive from her glass and popping it into her mouth.

"Of course."

"What is it?"

"You really don't know? I thought you were just ignoring it, which was why you didn't report it or come back. Or maybe you really don't care anymore."

"Care about what?"

"Keeping the world safe from harm?" he said lightly.

Mimi rolled her eyes. "As if I ever cared about that." Everyone was so *dramatic*. She had done her duty in the War, but it made her uncomfortable when people called her a hero.

"You did once," he said heavily. He looked down at the shiny white table and wouldn't meet her eyes.

She shrugged. Had she cared? She supposed she had, once, just like he said, just as she had cared about him. Although she still cared about him, she really did, even if she was the one who had left, but as for the rest of the world—well, that was another story. The vampires had been saved, the Coven reborn. They didn't need her anymore. They were even mounting a Four Hundred Ball. Everything was supposed to be peachy, with a slew of happy endings for all after Lucifer's defeat. Even Jack Force, her twin brother, had risen from the dead to live the rest of his immortal life as a vintner in Napa, happily married to Schuyler Van Alen. What was up with all the former Venators retiring to toil the earth and work with their hands? Kingsley and Jack had been Angels of the Apocalypse, hell-raisers, and now the only things they were raising were...seedlings.

"Well, are you going to tell me what it is or am I going to have to get it out of you?" she asked, giving him her sultriest smile, hoping to remind him what he'd been missing.

Kingsley leaned away from her and looped a long arm over the back of the booth. "It's Hell's Bells."

Mimi raised an eyebrow. "You're joking."

"I'm as serious as our troubled marriage," he said. "Hell's Bells is an alarm system, one of the most ancient ones. It means something's gotten out that shouldn't have. It's an alert...a warning."

She chose not to comment on his first mention of the status of their relationship. Troubled, was it? She supposed he was right to call it that (they were separated after all), and living together had been a *trial*. How did people do it? How did they hang on to love when routine was so deadening? She wondered if their friends had fared better, if Jack and Schuyler were going through the same struggles, and she felt a wash of bitterness at the thought of the two of them ecstatically happy while she and Kingsley had found their happy ending turned to ashes. It wasn't supposed to be this way between them.

Kingsley shifted in his seat. "A human girl was murdered over the weekend. Venators found her body in the sewers. She was killed by a vampire."

"You're in touch with the Coven?" she asked, unable to keep the surprise from her voice. That was interesting, since back in the underworld, he had shown no interest in the news of life aboveground.

He didn't reply, which meant if he was in touch with them, it wasn't through official channels. Of course not—Kingsley had never once worked through official channels.

"How long have you been back?" she asked suddenly.

Once again, he remained silent, continuing to look guilty.

"That long, huh?" It made her jealous, that he had gotten in touch with his old friends but had not seen her until now. He was so infuriating.

"Listen, darling, I meant to see you earlier... but things got in the way," he said.

"For sure," she said, put off but trying not to show it. Since they were separated, it wasn't too hard to imagine what he was up to. The city was sure to awaken his old vices and desires. New York held a myriad of delights that appealed to Kingsley: nightclubs, bars, after-hours clubs, shady gambling dens, beautiful girls of every stripe.

Kingsley raked his fingers through his dark hair in frustration. "Let's not fight, my love. I came to ask for your help."

"And what makes you think I'll give it to you?" she challenged.

He smiled at her. "Because. It's you. I know we're having problems, but I was hoping we could sweep that aside for now and work together like we used to. I need you. I wouldn't be here if I didn't."

Feeling a bit mollified by the smile and his admission, Mimi got down to business. "All right, then. A mortal—murdered by one of us, are you sure?" she asked.

"Positive," he said, his dark eyes cloudy and angry.

Mimi took a sharp breath. "But it can't be, no one would ever do such a thing; it has to be something else... someone else," she said, feeling a familiar dread at the thought of their enemies. "One of Lucifer's demons maybe. Oh." She realized now why Kingsley was so worried about Hell's Bells ringing.

"You think someone's escaped from Hell?" she said. "And you blame yourself."

"I thought I must have missed something," he brooded, his tone bleak. "When the bells began to ring, I went back immediately to check. I made the rounds, checked every cell, and no one has escaped from Hell. Not on my watch." His forehead crinkled in annoyance. He kept silent, but Mimi knew he was right. She had seen him crush demons underneath his heel, thrust his sword into their hearts, toss their bodies into the Black Fire, leaving them to burn. Those who had begged for mercy had been locked into their eternal prisons. No one was getting in or out of the underworld without his permission.

She nodded. "So what could possibly have set off the alarm?"

"I don't know, and that's what's troubling," Kingsley said. "Whatever it is, we need to send it back where it came from."

"We?" Mimi asked. "Let me remind you that I haven't said yes."

"Well, it's the only way to get rid of that infernal noise in our ears, and I assumed, at the very least, you'd want that, too. Don't you?" he asked innocently.

Mimi almost smiled. She drained her drink and motioned for another round. He had been back in the city for a month and only came to her now, which meant he was either in terrible trouble or still held hope for their marriage. At the moment, she didn't care what the reason was. Hell's Bells were ringing, and Kingsley Martin was out of the underworld and back in Manhattan.

It looked like she'd been granted her wish.

7 | **MEAN GIRLS**

*T*HE VENATOR-WIDE MEETING was held in the conference room the next day. All units reported in, from day to graveyard shifts. Sam Lennox stood in front of the podium with the Regent of the Coven as the Venators clustered around, talking in groups and exchanging notes. Ara and Edon found a place in the back, and she leaned against the wall with her arms crossed. Ara noticed Deming was sitting in the front, chatting with Sam and Oliver. She caught her eye and Deming looked away with a frown. Ara wondered if Deming would ever let it slide, and she thought the answer was definitely in the negative, at least for now.

Sam approached the podium and cleared his throat, and the room immediately went silent. "Here's what we know about the victim. Her name was Georgina Curry and she hadn't been seen since she left a party last Saturday night. She was a Holy Heart girl. A junior. Sixteen years old, mortal. Her family isn't part of the Coven; they aren't registered Conduits or familiars. We don't know how she came in contact with a vampire. This could be a random attack or a secret liaison."

So the girl was young, so much younger than Ara had first assumed. And it was such a horrid way to die, Ara couldn't stop thinking about it. She had been sucked dry and bled to death, then dismembered and stuffed in a hole.

The chief told them the autopsy showed that the girl had been killed sometime over the weekend—Saturday night, most likely. Day shift had found the pentagram on Sunday morning, and Ara and Edon had found the body on Monday afternoon. Ara hoped that the girl had died quickly and painlessly, that the euphoria that was part of the Sacred Kiss somehow shielded her to the violence that had been done to her.

Looking around the room, Ara wondered how many of the Venators were thinking about the last time a teenager associated with the Coven had died, although it was vampires who had been killed then, not mortals. She remembered the panic that had almost destroyed the Coven when the vampires went back underground, some to sleep forever, choosing not to reincarnate. It was different this time, but just as troubling if not more. The Coven had made the health and safety of its human familiars a priority in order to keep the vampires' existence a well-guarded secret from the rest of the world. The spell from the Sacred Kiss kept familiars from revealing their status, while human Conduits came from families that had served the vampires for centuries, their loyalty unquestioned and ingrained into their nature. Ara shuddered to think what would happen if the mortals ever discovered the Conspiracy was a lie, that real vampires lived among them and had been since the beginning of time. The mortal world could be as cruel and violent as Lucifer when it wanted to be.

"We're keeping this quiet for now. We're holding the body until we can find her killer. So far all the NYPD knows is that the girl is missing. They're conducting their own investigation. Scott and Marrok are leads on this case. They'll be going to the school, talking to her friends, her family, to find out whom she was hanging out with, how she might have met this vampire. As you're aware the blood bond doesn't match anyone in the Coven, so whoever did this was a stranger. I don't want to remind you of that Nephilim ring we broke up not too long ago. I'm not convinced this is related to that, but we can't be sure. That means the rest of you need to bring in every renegade in the city. I want every unregistered immortal brought in for questioning. Every. Single. One. We're going to get this guy. We always do." He moved to let Oliver speak.

Ara had only seen the Regent a few times in the past. She had seen him on television, of course, talking about the economy and politics, and his picture was all over the magazines, as he and his beautiful human familiar were regulars at swanky social events. But this was one of the few times she had seen him in person, which meant the Coven was treating the mortal girl's death seriously. She had heard the same things about him that everyone in the Coven knew—that he used to be mortal, but that he was special, having been the human Conduit and familiar to the most powerful vampire during the War. Oliver Hazard-Perry had the dignified air and stately bearing that one expected in a leader, handsome but not pretty, serious without being nerdy. His face was somber, but his tone was confident.

He cleared his throat. "First of all, I want to thank everyone for their hard work on this case. It's deeply troubling to find this kind of violence in our midst again. And I just want to stress what you all know. The murder of a mortal by a vampire is a crime punishable by death. If you know anything about this case that can help us, please speak up. We appreciate your efforts, as you are all aware that the Four Hundred Ball is coming up on Saturday. I can't help but think that this might be related to the fact that we are celebrating the Coven's survival. This isn't a random act of violence. This is a message. Let's let our enemies know we reject it."

Sam nodded. "Dismissed."

"Let's hit the kids first before her 'rents," said Edon, slipping the case file back into its folder and tucking it under his arm. "See if any of them can tell us about this party."

Private School Row, the blocks from Eighty-Fifth to Ninety-Second Streets between Madison and Park Avenues, was famous for its concentration of the best independent schools in the city. These elite institutions of learning were housed next to each other in former mansions and town houses or, as in the case of the French Institute, in new buildings built after razing four brownstones and annoying all its neighbors. Merryvale Academy was the preeminent all-girls school that made up the trifecta that also included Holy Heart and Tallywood-Sparrowfinch. For boys, there was New York Latin School, Bournemouth, and Westbury Prep. Duchesne School was the classic Blue Blood choice; it was the place where many generations of the Coven's finest were educated. It was coed, progressive, and cutthroat, pun intended.

While they walked from the Eighty-Sixth Street and Lexington subway stop, Ara ran down the list, enumerating the minutiae of differences for Edon. "Merryvale girls are the snottiest because they're the smartest. The First Lady is a Merryvale girl, as is the governor and our senator." Turned out there were parts of her old life that she was proud of; she hadn't realized that before.

"Yeah, yeah, yeah, I get it. You went to the stuck-up school," Edon said, scoffing at Ara's Private Schools 101 lecture. "So how'd you fit in there?" he teased. "Can't see you in plaid and pearls."

"I had to wear a uniform. It was required," she said primly and continued on unperturbed. "Tallywood has the models and the actresses, the Oscar winners. The prettiest sister, so to speak. They go out mostly with the Westbury boys, the hedge fund crowd. The Latin School is full of nerds, and Bournemouth is hippie. But Holy Heart girls are something else."

"Yeah? What?"

"Let's just say there's nothing holy about those chicks' hearts."

In Ara's day, Holy Heart had the bad girls, the ones who wore their skirts too short and their blouses unbuttoned a little too low, the girls who smoked in their uniforms and had affairs with their Latin teachers, the girls who were rumored to host orgies in their palatial apartments when their parents were in St. Barts. There had been so many rumors about the Holy Heart girls—blow job clubs, pregnancy pacts, cutting cliques—and at the time, Ara had believed all of them. Now that she was older she wondered if the school's reputation—easily more sordid and a whole lot dirtier than the usual exclusive private school scuttlebutt—was concocted by the Holy Heart girls themselves in order to make everyone forget that they essentially went to school in a convent and that morality clauses were part of the school contract.

Holy Heart was housed in a large, forbidding mansion that looked like a fortress behind iron gates. "Easier to get into the underworld," Edon cracked as Ara flashed her badge to the school camera.

A long, loud buzz sounded and they were let inside. They garnered a few curious looks from the student body as they entered the marble halls of the exclusive girls' school. The mansion was the former home of a millionaire steel baron from the turn of the century and had all the appropriate grandeur. Ara wondered if she should have made Edon change his clothes, or if she should have combed her hair. Not that either would have helped them pass muster with the headmistress, who would have been prejudiced against them from the beginning. If the school was a fortress, the headmistress had the look of a dragon slayer.

Mrs. Cecilia Henry ushered them into her office, a warm, cozy space lined with books and portraits of headmistresses before her. She offered them both tea, which they declined. After a few pleasantries, during which Ara divulged her own association with the insular private school world, Mrs. Henry got down to business. "The police have already come by and questioned several students. We have cooperated fully, and I'm afraid that is all we can do. Having more law enforcement here would upset the parents. They are nervous enough as it is with Georgina's disappearance."

"I understand, and I assure you, we will be very discreet," Ara said, explaining that she and Edon were from an elite secret organization within the police department, which was true enough. "We'd like to talk to a few of Georgina's friends, if that's possible."

Edon was slouched low in his chair, his eyes slits. He hadn't said a word so far, and when the headmistress looked in his direction, he seemed to glower. Ara wanted to kick him in the shin, and Cecilia Henry glanced at him sharply, as if he was a truant in her office. They glared at each other for a long time until Edon barked, "What's the matter? Not interested in finding her?"

The headmistress bristled. "Fine. You can talk to the girls during free period, but I will have to get their parents' permission, of course."

Ara nodded. "Of course."

They were escorted back outside, near the back stairs, where the receptionist offered them cookies. Edon took one from the delicate floral plate. "Why were you so hostile in there?" she asked when they were alone.

"These places give me the creeps," he said. "All pristine and stuck-up outside, and a den of iniquity inside."

"Den of iniquity?" she repeated, amused.

"Yeah." He shrugged. "At least the Nephs are honest—dirty business in and out."

"That cell you busted, what were they into?" she asked.

"The usual banality—human trafficking, running numbers, prostitution. What about the one here?"

"Running some kind of drug operation, manufacturing and selling crystal on the streets most likely, since we found traces of it before we torched the place."

He nodded, then eyed the girls walking through the stairway. She shot him a look.

"What?" he asked. When his gaze lingered a little too long on a few of them, this time she did kick his leg.

He yelped. "Jeez, I was just trying to get a read on them. Settle down. I don't do jailbait."

The headmistress came out of her office. "According to her teachers, Georgina had two best friends: Darcy McGinty and Megan King. I've contacted their parents, and they have agreed to let you speak to their daughters. You can use the library."

The library was a large and airy space in the addition built behind the school. Ara and Edon found a quiet nook in the back, and a few minutes later the first student, Darcy McGinty, entered. Darcy was a self-possessed platinum blonde whose lacy black bra peeped out of her uniform shirt and whose tiny plaid kilt barely covered her behind. She twirled her hair with her fingers and smirked at Edon, who winked at her.

Ara frowned and began her line of questioning, adopting a no-nonsense tone. Darcy reminded her a little too much of a few former friends of hers, those who had been fifteen going on twenty-nine and liked to adopt a jaded and skeptical air, although they were a lot more innocent than they looked. And according to her notes, Darcy McGinty was the host of the party Saturday night, where Georgina was last seen.

"You were friends with Georgina Curry," she said. "She was at your party last weekend?"

"Yeah, so what?" Darcy said as she crossed and uncrossed her legs. Her white socks were pulled up to her knees, and with her short skirt and high-heeled Mary Janes, the whole effect was that of a stripper costume or a certain rock video fantasy of the slutty private school girl.

"It was the last place she was seen," Ara said, checking her notes.

"Okay."

"Was Georgina dating anyone?"

"Not really."

"No?"

Darcy rolled her eyes. "No one 'dates' anymore. Everyone just… hangs out."

"Who was she hanging out with at your party?"

"The usual crew. No one special."

"You posted some pictures from Saturday night online. Care to walk us through them?"

"Do I have a choice?" Darcy blew a bubble with her gum and popped it.

Ara opened her laptop and shoved it toward Darcy, who started IDing the boys. "That's Jax, he goes to Westbury; that's Tommy, he's at Bournemouth; that's Henry, he goes to the Honors Program at Williams…" They clicked through all the pictures, and Ara shook her head slightly at Edon. They were all mortals. None of the boys were Blue Bloods. The Coven was a small community, and Ara knew almost everyone by sight if not by name.

"You seem to know a lot of boys from different schools," Ara said.

"Yeah, mostly from the Committee."

"The Committee?" Ara asked. There was only one Committee that mattered in New York. Only one Committee that they called "the Committee." Ostensibly it was the New York Blood Bank Committee, but in reality it was run by the Coven to educate its younger members.

"It's like a secret society that a few of my friends are in." Darcy smirked.

Was this how Georgina met her vampire?

"Who's that?" Ara asked, noticing a handsome, dark-haired boy next to Georgina in a few of the photographs. He looked as mortal as the rest, but he had an otherworldly beauty that could mark him as one of the Fallen. There was something compelling about him.

"Oh, that's just Damien Lane," Darcy said, shrugging.

"Who's he?"

"Some kid we know."

Ara enlarged the picture. "Did Georgina know him?"

"Yeah, of course. I told you… we all just hang out. Gigi might have been hooking up with him, yeah, maybe. I don't know."

"I thought girls told each other everything," Ara said as she tapped her pencil on the desk. "She didn't tell you what was going on with them?"

"No," said Darcy, her voice flat and toneless.

Edon and Ara shared another exasperated glance. "All right. I'll ask an easier question. Where does he go to school?" she asked.

"I don't know. I think he might be homeschooled."

"Did he leave with her on Saturday night?"

"I don't know. I don't remember," Darcy said, her face turning pink and her forehead becoming sweaty. "I'm not sure. Maybe?"

Ara let it go, wrote down "Damien Lane" and a question mark. She asked Darcy if there was a printer close by and the girl nodded. Ara sent the information and the girl went to grab it from the library printer.

"Is she dead?" Darcy asked, coming back with the picture and placing it before them on the table. She had her color back and looked more composed.

"Why do you say that?" Edon asked, crossing his arms and frowning. He tipped his chair back. "You know something we don't?"

The girl shrugged. Ara thought she would be pretty if she weren't trying so hard to be cool. "Otherwise, what's the big deal? Sixteen-year-olds go missing all the time," Darcy said.

"Not from the Upper East Side," Ara pointed out.

"Well, that's the thing, isn't it? Because she's not from the Upper East Side," Darcy retorted.

"Think she's lying?" Edon asked as soon as Darcy left. "About not knowing anything?"

"Yeah, she's definitely lying. She's hiding something. We have to find out about this Damien character," Ara said, paging through the papers in front of her. "Well, Darcy wasn't lying about everything." The file confirmed that Georgina Curry was a financial aid student, a scholarship kid with work study on her schedule, which meant she was a teacher's slave/errand girl.

"Her parents live in Hell's Kitchen. Dad's a chef, Mom manages the restaurant." She had been dreading meeting the parents. That would be their sad duty later, and it made her even sadder to discover that Georgina's parents had worked so hard for their only child. A girl who was now on a slab in the basement offices.

Edon glanced through the pictures of Georgina. She was a lithe-some blonde who wore her hair long and straight, with a tiny, delicate gold chain on her neck, diamond studs in her ears. "Funny, she looks just like them—a poster kid for the *Gossip Girl* set," he said. "Right?" He held up Georgina's yearbook portrait.

"You can never tell—girls go out of their way to fit in," Ara said, feeling sorry for Georgina all over again. It wasn't easy going to a school like Holy Heart when your parents couldn't afford the things everyone else could. School wasn't simply an academic experience but a social one as well. Ski trips, beach trips, blowout birthday parties, exclusive dances, and the extracurricular activities were numerous and pricey for this kind of education. If Darcy knew about the Committee, it meant she was part of the Red Blood elite who were human Conduits or human familiars of the vampires. The question was, how far had Georgina gone to fit in? Far enough to get herself killed? And who was this Damien Lane?

Megan King was a chubby, freckled girl, the complete opposite of Darcy McGinty. If Darcy looked like she was already in her late twenties and had the stories and the experiences to prove it, Megan looked much younger than her years. If they hadn't known she was a senior in high school, Ara would have pegged her as twelve years old.

Edon slouched lower in his seat, adopting a studied nonchalance, which Ara thought might work when interrogating Nephilim but was a little too much around these teenage girls. Megan glanced at him fearfully. Ara tried to project a warmer air, taking note of Megan's gold tank watch and her battered leather bag, along with her perfectly straight teeth and shiny hair. Megan, unlike Georgina, was not a scholarship student. Her family had money and status, and unlike Darcy, whose overt and aggressive sexuality on display was a rebellion against her family's good name, Megan appeared to be more than happy to be an example of her parents' good breeding.

"You were a friend of Gigi's?" Ara asked.

"Georgie's," Megan corrected. "The only one who calls her Gigi is Darcy, and Georgie hates it. Darcy overheard her parents calling her that one day and started using it."

Ara made a note. Sounded like Georgina was a little ashamed of her background maybe. "You were at Darcy's party Saturday night?"

Megan's cheeks turned pink. "No, I wasn't invited. Georgie and I were sort of friends apart from Darcy, if you know what I mean. Darcy's friends with those C-girls, and they all sort of stick together."

"Committee girls?"

"Yeah. I don't know what the big deal over etiquette classes is; we already had those in fifth grade," Megan said.

"Do you know about a friend she had, a guy named Damien Lane?"

"Yes."

"How did they meet? Did she tell you? Darcy said he's home-schooled."

Megan picked her cuticles. "I think they met at some club."

"What club? The Bank or Block 122?" Ara asked, naming a goth dance club and an exclusive, members-only nightclub that was popular when she used to go out to places like that, when she'd had the time and inclination to dance and have fun.

Megan shook her head. "Never heard of those places."

Of course not; they had been shut down long ago. Ara felt old all of a sudden. "Where do kids go now?" she asked.

"The Sundae Shop in Williamsburg for indie music, the W-Bowl for, um, bowling, Members Only for the afternoon techno party. Outcast or Smithy, if you want to get high."

Not so innocent after all, Ara thought. Who knew that behind that milk-fed facade was a girl who knew her way around New York nightlife?

"Yeah, I think she met him at Outcast one night."

"Was he her boyfriend? Was she in love with him?" Ara asked.

"I don't know. . . . I mean, she was at his house a lot. So maybe. All she told me was that he was nice and that she was helping him with something."

"Helping him with what?"

"I don't know. Georgie wouldn't tell me. She was weirdly tight-lipped about the whole thing, but . . ."

"But what?"

"Well, it just seemed she was—scared of something."

"Scared?"

Edon sat up straight and shot Ara a look.

"She told me on Friday at school that she knew some secret, and it was bad, and she was in trouble. She said she couldn't tell me what it was, because then I'd be in trouble too. But she said Damien would make it okay. That's all."

"Thanks, Megan," Ara said, writing it all down.

"Do you think Damien did something to her?" Megan asked tentatively.

Edon leaned back lower in his chair, his eyes appraising. "Why do you say that?"

"I don't know, why are you questioning me unless Georgina's dead?"

"You think Georgina is dead?" Ara asked.

"Isn't she?" Megan asked, eyes darting between the two of them. "Isn't that why you're here?"

8 | PICTURES OF YOU

*F*INN OFTEN TEASED HIM that he lived in what she called, not so jokingly, the "billionaire bubble," a cozy, protected, comfortable space where every joke he made never fell flat, every project he touched was immediately praised, every inconvenience or minor annoyance he experienced was quickly fixed and sorted by people eager to please, eager for praise, eager for a moment with the Great Man. Take right now, for example. Oliver was standing with Finn in the lobby of the Museum of Modern Art, which had closed early on what would normally be a busy Tuesday afternoon at his request and at great expense. He had asked the curator to accommodate his schedule, and so the usually bustling space was empty and silent in the middle of the day, aside from a few archivists and docents who were helping with the installation. Of course, they could have waited until the museum was closed for the day, but Oliver had not wanted to wait.

Was Finn right? *Did* he live in a bubble? Was he getting soft? Did he take his position for granted and become used to the bowing and scraping and jockeying his presence created? And if he did, was it so wrong to enjoy it? The city's snootiest art maven was hanging on his every word; the man was almost trembling from excitement as Oliver dangled the possibility of the Overland Foundation dedicating a portion of its annual budget to financing the latest wing of the museum. Just as a way of thanking the man for taking the time and the trouble to mount this exhibit, of course.

"Shall we go see the space on the sixth floor?" the curator asked. "We're almost ready for Saturday."

"All the way up there? I was under the impression the paintings were going to be displayed in the contemporary galleries on the second floor. They're much easier to access," said Finn.

"The galleries on the second to fifth floors are reserved for our permanent collections," the curator explained. "Special exhibitions are installed in a wonderful space full of light on the sixth floor and that's where we have started to install it."

"But the party will be in the sculpture garden," Finn pointed out. "Do you really expect our guests to make their way up so many escalators to go see the exhibit? No, the sixth floor won't do."

The curator was starting to sweat. Oliver could smell the fear on him. He felt pity for the man and placed a warm hand on his shoulder. "The contemporary collection can be moved for a while, can't it? If it's a matter of expense, I'm sure we can take care of it."

"Of course, of course," the man said weakly. "We will move the collection for the exhibit. It will be a tight squeeze as the party is only a few days away, but we will—manage. However, if you would like to see the paintings, we will have to go to the sixth floor for the time being."

"I think we'd like to see them," Oliver said, nodding.

As they made their way to the top of the building, Finn peppered the curator with more questions concerning party logistics. Oliver zoned out of the conversation, his mind elsewhere. It was one thing for the Regent to throw his weight around for a special party, but it was another if it blinded one to the darker forces at the fringes of their society. There was a reason the Coven had nearly come to ruin once before, and Oliver made a point of remembering that the purposeful blindness and arrogance of the former Regis to the truth of their enemy's existence and intent was a huge factor in the community's near demise.

Oliver didn't believe that the Nephilim drug ring and the dead girl's murder were random, unrelated events, no matter what the chief believed. Something was going on, and as Regent he had to get ahead of it. It was his job to keep them safe. Their immortal lives were his responsibility, and soon their fate would be tied to his own.

It was a daunting prospect, and Oliver had had a few sleepless nights wondering if he was up to the task. He comforted himself with the knowledge that while he might have become used to the trappings of power, he had a pretty good ear for bullshit. It was one of the advantages of having been born mortal and something of an outsider in high school.

He returned his attention to the conversation in front of him. The curator was used to being interrogated by rich ladies with opinions, and while he was being respectful of Finn, there was a hint of condescension in his tone as they took in the sixth-floor space. Oliver decided it was time to step in and have a little fun. "Why can't we have the DJ set up in the other tent?" he asked, when Finn asked why the second tent, for the younger members' after-party, had not yet been approved. The plan was to have the Lester Lanin Orchestra play in the main tent, with a downtown DJ in a smaller one across the courtyard.

"The city has very specific noise ordinances," they were told. "And this is a very strict neighborhood."

"The mayor is a friend," Oliver said grandly. "Besides, when we begin construction on the new building, your neighbors won't be very thrilled, either."

The curator's smile froze on his face. "I will have the caterers set up the second tent immediately."

"Thank you, we appreciate it." Oliver smiled. He winked at Finn, who looked bemused. "Thank you for having us here today," he said in a tone that indicated the curator was dismissed.

When they were alone, they burst into quiet laughter. "Nice work. I thought he was going to faint when you told him to move the permanent collection," Finn said. "Oliver, do you think we're asking for too much? I mean—they're doing a lot to accommodate us. Maybe we should revisit our plans?"

"No, we should get what we want, shouldn't we? We're paying for it," he said. It was the way the world worked, after all. That much he understood from the beginning. As far as Oliver was concerned, they weren't spending *enough*. He would have preferred they had built a brand-new building just for the ball, the way the Coven had in the past. But the city was crowded, construction permits dragged, and he didn't want to wait another year. Besides, he liked the idea of having the party in the museum, surrounded by the things the Coven valued and prized—civilization, art, and high culture.

Only a few of the works that would be part of the exhibit had been hung. They stood in front of a large-scale photograph of a vast ninety-nine-cent store, the detergents on display a bright shade of red. "You know I started collecting when I was a freshman in high school?" he asked.

"You told me—a Warhol, was it?"

He nodded. "A drawing. At auction. I paid for it out of my allowance."

"Of course you did," she said with a faint smile. "Oh, look— there's Dad's stuff."

The first time he'd seen these paintings was in Finn's dorm room ten years ago. He had been drawn to them then, and now, arranged and exhibited in one of the most prestigious museums in the world, they were even more striking. Each and every one was of a beautiful and haunted girl, with blood dripping on different parts of her body, as wounds on her neck, tears on her face, or streaming down her torso.

Finn moved on to the next painting, but Oliver remained in place, transfixed by the red portrait. He looked closer at the surface of the canvas and noticed a small, five-inch hairline scratch in the blood, as if someone had taken a nail and scraped it. He studied the other paintings and found the same deliberate scratch on each one. Was it some kind of signature? It bothered him, although he didn't know why. But he didn't have time to think about it as Finn was waiting for him to catch up to her.

"Have you heard the latest?" she asked. "Since they can't prove that Allegra is dead, they've moved on to complaining that the museum and Overland are championing a dead artist instead of investing in young, emerging artists who are alive."

"But your father isn't the only artist in the exhibit. Ivy Druiz, Jonathan Jonathan, and Bai Wa-Woo are all alive," he said, still distracted by those long, odd scratches.

"They don't let facts get in the way of their editorials, that's for sure."

"Let them talk...it doesn't matter," he said. He turned back and looked at those empty white scrapes. "Finn—did you notice—" he said and pointed to the marks on one of the paintings. "What do you think that is?"

She leaned in for a closer look. "I don't know.... Wait—do you think it might be sabotage?" she asked, her voice rising. To his surprise, she was almost shaking and Oliver strove to soothe her. It took so little to rattle her these days. The stress of planning this party and mounting this exhibit was clearly getting to her, and Oliver wished once again he had never agreed to it.

"No, no...I think it's okay. I just thought it was strange. I'm sure it's nothing," he said, even though he had seen the paintings many times and had never noticed them before.

"You know Chris Jackson cornered me last week at the ballet opening and chewed my ear off about what a bad idea the ball is. She went on and on about how there's too much attention, bad press, and it's bad for the Coven," Finn said suddenly, her voice heated.

"Chris Jackson is a headache," said Oliver. From one of the finest New York families, and one of Manhattan's most visible social doyennes, Christina Carter Jackson was the head of the Committee, the Coven's organization that taught young vampires how to use their powers and live according to the Code. And one of the conclave's more vocal members. When Oliver had taken over as Regent, he had largely been accepted as one of them, even though he did not have their same pedigree and background. Although no one had ever publically questioned why the Almighty had bestowed the gift of immortality upon him, for a while there was talk that some might splinter off from the Coven. But so far, no one had done anything but grumble, and Chris was one of the loudest grumblers.

"You know that cliché, 'Keep your friends close and your enemies closer,'" she said. "But maybe she has a point?"

He turned to Finn. "Darling, do you not want to have this party?" Finn paled. "No...I..."

"I can handle Chris. The Venators are loyal to me," he said. It was a thorn in his crown, the fact that there was anyone who doubted him, doubted his fidelity to the Coven, doubted his leadership. He had given his mortal life to the Coven and would dedicate his immortal life to its safety forever. Sometimes he wondered if he had asked for the right thing—if his transformation had truly been a gift. Another old cliché came to mind, the one that said you get what you wish for.

Oliver stared at the painting in front of him. Allegra Van Alen was the age he was now. It was the one picture where Stephen had painted himself in the portrait as well. The two of them gazed out from the canvas, captured in their youth and beauty, radiant with love and happiness.

Finn rested her head on his shoulder. "We're just like them, don't you think?" she asked, loving and sweet once more.

He kissed her forehead. "Yes," he answered, but he found it odd that Finn would say that. Stephen and Allegra's love story was a tragic one. He died young, and she fell into a coma, and their child— Finn's half sister, Schuyler—had grown up alone, misunderstood and neglected, with only one friend to her name: Oliver. Unlike Sky, Finn had grown up away from the Coven, with no knowledge of the secretive vampire world. When he met her, he had immediately wanted her lightness and gaiety for his own. She was so *normal*, and he remembered their courtship as a respite from the growing darkness and full of ordinary things that young people did, like college keg parties and picnics in the park. When the time came, he had taken her as his human familiar, just as Allegra had taken Stephen as hers. But Oliver wanted more for himself and Finn than Stephen and Allegra had had, and he would do whatever he could to escape repeating the mistakes they had made, to forge a new future for them instead of following in the footsteps of their tragic past.

He stared at the portrait of the doomed Allegra Van Alen and wondered if she had truly found happiness and salvation at the end. In the corner was that strange white scar, almost unnoticeable unless one looked very closely. Why would someone take paint, or actually blood (though despite the rumors few people know it was exactly that), from the canvas? It was creepy to think that these canvases were covered in Stephen's blood, but a thought occurred to Oliver now: What if the reporters were right? What if Allegra's blood was in the paintings as well?

Angel blood.

The blood of the most powerful angel the world had ever known.

He shook his head. He was being paranoid.

Still, the trepidation he was feeling was starting to grow. Maybe as a survivor of the War, he knew the signs when they appeared.

That pentagram he'd seen in the glass doors of his building yesterday morning was still there. It was a pentagram all right, and the building staff apologized, but they couldn't seem to get it off. They were trying with several industrial cleaners, but nothing seemed to work.

He saw it again that morning, and Oliver had a feeling it would remain there until the Venators figured out exactly what it meant.

9 | OLD FRIENDS, NEW ENEMIES

*K*INGSLEY CAME BY ON Tuesday night after she got off work again, and they repaired to the same bar. He was wearing different clothes, and he had showered, which meant he had a place somewhere, a Venator safe house, maybe—he knew every one in the city. She managed to resist asking him where he'd been last night, and he didn't offer. He avoided any more talk of Hell's Bells and refrained from repeating his plea for help, even if it was clear from his presence that he needed her. Mimi hadn't decided if she would help him. She thought she would, but she also thought it would be fun to torture him a little. Let him beg. She just wanted him to admit he missed her. That he wasn't just asking for her help, that he wanted to spend time with *her*.

"What's your favorite thing about being back?" she asked.

"In New York? I don't know, everything's so different."

"Exactly."

"I like the new starchitect-designed buildings. It's great to see something new again, something eye-catching," he said.

She smiled. "Me, too."

She was still waiting for him to say something about the dead girl and Hell's Bells, but instead, he kept his cool, and at the end of the evening, he got up from his seat and tossed several twenty-dollar bills on the table so they fell on the leather-bound check cover.

"That's it?"

He raised an eyebrow.

"I mean...I thought you said you needed my help."

"Well, you don't seem very interested," he said.

He had a point there, but Mimi couldn't believe he was just going to walk away again. "So why'd you come by again? You're not even going to try to convince me?" she asked.

"What's the point? I could never get you to do anything you didn't want to do, not even when we were together," he said with a smile. "And is it a crime to spend time with my wife?"

It was what she wanted to hear, but she had a feeling he was just placating her. "Where are you going?" she asked, curiosity getting the best of her.

His cool gaze was maddeningly familiar. "Do you really think you can ask me that anymore?"

That Kingsley. In one breath he was calling her his wife and she was feeling everything for him again, and with the next he was pushing her away.

She flushed and would have let it slide, but that was their old pattern—before they were married: letting things slide, never being honest with each other about how they felt, doubting each other, distrusting each other. Marriage had changed that pattern. They had been loving, supportive, honest, and open—and bored, so terribly *bored*. Mimi felt the spark of a challenge, felt the passion she had felt the first time they had met, when he had been unknowable, his heart a mystery and closed to her. "I just thought..." She shrugged.

He raised an eyebrow. "Are you asking me to come home with you?"

She looked him square in the eye. "Yes." Why not admit it? It was what she wanted, and she wasn't afraid of telling him the truth. Maybe they could pick up where they left off, maybe they could start over again somehow—or maybe they could just have a little fun together. Why not? And maybe she would help him with the Coven, with that murder. Maybe.

Kingsley put on his jacket and thought it over. "Well, I don't see how I can refuse."

She tried to hide her smile of victory.

They walked out together into the dark of the city, and Mimi felt confident enough to slip her arm through his. He didn't flinch, but he didn't squeeze her arm affectionately like he used to, either, or take her hand and keep it warm in his jacket pocket.

"Nice digs," he said, when they arrived at her place. "You do look good in white." She lived in a white box in the sky—the loft was kitted out with white shag carpeting, white leather couches, white modern canvases on the white brick walls. Maybe it was a reaction to their former home, or maybe it was as Kingsley had said, she looked good in white, and so she had created the most flattering domicile for herself.

She took off her shoes and her feet sank into the soft white carpet. "Nightcap?" she asked, walking to the bar cart and picking up a bottle of his favorite Scotch.

"Sure," he agreed. He looked out the window for a while, at the lights and the cars on the West Side Highway: headlights making ribbons in the air, the taxis all bright yellow streaks. "New York, New York."

"So nice they named it twice," she said, handing him his glass. "Cheers!" She clinked hers to his and sat down on the couch.

Kingsley moved from the window to study her collection of paintings on the wall. "Interesting," he said, staring at the small brown square.

"It's one of our artists. Ivy Druiz. Her work is part of some exhibit they're having at the Modern for the Four Hundred Ball—a show called *Red Blood*—isn't that rich?"

He nodded and didn't seem to be too surprised to find out that the Coven was having a Four Hundred Ball again.

"You know who else is in the exhibit that I just found out?" she asked.

"Who?"

"Stephen Chase. All the paintings he did of Allegra are being featured. Sort of disgusting when you think about it. Painting her portraits and using his own blood in them."

Kingsley looked up at her. "Did he ever—Did he ever use *her* blood in his work?"

"Allegra's?" she asked. She thought about it. "I don't think so, no. Pretty sure it was all just his. Why?"

Kingsley looked relieved. "Nothing—I was just—Nothing." He lit a cigarette and she didn't protest, although she pointedly opened the glass doors to the balcony.

Then they heard it again, both at the same time. The bells.

"Shit, Kingsley, what are we going to do?"

"I don't know, but we have to do something." He stubbed out his cigarette and paced across the room; with his long limbs he looked like a cat, a black jaguar, sleek and graceful. "Helda told me there's a book that might help figure it out, one that holds all of the knowledge and history of Hell. It was stolen from her archives a long time ago, but she thinks there might be a copy in the Repository."

"And you trust her?" Mimi frowned. The queen of the underworld was a tricky, manipulative little wench. Helda and Kingsley shared power over their domain, but it was an uneasy alliance. "She lied to us once. How do you know she's not doing it again?"

"Maybe, but I can't exactly accuse her of lying," Kingsley said, holding up his arms in a helpless gesture.

"Isn't it always in some book?" she said with a dry smile. "Why not ask the Coven for help? Surely their historians would know something about it? If it's that important?"

"No!" he said, shocking the two of them with his outburst. He leaned back, shrugging. "I want to keep the Coven out of this for now."

"You're not going to warn them about the bells? Not even *Oliver*?" she asked. "I mean, I know I haven't gone to say hi or anything, but he was a friend of ours. Don't you think he deserves to know what's going on? He is Regent, after all."

Kingsley brooded and didn't reply.

"Oliver practically *saved* the Coven," Mimi pointed out. "He rebuilt it, contacted everyone who was left, made it what it used to be."

"I said no," he said sharply. "We can't tell him. We can't tell anyone in the Coven until we know what's really going on."

"Why not? Is there something you're not telling me?" she asked. "There is, isn't there? You know something about the Coven. You know who killed this girl."

Kingsley slumped back in his chair. "No, I don't," he said. "But I have my suspicions."

"What are they?"

He shook his head. "I can't say. Not until I'm sure."

"Not even to me?" she said petulantly. "I thought you said you needed my help."

"I do," he said. "But I'm also trying to protect you as much as I can."

"So you're going to break into the Repository, is that it?" she asked.

He shrugged. "Maybe."

"Well, whatever's going on, Oliver is innocent," she said loyally.

She liked and respected Oliver Hazard-Perry. They had been adversaries at first—okay, fine, she'd admit she wasn't very nice to him when they were teenagers. She had been cruel and thoughtless, and Oliver hadn't done much to help himself socially. He had been a nerd and Mimi the queen bee, but somehow they had become friends in the end, before she and Kingsley left for Hell. She had missed their friendship and had been planning on letting him know she was back, but she just hadn't gotten around to it yet. In any event, Oliver worshipped the vampires; it was why he had wanted to become one of them, because he wanted so much to be part of it. She didn't think Kingsley was right to doubt him, but she didn't feel like arguing with her husband, who could be stubborn.

"Well, if you're not going to tell me what's going on, why'd you even come here?" she asked, irritated now.

He smiled and put away his drink, his dark hair falling into his bright blue eyes, that slow smile of his making her melt a little. "Because you asked me to."

Damn it. He had her there. And it was getting late. They might as well get on with it. Mimi yawned casually and stood up. "Unzip me?" she asked, turning her back to him and lifting her thick hair above her neck so that he could reach the zipper on her dress. She waited, but he didn't move, and when she looked down, he was just sitting there, looking up at her with that smile on his face.

Finally, he stood up and placed a hand on her back, took the zipper and slipped it down slowly, so that his fingers brushed her skin, and she knew he noticed she wasn't wearing a bra. She waited for him to do something—she was practically offering herself up to him, waiting for him to make a move—and she was almost trembling from excitement and anticipation. "How about we have a little fun?" she whispered, her voice husky. "Celebrate our anniversary?"

"I don't think that's a good idea right now," he said, brushing his lips against her ear and sending shivers down her spine. "Good night, darling," he said and walked away from her toward the guest room.

Mimi held the dress against her chest, annoyed and exhilarated at the same time. So he was going to play that old game, was he? That old dance between them? Well, she hadn't forgotten the steps. She could dance, she could parry. She could pretend she wasn't feeling what she was feeling.

"Good night!" she yelled across the apartment, and when he turned around, she let the dress drop to the floor so he could take a good long look. "Don't let the vampires bite!"

10 | SURVIVAL OF THE FITTEST

*S*ITTING IN THE BACK of his town car, staring out at the city through the tinted windows, Oliver couldn't help but ruminate on the danger that lurked right below the hustle and bustle of metropolitan life. New York was a dangerous town, even without the Nephilim. He had just left a tiresome meeting with the city's mayor to discuss closing the streets surrounding the museum on the night of the Four Hundred Ball. The mayor hadn't been too happy about it, but he'd caved in the end. Oliver didn't like feeling like a douche, but it came with the territory. That was one of the parts of the position he could do without—the conclave meetings that droned on, and the petty trivial bickering behind the scenes were also atop that list.

But there were parts of his position he did relish, like hanging out with the Venators. As a mortal he'd had a healthy fear of their abilities, but as Regent, Oliver had developed a keen appreciation for their kind. A few years ago he had asked Sam to let him take the test. Just to see if he could pass. If he was going to send them into death and danger, he needed to know what they were up against, if he could do what they could. And so he had walked into dreams, had manipulated human minds, and had shown he could take control without abusing the ability. Sam had assured him he would have made it into the Venator ranks, as he had done well in the exam, and Oliver was proud of that accomplishment. It was good to see his old friends, too. He had never been especially close with Deming and Sam before the war, nor Edon for that matter, but it was good to see their familiar faces during the briefing yesterday. They were part of the team who had defeated Lucifer, and Oliver felt confident that they could do it again, that the hidden enemy—whomever or whatever it was—would not remain hidden for long.

The dead girl weighed hard on his conscience.

His mind churned with possible suspects. It had to be the work of a renegade, a lost and wounded soul, one who had succumbed to the temptation that throbbed below the surface of the Sacred Kiss. It was right there.

The ability to kill.

Life and death hanging in the balance.

It was so easy to tip the other way.

The miracle was that this had never happened before.

Chris Jackson was waiting for him in his office when he arrived back at headquarters.

"Chris." Oliver smiled tightly, trying to be gracious. "I'm sorry—I didn't know you were here. I hope you weren't waiting very long."

"Not at all," she told him. Christina Carter Jackson was as elegant and frosty as her impeccable designer suit and sharp black bob. She looked exactly like the cold-blooded barracuda she was, which meant she looked almost exactly like she did in high school. She ran with the fast crowd, the beautiful people, the teenagers who were hooking up with party promoters and movie stars at nightclubs like Block 122, while his presence was merely tolerated at school dances. He had a feeling that her obvious dislike for him stemmed from his own humble origins, that she took offense to his lofty position as Regent while she remained a mere conclave member.

Yet she had been an ally once, one of the most vociferous proponents for changing the Code to punish vampires for human abuse. *The mortals are of utmost concern*, she had said time and again. *Our survival depends on theirs. We are locked in a symbiotic relationship with them.*

On this point, she and Oliver firmly agreed. Vampires had written and shaped much if not all of human history. The mortal and the immortal world were bonded to each other in a million intractable ways. The Coven would not survive if the mortals discovered the truth of their existence. There were too many of them and too few of the Fallen, so keeping the mortals in fascination, fear, and admiration for their immortal brethren was key to the Conspiracy's success and the Coven's safety.

Oliver regarded her current opposition as a personal affront. He had counted on Chris to be an advocate, not a rival. When he had been elected Regent of the Coven, she could have been a contender for the position, but because of her ties to the former regime—the one that had been corrupted by Lucifer—she had decided to campaign *for* Oliver instead of run against him. Without her influence, he would never have ascended so high. He was perplexed and irritated by her inability to agree with him on the issue of the Four Hundred Ball, among other things.

"I hope you don't mind, but the fire in here is much more comfortable. Fletcher insisted I wait outside, but I made him come around to my way of thinking," she said with an icy smile.

"I don't mind at all," Oliver lied, making a mental note to can his assistant, who couldn't even keep an unwanted guest out of his office. He put his folders away in the file cabinet and took a seat at his desk across from her. "So what can I do for you, Chris?"

"It's such a shame about the Holy Heart girl. Do they have any idea who did it?"

"Not yet."

She fiddled with the pearls around her neck. "Do you think we'll find him?"

"I have no doubt."

"You really believe in Lennox, don't you?" she said with her alligator smile, the one that didn't reach her eyes.

"Why shouldn't I?"

"I suppose he was Kingsley Martin's man all those years. But I heard he's gotten soft... There was that incident with one of the new Venators not long ago... He showed a terrible lapse in judgment, I would say."

"It was taken care of," Oliver said, annoyed that the gossip had gotten out to the Coven at large. He had thought Sam had been able to keep it quiet, but it seemed Venators had big mouths just like everyone else. People thrived on gossip. "In the end there was no harm done to either party." Although try telling that to Deming, he thought, but kept silent.

"I'm sure. You know some in the conclave say he's been a little…unstable lately. Letting the noovs get a little out of hand. The Nephilim raid, for instance. Why was the compound burned? We could have gleaned information out of it."

"Sam felt strongly that it needed to burn, and he's the chief of police. It was a good call. The premises were cleansed so that nothing could survive," Oliver said, his voice as cool as the holy water that had burned down that demon hole. "Apologies for being blunt, but why exactly are you here, Chris?"

She crossed her legs and leaned forward. "You need to cancel the ball. As I told Finn the other day, this is wrong. It's not the right time for it; it brings too much attention, creates too much of a spotlight on us; it's so public—I think it might be the reason this is happening."

"This?"

"The dead girl," she said. "Our enemies attack just as we celebrate our victory. It's not a coincidence. This is the work of Lucifer's survivors. It has to be. Why are the Nephilim suddenly back in the city? They're crawling out of the shadows. There's a reason for it! We can't ignore it. They're planning something. It's just like Lucifer, to hit us just when we stopped worrying about him. Don't you remember what we learned from the War? *The greatest act of the devil was to convince people he didn't exist.* For hundreds of years the Coven kept its head in the sand and denied what was right in front of us. We discovered the truth almost too late."

"Lucifer is dead," Oliver said a little too forcefully. "His remains— what's left of them, anyway—lie in a blood-locked safe in the Repository. We *won* the War." He was irritated, even though what she was saying was exactly what he had said to the Venators earlier and exactly what he believed. But he wasn't about to admit it, especially to Chris Jackson, who only wanted to see him fail, to let the Coven know they had made a mistake in crowning him Regent and delay his investiture as Regis.

"I'm not going to call it off. It is ludicrous to show cowardice instead of strength, especially at this time."

"Not cowardly, cautious," she said. "Put off the party until we've found the killer."

"No," he said more forcefully than he had intended. Oliver smoothed his necktie, willing himself to remain calm, and not to allow her to see how scared he really was. Because what if what she was saying was correct? What if the Four Hundred Ball was the biggest mistake of his Regency? He was beginning to suspect that the party would be his downfall, he saw gloom and doom in every corner, and it made him furious to hear his secret fears articulated. Chris was wrong. Chris had to be wrong. The War was over and Lucifer had been defeated. There was nothing—absolutely nothing—to fear. Except his wrath, he thought. "I'm sorry, but no. The Venators have assured me that security at the party will be at maximum force; no one from outside the Coven will be able to get inside. We will be perfectly safe."

"But what if the danger is *inside?*" she said softly. "What if it's already here? Remember what happened the last time."

"How can I forget?" Oliver asked drily.

Finally, she bowed her head. "I didn't think you would agree," she said finally. "But I had to try."

"Is that it, Chris?"

"Well, if you won't listen to reason, I suppose I should go back to training the younger members."

"Thank you."

"Good day, Oliver," she said as she gathered up her gigantic handbag and headed for the door.

"Good day," he said to her back.

Oliver stood up from his desk and walked toward the bookshelves, which held his vast collection of classic books as well as a few photographs in sterling silver frames. He didn't keep very many from his past, but he did keep the one of himself and Schuyler from one summer on Nantucket. The two of them, sunburned, skinny, and young, ice cream running down their chins. Schuyler looked so much like her sister Finn in the photograph; at nine she'd had the same sunny smile, even a few of the same blonde highlights in her dark hair. He picked it up and set it down. Schuyler had not wanted to be part of the new Coven, had wanted peace and quiet after the War. She would have been the queen of the Coven had she stayed. He respected her wishes for distance from the past, and the two hadn't been in touch in some time. The last time they saw each other was at her college graduation, and that was almost seven years ago. Some days, he wished he, too, spent his days lolling in a vineyard, stomping grapes, and bottling vintages instead of carrying everyone's fate on his shoulders.

Sighing, he placed the frame back on the shelf, and a slip of paper fell from behind the photograph onto the floor. It was a note from Sky that he had always kept out of sentiment, the one where she told him she loved him and would always love him, friends forever, that he could come to her whenever he needed her, whatever happened to him. He was hit with a pang of loss, struck by how much he missed his old friend. He wondered what she was doing now, if she ever thought about him and Finn and worried about them. He bent down to pick up the note and noticed that the rug was slightly askew. As he knelt to straighten it, something caught his eye, something under the rug. A dark shadow that looked like dirt or paint. He pulled back the edge of the carpet to examine it more closely and the shadow grew and grew, finally revealing a dark shape.

A pentagram.

Burnt into the wood floor, its sinister outline was branded into the center of his office. He inhaled sharply. Someone or something was here. His inner sanctum. *How was that possible?* He felt his heart beating wildly in his chest. Chris Jackson had asked him just moments before in her raspy smoker's voice, what if they were already *inside? Just like before?*

Fletcher entered, looking rumpled and sheepish. Oliver quickly covered up the pentagram, putting the rug back in its place and smoothing out the bump with his shoe.

"Sorry, sir—she put a spell on me. She used to be a Venator, did you know?" Fletcher asked.

"I know."

"Everything all right, sir?"

Oliver didn't answer at first. He was recalling his conversation with Sam Lennox after the briefing, when they had discussed the pentagrams all over the city.

"Pentagrams amplify one's power, but there are other uses for them," Oliver had said. "Let's think it through."

"Well, traditionally in dark magic, pentagrams are used to call up a demon, to trap a dark spirit to do your bidding," Sam said.

"So whoever is doing this is trying to trap a demon?"

The Venator chief had sighed heavily. "Or let one out of Hell."

But Lucifer was dead. Schuyler had seen to that.

The greatest act of the devil was to convince people he didn't exist.

"Sir?" Fletcher asked. "You don't look well."

"I'm fine," Oliver said, stepping over the carpet with a smile. "Everything is fine."

11 | A NIGHT AT THE HOLIDAY

FAR DOWNTOWN, at a bar that Oliver used to patronize when he was a mortal teenager but not since moving up in the world, Ara sat on a creaky leather barstool and glowered at her full beer stein. She didn't want to be there—the place brought back too many bad memories—but Edon had made her.

The Holiday was an East Village landmark, harking back to the days when transgendered hookers, drug dealers, and poor artsy kids who might be one or both dominated the area. Manhattan today might be filled with slick, trendy watering holes that boasted arty "mixologists" who were obsessive about their custom cocktails, made with pureed fresh fruit, homemade bitters, and stovetop sugar syrup and priced in the double digits, but there was none of that at the Holiday.

It was a small, cheerful, shabby little bar, aptly named because it was Christmas year-round, with twinkling lights and garlands across the mantel. It was also owned by a witch who was privy to the vampires' secrets, which made it a safe haven and thus a go-to watering hole for off-duty Venators. The beer was cold, the chips were crisp, and if the bartenders didn't know your name, they were at least sympathetic to your problems.

"Mixologists my ass," one of them said as he pulled the tap, filling a frosty mug with a dark, rich brew and placing it in front of Edon. "We're slingers. We *slaaang draaanks*," he crooned.

Edon lifted his mug in acknowledgment and turned to Ara, who had yet to take a sip from her glass. "You all right?"

"I'm great," Ara said sullenly, her mind on the case. So far all the boys at Darcy's party had checked out—the Blue Bloods among them didn't match the blood signature on Georgina. But then that wasn't a surprise, as they were Coven members and the Venators already knew whoever killed her wasn't registered.

Ara should have been working, not drinking, but Edon had insisted they needed a break. "Do we have to be here?" she asked, raising her eyebrows at a bunch of noovs nearby using their crescent blades as darts and hitting the bull's-eye every time.

"Looks fun," Edon said, shrugging. "You've been a Venator how long? And you've never been here?"

"That's not what I said. I've been here. Many times." She glowered. Too many to speak of, not to mention that one particular night just the other month.

"Okay, then." He finished his drink in short order and another materialized just as quickly. More Venators entered—shuffling in a sea of black, greeting each other heartily, and calling out their drink orders—but none of them made their way to Ara, and most seemed to either avoid or deliberately ignore her. Nor did she wave any of them over, either. Ben Denham caught her eye and smiled, but she turned away from him without returning it. It was true, she didn't pal around much, and especially after what happened, she had a feeling she wasn't too welcome. Ben would find out the gossip about her soon enough and learn to avoid her, too.

"It's not such a bad thing to have friends, Scott, to have people who've got your back," Edon said, wiping the foam off his mouth with the back of his hand.

"Like the boys Deming asked you about?"

Edon nodded. "My brothers, yeah. When I'm done with whatever this is here, I'll go back to them."

"Back to keeping time."

"Someone has to," he said dismissively.

Ara sighed. She hadn't meant it as a dis; she was just trying to take her mind off the case. She could see it again even with her eyes open—the girl's neck, the twin deep, open wounds. She'd been savaged, not kissed, and the blood, so much blood... it was shocking to see how much blood one person could hold, could lose. A monster had done this to her. But vampires were not monsters. The notion that they were creatures to be feared, the devil's minions, was the work of the Conspiracy, to keep mortals from knowing the truth about their existence. Coven rules concerning behavior around and toward humans were even stricter now. Mortal life was more sacred to the Coven, and familiars were cherished more than ever.

Ara had yet to take a human familiar for her own, to perform the Sacred Kiss, the ritual sucking of blood. It was an intimate act, and the first time it was performed it would bind a vampire and a mortal for life—so she wanted to choose wisely. Human familiars were not necessarily romantic relationships, and in the past taking one's human familiar as a bondmate had been forbidden. But the practice was commonplace now, since so many vampires had lost their immortal mates in the War and its aftermath. The rules had changed out of necessity, and the Regent himself was about to take his familiar as bondmate. Rumor had it that it was only a matter of time before they made it official.

Speaking of intimate acts, her mind wandered to the last time she had been here, when she had been sitting at this same booth, but with a different person. It all got so murky—love and blood and sex and mortality.

"She probably thought it was fun," Ara said bitterly, voicing her thoughts. "Being chosen to be a familiar, having a vampire for a boyfriend. They all want one now, and we only have ourselves to blame. Fucking Conspiracy. I don't know who we think we're fooling."

"What about a wolf boyfriend?" Edon joked. "I heard we run hot rather than cold and tend to take our shirts off at every opportunity."

"You're not supposed to use someone so young, to bind them to you so early," she said, ignoring him.

Edon shrugged. "But people do it all the time."

"People suck."

"No, vampires suck," Edon said reasonably. He motioned to the bartender to pour another drink.

Ara remembered the trace memory on the blood she had licked—the girl's fear, the narrow tunnels—the girl knew she had been brought down there to die. She knew. She had died with her eyes open, screaming. Someone's little girl.

Meanwhile, in the back of the bar, someone else's little girl was lying across a table while vampires took turns sucking blood from a thin line on her exposed belly. She was willing and eager, and had pulled up her shirt to just below her bra, displaying a taut, toned abdomen. The vampires who surrounded her weren't Venators, and they weren't taking enough blood to bind her to them, just getting a taste and chasing it down with a slug of tequila. It was a party trick. A "bloody shot."

"Didn't take you for a prude," Edon said, when she grimaced in distaste.

"Why are we here, Edon?"

"Camaraderie."

She sniffed. "Right—because I'm so popular, as you can see."

"Why the bad blood between you and D?" he asked, as the woman in question stalked in and pointedly waved to Edon while snubbing Ara. They watched, somewhat admiringly, as the crowd parted for the beautiful Venator, and Deming was welcomed with open arms and loud exclamations of affection from the group of hard-boiled demon chasers. Ara felt a sharp pang of jealousy and had to tell herself that really *she* was the one who'd been wronged. She was the younger party, the innocent.

"You ever gonna fess up?" Edon prodded.

"You really look like that because you've been working under-cover?" she countered. "You know what I think? I think you work undercover because it's an excuse to look like that. Why aren't you with the wolves? What are you doing hanging out with us bloodsuckers?"

It was Edon's turn to glower and look away.

"Aha, so the wolf's got secrets, too."

"You don't know what you're talking about," he said quietly.

I know they said you were beautiful and golden and glorious, she thought. *And now you're a wiseass wreck with bad teeth.*

"They said we won the War," Edon said finally. "But mine was a hollow victory." He looked so crushed and so sad that she wanted to take back her teasing. She knew what it was like in the War's after-math, how much the victory had cost her. Sometimes, she wasn't even sure what they had won.

"I'm sorry," she said.

"It's all right, angel," he said, giving her his crooked yellow smile again, and his eyes crinkled in a way that made her heart jump, just a little.

Ara looked at him and then picked up her beer glass and downed the amber liquid in five gulps. "Damn it," she said as she slammed the glass back on the bar and she stood from her chair.

Fuck this. Fuck all this. Pentagrams all over the city, dead girls stuffed in dark holes, her partner's bleak sadness, and her own recent and tawdry past. It was too much to think about at the moment. She longed for oblivion, to forget for just a little while, and maybe those noovs had the right idea. "Come on, dog. Let's see if we can get one of those bloody shots."

12 | SPEAK, MEMORY

*K*INGSLEY WAS GONE when Mimi woke up the next morning. The apartment had a lonely, abandoned quality it didn't have before, with highball glasses left on the coffee table, her shoes strewn on the rug, along with her dress, crumpled and discarded. He hadn't left a note, not that she had expected him to. He always came and went as he pleased, even when they were married. It saddened her to realize she was thinking of their union in the past tense. Mimi tried to put it out of her mind for now, knowing he would show up when he wanted; he knew where to find her.

She tried calling Ivy's number again, but there was no answer, and the voice mail was full and not accepting any new messages. Mimi remembered that Ivy had a roommate, Jake Littman, a photographer who wasn't quite as successful as she was, but was nonetheless represented by Murray. She logged into the gallery's database to find his number and dialed. Jake told her he hadn't heard from her in a week or so, but that was Ivy. She did this, disappeared once in a while. "She'll turn up soon enough," he said. "Her mom told me she's been like this since she was a teenager."

Mimi explained that it was a little more serious this time—Ivy was expected at a patrons' dinner on Thursday evening, and the museum had been trying to reach her so that she could approve the copy they had written to describe her work.

"Okay, I just noticed her Twitter hasn't been updated since last

Sunday," Jake said, typing in the background. "Or her Instagram. That *is* weird. Ivy's an attention whore. Hmm. Now I *am* worried. Will you call me if she checks in?"

Mimi promised she would and went to work at the gallery. Murray was attempting to soothe an irate client who had called to complain that the price of a painting he'd purchased from them had sold at auction for much lower than he had paid for it, which of course Murray tried to explain was out of his hands; he advised clients to purchase art for love, not the fickle tastes of the art market. She shook her head at the nerve of some people.

"Dear Lord, I thought he would never get off," Murray said when he finally hung up the phone. "Why is it my fault? I didn't tell him to sell it!"

She asked him if he had heard from Ivy, and of course, he hadn't, either. "She'll turn up for the dinner," Murray said, fanning himself with a price sheet. "She never turns down a free meal. Artists!"

They had a shared chuckle over that, and Mimi went back to work, although it was hard to concentrate, distracted as she was, wondering what Kingsley was up to all day. He was somewhere in New York, but what was he doing? He was in deep with something, but he wouldn't tell her what it was, even as he so desperately seemed to need her help. His reckless and rebellious nature had been tamed by love and marriage, but Kingsley had a wild streak in him and could go off the edge. What had he gotten himself into this time? And why didn't he trust the Coven?

Mimi had never been the kind of girl who waited by the phone, and she was annoyed to find she kept waiting for Kingsley to turn up.

When he finally did at the end of the day, she was more than a little huffy. He offered no explanation for his actions, as usual. But he seemed more cheerful than the night before. "Hello, darling. Miss me?"

She snorted. "What's going on now?"

"I read the book. New headquarters is something else, isn't it?"

Mimi was impressed despite trying not to be. Not many people could break in and out of the Repository as if it had a rotating door. "So?"

"But the page I need is locked, and I can't read it without your help," he said with a broad grin.

She crossed her arms across her chest. "Really."

"Well, are you coming or not?" he asked, walking away.

After hesitating for only a brief moment, she followed him, motioning to Donovan to cover the phones.

Kingsley led her to a small coffee shop, where he ordered his usual tall latte with an inordinate amount of sugar. "So, where's this book?" she asked.

"In here," he said, pointing to the side of his head.

"Come again?"

"The book, *Arcana de Inferno*, it's here," he said, tapping again. Of course, he was talking about the vampire sight, the photographic memory that was part of their supernatural abilities. Truth was, Mimi rarely read anything beyond *Vogue*, and there was no reason to recall the articles verbatim, even if the fashions were sealed in her memory.

Kingsley stirred his coffee slowly. "I didn't have much time, so I just scanned the whole thing. But now we can take our leisure inside my memory palace to read it."

She nodded, relieved he had been working instead of carousing. A "memory palace," Mimi knew, was a mnemonic device used to preserve and improve memories. It had been popular practice during Greek and Roman times, as a way to replicate what the vampires did naturally, without even thinking.

"Let's go down the rabbit hole," he said.

"Right now? Here?"

"They won't notice. We'll be back in a second," he said and reached across the table to hold her hand.

Mimi supposed she didn't have a choice, and after a moment's hesitation, she looked deep into his eyes and slipped easily back into the shadow world, the world where Venators walked into dreams and read minds, where they could access another's memories. All these years together, and she had never been inside his mind, and part of her was like a kid in a candy shop, excited to finally be privy to all of his secrets, to his dark dreams and twisted ambitions. She fully expected it to be a full-time bacchanalia or resemble a hazy opium den. He might've turned into a boring homesteader in Hell, but Kingsley had lived a thousand lives on earth, chock-full of excitement and wickedness. So she was surprised and a bit touched to find that the inside of his mind was like stepping into a cramped apartment full of books. He was being too modest—there were hundreds, if not thousands and thousands of books in here, and she picked her way carefully through the ziggurats of hardcover tomes.

"Over here," he called, waving from the open doorway that led up to a spiral stairway.

She followed him but hesitated, hearing music through a closed door on the other side of the room. The melody was familiar, and she was drawn to it, feeling a mixture of dread and curiosity. She turned away from him and toward the sound instead. When she reached the door and peered through the peephole, she was not surprised to discover a vision of the two of them on their wedding day. This was his memory of that moment. They had forsaken a big wedding and had exchanged vows with only each other as witnesses. Mimi stood watching for a while, entranced by the sight of the two of them, how happy they looked. She remembered the words he had whispered in her ear that day, and what she had said in return, and how her breath caught in her throat for a moment when she saw the light shining in his eyes.

"Hello?" Kingsley—the real Kingsley—called from upstairs.

"Coming!" she called back, wrenching herself away from their past, her heart racing, and as she ran toward him, she saw something else, something hovering in the hallways of his mind—an image that would haunt her later. For now, she attempted a casual smile.

"Snooping?" he asked pointedly.

"Don't flatter yourself," she said.

He smiled to let her know he still found her sharp tongue amusing. "This is where I keep the rare and important books," he told her, motioning to a tidy bookshelf where the books were arranged by color, from pale to dark, a rainbow of spines. Kingsley drew out the first book on the highest shelf. It was white with gold lettering on the front. Upon closer inspection, the gold embossing on the cover also showed a serpent with a forked tongue coiled around a gate. Mimi recognized that gate. It was the one that kept souls trapped inside the underworld.

The book contained all the knowledge of the underworld, the history of Hell, the secrets lost to Time. It would tell them why Hell's Bells were ringing and what kind of monster had been unleashed from the abyss. Or so they hoped.

"What is it?" Mimi asked, when she saw the page Kingsley had opened to. It was completely white, with nothing on it. "It's blank."

"Because only the Angel of Death can unlock the secret of this page. The last page in the book of Hell."

Mimi knew what to do. She removed her sword and made a small cut on her wrist, letting her blood bleed on the page. It absorbed it, and the paper was awash with her sapphire-colored blood, until the page revealed words in the Sacred Language of Angels.

In morte vita est. Regulus Mane resurget.

In death is life. The Little King of the Morning will rise again…

Underneath the writing was a silver pentagram.

"Kingsley, what is going on?" she asked, with a feeling of dread and dark premonition as he bound her wrist with a bandage he removed from his pocket. He was prepared as always.

But Kingsley shook his head to indicate he wanted to concentrate as more words were appearing, dark words of a dark prophecy, and together they began to read.

Mimi opened her eyes. They were still sitting in the same coffee shop. Only seconds had passed since they had entered Kingsley's memories. He opened his eyes more slowly than hers and released her hand. His face was troubled and grave. She remembered his face on his wedding day, his laughing eyes, his soft, fervent declaration of eternal love. She wanted to tell him that she regretted every moment away from him, and sitting across from him right then, watching the shadows fall on his face, she wanted nothing more than to take it all back. There had to be some way to fix what was broken between them, a way for them to be together without giving up her own life. There had to be. They couldn't just give up on each other.

"Kingsley…," she said, then remembered the other image she had seen—and her doubts returned, just as quickly brushing away any thoughts of romance or reconciliation for now. They had a lot to sort out, and on some level Mimi knew this conversation, this mending of their relationship, couldn't be rushed.

"Yes?" he asked, busy writing notes on his napkin. He was translating a few more sentences from the page they had just read.

"Never mind," she said, just as he shoved the napkin across the table to show her what he'd written.

In death is life. The Little King of the Morning will rise again as the White Worm brings eternal darkness to poison the gift of the Heavens.

"There's no mention of Hell's Bells?" Mimi asked.

"Hmm, that is odd," he said. "But the Little King of the Morning is the Prince of Heaven, Lucifer, of course, the Morningstar, the Lightbringer."

"What's his white worm, though? A worm on the loose in the city? Like alligators in the sewers?" She smiled.

Kingsley smiled. "*Worm* is a common name for devil, demon. Which means it could be anyone—a dark angel bent on revenge," he said. "A demon loyal to Lucifer who seeks to avenge its fallen master."

" 'In death is life,' " she mused. "But Lucifer is dead. Schuyler fulfilled her prophecy. There's no way for him to return. He's gone."

"Or so we believe," Kingsley whispered.

"We saw it with our own eyes," Mimi said. "We won the War." Hadn't they? Or was their victory so short-lived?

"Yes," he said, troubled. "But what if we missed something? What if there was something else?" He stared down at his glass, and when he looked back up at her, she saw the pain and sadness in his eyes from the first day he had sought her company. He needed something from her—he was guilty of something, but she didn't know what—and if he didn't tell her, then she wouldn't be able to help him. She wanted to tell him he could trust her, she would be there for him, but the words were caught in her throat.

"Kingsley..."

"No. I'm sorry. I made a mistake. I shouldn't have bothered you with this. It's too dangerous. I should never have involved you," he said, looking at her mournfully. Then his face changed, and his jaw was set, and Mimi felt suddenly afraid.

He stood up from the table with an apologetic smile. "Don't worry about me, darling, you know I can take care of myself. Thanks for the help with the book."

"But—" she said. *But what about us?*

Was this good-bye? Truly? If Lucifer was back to menace the Coven, didn't he need her help? Wasn't that why he had sought her out in the first place?

What was holding him back?

Mimi wondered if she should call out after him and ask him where he was headed. But his words from the other evening rang in her ear. *Do you really think you can ask me that . . . ?*

She had left him and so she had no right to ask him anything. No right or claim to him at all. And so she watched him walk away without knowing when she would see him again.

13 | THE SECOND WORST

*T*HE BANGING WAS *NOT* IN HER HEAD, Ara realized, even though it sure *sounded* like it was in her head, because she could *feel* her head throbbing, but that heavy thumping that had escalated to a barrage was actually the sound of a fist knocking on her door. She dragged herself out of bed and opened the door a crack to find a pale yellow eye staring back at her. She jumped back. "Edon, what the fuck? I'm off duty," she groused, unlatching the chain and letting him inside. He was holding a brown paper bag and two cups of coffee in a cardboard carrying tray.

"Venators are never off duty. Haven't you learned that by now?" he asked, entering the room and shoving one of the coffees her way.

She accepted it, took a sip, and was glad to find it was made with a copious amount of milk and sugar. "Thanks," she said, shutting the door behind him.

Edon took a slurp from his cup and looked her up and down as he dug into the bag and pulled out a cruller. "Maybe you should think about putting some clothes on?"

Ara looked down and realized she had answered the door wearing only her black tank top and underwear. "Didn't take you for a prude," she mimicked. She walked toward the alcove where the bed was hidden and rescued a pair of sweatpants from a dirty pile on the floor. "What?" she asked, when she walked back to the main room to find Edon shaking his head at her.

"God, Scott, you really tied one on last night, huh?"

"What do you mean? Ouch, my head hurts," she groaned, closing her eyes.

"You're having what the mortals call a hangover. Comes from drinking too much alcohol. Told you to drink some water with each cocktail, but you wouldn't listen."

"Alcohol isn't supposed to affect vampires," she said, rooting through the brown paper bag he had brought and picking out a jelly doughnut. It was sticky and sugary and exactly what the doctor ordered.

"Riiight." Edon clicked his tongue. "What other fairy tales do you believe in? Santa? Easter bunny? No, tell me, I'm curious."

"Shut up! It's common knowledge that vampires can eat and drink whatever we want and it doesn't affect us."

"Seen Lennox lately?"

"So he's gained a few," Ara said. She thought about it and wondered if Edon might have a point—and if so, maybe having another doughnut wasn't the best idea. Then she decided she didn't care; she had other, more important things to worry about than what she ate. "I've never had one before. A hangover, I mean. I see why mortals complain about it all the time. It's awful."

"Maybe you've never had so much to drink before," he said reasonably. "You *were* putting them away last night."

"Or maybe there was something else in the drinks?" she asked.

"Or maybe you're just a lightweight."

"Fuck you."

"Gladly."

She stared at him, a half-eaten doughnut shoved in her mouth, speechless for once and unsure of how to respond. It had been a while since anyone had noticed she was a girl, and the last time it had happened hadn't turned out all that great for her, come to think about it.

"I'm kidding. Don't get too excited. You're not my type." He wiped the edges of her lip with a napkin, showing her that it was caked with powder. "Where's the garbage?" he asked, balling up the bag and his empty coffee cup.

"Over there," she said, motioning to a dark corner of the galley kitchen.

Edon opened the garbage bin and made a face. "Jeez, think

about cleaning up a little, will you?" he said, as he pulled the overflowing trash bag out of the can, pulled the corners up, and tied them together. He moved to the sink and began to wash the dishes, running hot soap and water over the crusted pots and pans. "How long have these been in here? You're lucky you don't have bugs."

"Go ahead, make yourself at home," she muttered. "I'm going to take a shower."

When she came out of the bathroom, he had taken out the garbage, wiped down the counters, stacked the dishes, and was kneeling on the floor wiping down the linoleum. He looked up at her and showed her the huge ball of gray fuzz he had peeled from the walls. "This is disgusting. It's called being a grown-up, Scott. Try it sometime. You live like an animal. What are you, depressed or something? This is not a sign of a healthy mind."

"Tough talk from a wolf," she said grimly, even if his shot had hit the mark. She had been feeling a little low, she thought, and had sort of let things slide around here since...well...she didn't want to think about it. Her apartment was so much nicer now that it was clean. Edon was a puzzle. He looked like a deadbeat, but he obviously didn't live like one.

"Wolf dens are cleaner than this cesspit. If we're going to work together, you're going to have to keep a better house," he scolded, putting away the dustpan and the broom. "You don't even own a vacuum. Not even a handheld."

"Edon, why are you here, by the way? It's our night off. Unless you're freelancing as a maid on the side."

He looked sheepish. "Sorry. Chief found out what we were up to last night—" he said. "And he wants to see you in his office."

"Shut the door," Sam said, closing the venetian blinds on the interior windows so they could have privacy. Ara noticed a few of her colleagues shooting curious glances her way, and she flushed. She would never live down the past, and she hated the fact that there was now this awkwardness between them.

"What's up, Chief?"

Sam perched at the end of the table. "I'm disappointed in you, Ara."

She felt the flush on her face turn to a burn.

"I understand you guys need to let off some steam, but trashing a bar, harassing humans, and passing out is not condoned by this office." He coughed into his palm. "Bloody shots?"

"It was all in good fun," she said sullenly. Everyone else was doing it that night—even the untouchable Deming Chen, she wanted to add, but didn't.

"Right." He sighed. "If a witch didn't own the Holiday, we'd be in trouble. But thankfully she's the understanding type."

"Like you," she said.

He frowned. "Look, after everything that happened, I can't give you any breaks, Ara, and you know exactly why. Besides, your record is abysmal," he said, picking up a folder with her name on it. It was her Venator file, which included every infraction she had ever committed against the rules of the Coven. "Death Walks. Dream intrusion. Disrespecting a commanding officer. Noncompliance with standard safety procedures. Another black mark and you'll be kicked off the team. I won't be able to shield you this time."

"Yes, sir," she said, saluting him.

Sam sighed. "So far, what you've got is the second-worst conduct record in the history of the Venators."

"Who was the worst?" she asked, honestly curious.

"Kingsley Martin," he said with a hint of a smile. His former commander. Another legendary hero. Ara had quite enough of those.

"All right, get out of here."

She did.

14 | REGRETS ONLY

*T*HE LONG TABLE WAS SET IN A ROOM right off the garden, so
that the French doors looked out onto a beautiful landscape
and twinkling lights, which were complemented by the delicate floral arrangements, exquisite white roses and green pea tendrils in
square vases dotted by small tea light candles. The crystal and silverware gleamed, the linen napkins were folded and starched, and the
group—an exclusive and elite group that ran not only the Coven, but
the city at large—was laughing and smiling over champagne glasses.
Oliver caught Finn's eye in the center of the glamorous bunch, a wil-
lowy collection of New York's most beautiful art enthusiasts.

"What's wrong?" he asked when he saw the lines crinkle around
her eyes.

"Nothing, nothing…" Finn smiled brightly.

"Let me guess, Ivy hasn't shown up," he said.

Finn nodded.

"Maybe she's late," he said. "You know how artists are. Divas. And
from what you've told me, Ivy has a bigger ego than most."

It was a private dinner for the artists who were part of the *Red
Blood* exhibition thrown by their Blue Blood patrons. Everyone was
there: Jonathan Jonathan in his trademark plaid suit, Bai Wa-Woo
in a dress that looked like it was made of Big Bird's yellow feathers,
even ninety-year-old Hershel Song, the most seasoned and arguably
the most famous artist in the collection.

"Yes, you're right, that must be it," Finn said.

"She'll show up," he said. "You told me yourself she's flighty, and you only added her at the last minute because she begged to be included." Oliver was trying not to feel too agitated himself. Finn was a little touchy when it came to Ivy, who was a friend of hers from college—from her life before the Coven—something Finn kept reminding him of.

"Yes, of course, it must have just slipped her mind," Finn agreed. "This is so embarrassing, though."

"Let me talk to him." Oliver walked over to Murray Anthony, who was stuffing his face with little crab cakes.

Murray smiled at him nervously. "I know, I know. I'm sorry. I tried—we've been trying to track her down for days now. The museum wants to talk to her, too."

"Anything wrong? Does she not want to be in the exhibit? With all the controversy?" Oliver took a glass of champagne from a passing tray. He knew the flowers—roses, deep in bloom—were supposed to smell wonderful, but he smelled nothing. One day he would ask the Coven doctors what was wrong with him.

"No—you know Ivy doesn't bother with gossip and the tabloids. She loves a party."

"Find her, then."

"Will do. She'll be at the opening for sure," Murray assured, even though he looked as if he didn't believe it himself.

Oliver went back to Finn, who looked decidedly ill. "Oliver— about Ivy, there's something you need to know—"

"Yes?" he asked, distracted by the sight of Sam Lennox entering the party suddenly. The chief never came to these things. Something must be up. "Hold on, sweet..."

He made his way toward Sam but was interrupted by Chris Jackson barreling toward him. She greeted him with air-kisses on both cheeks. "What a wonderful party," she said. "Finn outdid herself. Is she all right? She looks a bit pale."

"She works too hard," Oliver said shortly. "I don't know what I would do without her." He returned her tight smile. This was the world he was part of, one in which empty smiles hid dark hearts. Outwardly his face was placid, but inwardly he was haunted by the image of the pentagram on his office floor. How long had Chris been in his office the other day? Was her visit a warning? A way to tell him that *she* was the one *inside*? And if she had been the one to do it, what did she want? And why kill a mortal girl to get it? What was her agenda?

"Well, I just wanted to say hello as I can't stay," she said. "It's the opening night of the symphony as well."

"Now who has a busy schedule?" Oliver smiled. "Good to see you, Chris. Excuse me," he said, finally making his way to the chief. Sam looked out of place in the beautiful room; his suit was shabby, and he looked older and grayer than ever.

"We've had a security breach," Sam said, without waiting for pleasantries. "None of the alarms were set off and the cameras didn't pick up anything, but I'm convinced someone broke into the Repository."

Oliver kept his calm. "How can you be sure?"

"There are a few seconds missing on the time stamp. Like some-one messed with it or caused it to skip. And here's the thing. It's happened before but we only noticed it now. We went through the records, and there are several unaccounted moments."

"What did they take?"

"That's the thing. Nothing. We can't figure it out. Nothing's miss-ing. We had all the clerks go through the archives. Everything is where it should be."

He frowned. "What do you recommend?"

"Lock and fortify."

"If we go into lockdown, whoever's behind this will know we're on to them," Oliver said, considering his options. "We can't show our hand just yet. Do everything you can, but do it quietly."

"There's another thing. We found another body."

"Mortal?"

"Yeah. Bitten. Just like the other one."

"Where?"

"Out by Fort Greene, not far from where we busted that Neph hive the other week. Another young girl. We're IDing her now. We've got a killer out there. Serial from the looks of it."

Oliver cursed. "Do you think they're related? Was there a pentagram?"

Sam nodded. "Big and bloody. We're keeping this one quiet for now. You still planning on performing the ritual at the ball?" he asked. "The investiture?"

Oliver nodded. "Yes. At midnight. The center of the museum will be cleared for the stage, and Finn and I will be in the green-room right before and then I'm to make a grand entrance Finn has orchestrated down to the last detail."

"We're going to have to double up on the Venators," Sam said. "I called in a few more from overseas. They'll be here by Saturday."

"Sam, so good of you to join us," Finn said, coming between the two men and putting a hand on Oliver's arm. "Are you staying? I'll have them set another place."

The Venator chief shook his head and looked uncomfortable. "No, ma'am, I'll be heading out in a bit. Just had some news to share with the Regent. Thank you, though."

"Well, you're more than welcome to stay," she said warmly.

"Thank you," he said.

They watched as Finn floated to the other guests. "You're a lucky man," Sam said to Oliver.

"Don't I know it." Oliver sighed.

"Some of us—Some of us aren't so lucky." Sam sighed, and Oliver knew that he was thinking of his life before the War. He clasped his friend's shoulder and squeezed it in sympathy.

"We all made sacrifices," Oliver said.

"Some of us more than others," Sam replied. But he gave Oliver a wry smile and left the party without further comment.

When Oliver walked inside the dining room, Finn was standing at the head of the table. In the candlelight, her beauty glowed, and Oliver felt a surge of pride. Finn made his life possible; she smoothed the relationships and the rough edges created by his position; she urged him to listen to people, to keep his mind and heart open. As for those who resented her high place in the Coven, especially snobs like Chris Jackson, he couldn't care less. Finn caught his eye before speaking, and he winked at her to let her know she had nothing to worry about. She had this.

"My dear friends," Finn began. "Thank you all for coming today to celebrate our upcoming *Red Blood* exhibit. One of the greatest mandates of the Overland Foundation is to promote the vibrant cultural and intellectual life of the city. All the artists in this collection work with blood in interesting and intriguing ways that allow us to more deeply appreciate our own mortality," she said with a knowing smile reserved for the vampires in the group. "My father, Stephen Chase, was an artist who used blood in his own paintings to display the fragility of the human condition, and it brings me great honor today to know that his paintings will soon be enjoyed by all."

After the applause had died down, Finn introduced each artist at the dinner, who spoke briefly about their work.

Once everyone had made their remarks, she stood up again. "And lastly, I would like to say a few words about Ivy Druiz, who I am very sorry to say cannot be with us today due to a personal conflict, but her gallery manager, Murray Anthony, is here to answer any questions. Murray assures us Ivy will be with us during the Four Hundred Ball and the opening of the exhibit. I have been drawn to Ivy's work for years, and I admire her passion for women's lives and troubles. It's a real testament of her courage and conviction to create art that gives voice to the voiceless, that finds meaning in our everyday traumas. Thank you for joining us, and here's to a life-changing Four Hundred Ball! To the artists!"

Glasses raised, crystal clinked, and the dinner party began in earnest with the delivery of the first course—a blood orange salad in a balsamic vinaigrette. Finn slid into a seat across from Oliver and whispered, "Did I do all right?"

"Perfectly," he assured. "Life changing?"

She laughed. "I really want the ball to be special."

"It will be," he said, nuzzling her cheek. "Wait till you see what I have planned."

The rest of the evening went as well as it could, with a few conclave members getting a little tipsy from the blood wine, and everyone staggering out to an uncommonly mild autumn night. Exhausted, but satisfied that the night went as well as it could, Oliver and Finn finally repaired to the limousine waiting for them by the sidewalk.

When they were alone, he told Finn what Sam had told him about the second fatality, the body the Venators had found in Brooklyn. "Maybe we *should* cancel," she said. "Maybe Chris is right. Maybe it's not time for a party."

Oliver sighed. He hadn't told Finn about the pentagram he'd found in his office or the one he saw tagged on their building the other morning, as he didn't want to add to her worries.

"No, the ball is in two days, you'll look ridiculous," Finn said, changing her mind when she saw the look on his face. "Chris Jackson is a frightened woman trying to scare you, make you doubt yourself. Show them your strength. Show them they can't destroy us. We can still have the party while we keep investigating and bring this killer to justice."

He loved her passion and ferocity. *Finn would make a wonderful vampire*, he thought. *Except that it's impossible, and so she will die, and when that happens I will mourn her forever.*

He brought her hand to his lips, planting a line of soft kisses, slowly from her wrist, up to her elbow, and past, until he reached her neck. She sighed and reached for him as well, bringing him closer to her so that she was almost on his lap. She turned to him with a sly smile, and Oliver raised the partition that separated them from the driver. Unbuckling his seat belt and hers, he laid her lengthwise on the seat of the car and slipped the straps of her dress off her shoulders.

"Darling, do you ever regret it?" he asked as he carefully undressed her. He unhooked her bra with one hand and took a moment to congratulate himself on that.

"What?" she breathed as their lips met, and she pulled his shirt out of his pants and began to unzip.

"All this...me," he whispered as he moved on top of her.

"Regret you?" she asked, just as he thrust his body into hers, and she shivered, drawing her knees around his waist.

"Yes," he said, his voice tight, as he rocked against her.

"Why would I do that?"

"If you had never met me, you wouldn't be part of the Coven, privy to its dark secrets." *You wouldn't be in danger from our enemies*, he thought, but couldn't admit it out loud, not yet. *They would hurt you to get to me.* The mortal body count was climbing. Instead he told her, "You would be safe. You would be—"

"—lost without you." Finn looked deep into his eyes and placed both her hands on his cheeks. "You are my life."

I have made it so, Oliver thought. *You don't have a choice anymore.* And with that thought, he sank his fangs deep into her skin, and soon they were both shuddering in ecstasy.

15 | SYMPHONY FOR THE DEVIL

*M*USIC WAS ANOTHER THING SHE'D MISSED, living in the underworld. Mimi had never been much of a fan when she'd lived on this side of the Gates of Hell, but after ten years underground, where cacophony ruled and dissonance was the only sound she could pick up on her radio, it was a relief and a pleasure to listen to music again. She had made a habit of visiting Lincoln Center to catch the New York Philharmonic, and the night after Kingsley had bid her good-bye, she was seated in her family's old box in the theater. Murray left the patrons' dinner early to join her, and they shared glasses of champagne in the lobby, admiring the newly renovated plaza (even though it was years old now, it was still "new" to Mimi) before heading inside for the performance.

"How was the party?" she asked, when he arrived.

"You know what they say, *the rich are bloodsuckers,*" Murray joked.

Mimi laughed as they made their way to their seats, thinking, *If he only knew.*

Settled in the plush velvet chairs, Mimi felt the anticipatory rush of the crowd moments before the show began. She wasn't a music snob; she was not one to prefer the obscure or the rare. For instance she had once fallen asleep to *Parsifal,* one of the more difficult-to-appreciate Wagner operas. She much preferred the Ring cycle or something even more pleasurable—*The Barber of Seville, The Magic Flute, La Bohème.* Her taste for classical music was the same as her preference for the well-known operas. She enjoyed Beethoven and Tchaikovsky and had once swooned to a particularly lovely performance of Ravel's *Bolero* that had made a memorable impression upon her soul. Tonight the orchestra was performing her favorite, Mozart's *Requiem.*

She let the music carry her away from her troubles, her worries about her absent husband, and whatever was happening with the Coven and Lucifer's worm. She had to admit, she was pulled into it, even if she had resisted at first. She thought she had no more desire to save the world, and yet there it was.

The conductor was waving his baton, and she followed the graceful flow of the music, the audience as attentive as she had remembered it. As a child her father had admonished her for being unable to sit still. During the coughing break, when the audience took the opportunity to clear their throats and unwrap their mints, the *crinkle, crinkle* of the foil was as effective as Proust's madeleine cookie as a gateway to her childhood. It was all there.

At intermission, she and Murray repaired to the mezzanine for more drinks. It was a practice she'd learned from her parents, who took her to the opera, the symphony, and the theater and took a glass of champagne before, during, and after the performance. When she was younger, she had looked forward to being old enough for the drinks. Now that she was older, she found she enjoyed the music more, but she continued the practice because it reminded her of being young and of her parents, who were gone now. They took their champagne flutes nearer the windows to watch the fountains dance on the plaza.

"Why, if it isn't Mimi Force," a cold voice said right behind her.

Mimi turned to see a slim, dark-haired woman in an impossibly chic cocktail dress appraising her with a cool gaze.

"So good to see you. It's Mimi Martin now," Mimi said automatically as she tried to recall the woman's name. She let the woman kiss her on both cheeks as she searched her memory.

"This is Murray Anthony," Mimi said, introducing her friend to the stranger, using an age-old party trick to cover up her ignorance.

"Christina Jackson," the woman said, offering her hand. "Didn't I just see you at the dinner at the Modern?"

"Yes, I represent one of the artists," Murray said, happy to have been recognized.

For her part, Mimi remembered her as well. Chris had been one of the women who ran the Committee with Priscilla DuPont back in the day. In fact, she looked like she hadn't aged since, and Mimi chalked up her inability to place her as just part of living alone with Kingsley in the underworld for a decade.

"Pleasure," Murray said. He downed his glass in one shot. "I'll grab us another," he told Mimi, exiting stage right.

"When did you get back to the city?" Chris asked.

"This summer," she said.

"You haven't registered with the Coven."

"My bad." Mimi shrugged.

Chris tapped her finger to her cheek. "I'm surprised the Venators haven't taken you in for questioning. They're very serious about rounding up renegades."

"Right." Mimi laughed weakly.

"I suppose you're here for the Four Hundred Ball."

"I wasn't aware I was invited," Mimi said.

"Now don't be silly. It's going to be quite a party."

Mimi craned her neck over her shoulder, pointedly giving Chris the signal that she was bored with this conversation. "How is everything with the Coven?"

"You know, everything changes and nothing changes," Chris said. "Wasn't the last Four Hundred Ball your coming-out?"

"I think so, I'm not sure," Mimi said, although she remembered her dress well. "How is the new crop of debutantes and their dates?"

Chris smiled thinly. "Rambunctious, as usual."

"And Oliver? How is the Coven faring under his leadership?" Mimi asked, because she had a feeling Chris wanted her to.

"He should take better care. Did you hear about the girl they found in the sewers?"

"Mortal, was it?" Mimi asked, pretending she didn't know very much.

"Yes. I told the Regent that it might be a good idea not to have a Four Hundred Ball at this time."

"And what did Oliver say?"

"He said it wasn't a time to show weakness."

"Understandable."

"The Regent is putting the Coven at risk," Chris said, fingering the necklace around her throat and looking at Mimi meaningfully.

"He's forgotten what it was like to be mortal. Perhaps someone should remind him that not even vampires are indestructible."

It was then that Mimi noticed that the charm hanging from Chris's link necklace was that of a serpent. A white gold serpent, with emerald chips for eyes, the color of Lucifer's Bane, the stone that was lost during the War. She knew the stone well, as she had once worn it herself, and only Kingsley had been able to destroy it and set her free. But it looked like someone had picked up the pieces, and she felt a shock to see it again so soon after the War. It was as if Lucifer were mocking her.

Chris squeezed her arm to bid her good-bye and disappeared into the crowd.

"Who *was* that?" Murray asked, returning with the drinks at last, just as the bells pinged to warn the audience to return to their seats. "She gave me the shivers. When I shook her hand, it felt like a shadow walked over my grave."

No, Mimi thought, not like a shadow, more like a snake, a worm. A viper with a warning on her tongue. *The Regent is putting the Coven at risk. He's forgotten what it was like to be mortal. Perhaps someone should remind him that not even vampires are indestructible.*

Murray wasn't the only one with shivers, as Mimi recalled a certain fact. Christina Carter Jackson was Forsyth Llewellyn's sister.

Forsyth, the traitor to the Coven; the one who had almost brought it to ruin; Forsyth, who was Lucifer's most trusted lieutenant.

16 | SAFE HOUSE

$\mathcal{T}$HEY SHOULD BE TOLD that their daughter is dead," Ara said, as she waited for Edon to pay for his coffee late on Thursday evening. "It's not fair to them, not knowing. Not knowing is worse than knowing."

"Haven't you heard that ignorance is bliss?" Edon asked, handing her his cappuccino so that he could take off his jacket given the unseasonably warm night. Vampires were real, but climate change was a myth. It was fascinating what the mortals believed. Everyone knew the weather changed on the whim of the Almighty or the random weather warden or two in the Coven.

"Not when it comes to missing children," she argued. "I would rather know. Not knowing is the killer."

"We can't let them know she's dead until we've discovered the killer. As soon as they know she's dead, they'll want her body for a funeral. But we need it for evidence, to match up the killer's blood bond when we find him," he said patiently. "Standard Coven procedure, you know that. I'm not a vampire, but I get it."

"Well, I don't like it."

"Neither do I, but I don't like a lot of things, and I never thought we had a choice on what we liked or not."

"True that," Ara said, realizing his lingo was rubbing off on her. "Did you hear about the other body?"

Edon nodded. It was found in an abandoned warehouse in the

far reaches of Brooklyn, not far from the torched Nephilim hive. The girl had suffered the same treatment—the left hand hacked off and a bloody pentagram painted on the wall above her. Deming and Acker were the leads on that one, and they were still trying to figure out who she was. "Two in one week can't be good," he said.

The Currys lived in a small apartment in a high-rise in Midtown. It was past midnight, but they could only meet then after the restaurant closed. They looked weary and anxious. There were dark circles under Frank Curry's eyes, and Madeline Curry looked pale and worn.

Frank was a short but powerfully built man, with the burned fingers and forest of intertwining tattoos on his forearms of a chef who had put in his hours, had paid his dues. "Have you eaten?" he asked, when they were seated at the family's small dining table. "I can make you something. Spaghetti?"

"No, thank you," Ara said, even as Edon was about to say otherwise. She couldn't bear to think of taking advantage of their kindness.

"Georgie is a good girl," Madeline said. "We are very close. She would never just run away. Your colleagues asked if there was any reason why she would want to leave, but there isn't. She had a test on Monday. She was studying for it. She loves the city. Where else would she go?"

"I'm sorry, ma'am," Edon said. "But we do have to cover all the bases. She's sixteen, and sometimes teenagers do run away."

"Not my Georgina. Like I said, she would never run away," Madeline said. "Never."

Ara scribbled notes in her book, trying to keep her face calm, trying not to give away what they knew. "We've spoken to her friends at school."

"You talked to Darcy?" Madeline asked.

"Yes."

"Wild Darcy." Madeline sighed. "Georgie's evil twin. We've been trying to separate them since kindergarten. She's a bad influence."

"Darcy said that Georgina had a boy she was close to," Edon said.

"Damien." Madeline nodded.

Ara was impressed. Not many mothers knew what was going on

with their teenage daughters, but Madeline Curry seemed to be on the ball.

"Yes. What was her relationship with him? Was he her boyfriend?" asked Ara.

"The kids—they don't call it that anymore. Did you notice? They're sort of…unlabeled. I wish I could tell you, but mothers are always the last to know. Why? Do you think he has something to do with this?" she asked worriedly.

Ara didn't comment. "Do you know where we can find him?"

"The other detectives already asked about him, but I don't have a number for him, I'm sorry. Like I told the officers, all I have is just an address. Georgie asked me to pick her up at his house once. Hold on." She got up from the table and rummaged in the kitchen drawers. "Here's that Post-it."

Ara took it and felt her heart stop when she read the address. She showed it to Edon, who let out a long, surprised whistle.

The two Venators stared at the building where Georgina's mother had sent them. They were standing at the corner of 101st Street and Riverside Drive, staring at the old Van Alen mansion, where Schuyler Van Alen had once lived with her grandfather.

"Who lives here these days?" Ara asked. "After they all left?"

"Dunno, I think the Coven owns it now."

"We were just here three days ago. Three days ago Georgina was still alive. You came here and I followed you. Why were you here?"

Edon didn't answer and showed her instead. "Look," he said, pointing to a pentagram etched on the dust of the glass windows on the doors of the brownstone.

She shook her head. She hadn't seen that when she was trailing him.

"Who the fuck is this Damien Lane and how does he get into *this* house?" she asked.

Edon kicked at a pile of leaves on the ground and jammed his hands into his pockets. Ara walked up the steps and tried to peer through the dark, boarded windows. She couldn't see anything. There were powerful wards around the house, too, which meant they couldn't go in, no matter how hard they tried. The house was protected, sealed, with deeper magic than they could conjure.

They headed back to headquarters, where Ara surrounded herself with all of the notes in the case file. She was missing something, but what? Ara studied the photograph of Damien Lane. Handsome, dark-haired Damien Lane, the renegade vampire and seducer of mortal girls.

"Doesn't he look familiar?" She squinted. The hair was shorter, but the smile—she had seen that arrogant smile before somewhere.

"How so?" Edon asked.

"I know I've seen him lately—but where?" Then she knew. She shot up and ran out of her office—there was a photograph that the chief kept on his desk that she had seen the other day.

She grabbed the photograph and brought it to Edon. "Look!" she said breathlessly, placing the photograph of Sam's old Venator team side by side with the printout. The hair was shorter, but the smile was the same cocksure one exhibited in the picture on the chief's desk.

Damien Lane was a dead ringer for none other than Kingsley Martin.

Red Blood

But first, on earth as vampire sent,
Thy corpse shall from its tomb be rent:
Then ghastly haunt thy native place,
And suck the blood of all thy race.

—Lord Byron, "The Giaour"

17 | SEVEN-YEAR ITCH

*S*HE DID NOT JUST HURL the contents of her wineglass in his face, did she? Yes, she did. Kingsley stood there with the wine dripping down his nose, his cheeks, and his chin. He ran his tongue over his lips and tasted the wine with a smile. "You're right, it is sour," he said and laughed. Because it was funny and because his wife was right—you couldn't get a good bottle of wine in the underworld, no matter how hard you tried.

It was just one of the many reasons why she was determined to go.

Mimi stared at him, her face white with shock and rage.

Kingsley tensed, uncertain what she would throw at him now. Her plate? The wineglass itself? Her sword, which she kept, charmingly, as a needle in her bra? How they had fought once, matching each other, steel for steel, the sparks between them as hot as their passion for each other. Where was *his* weapon, come to think of it? If she took hers out, he would be skewered in seconds, a little Kingsley kebab.

Was she really the only one on the attack these days?

Was he happy with how things were between them now?

Sour?

He thought she was going to scream at him again, but instead, she did the oddest thing. Mimi Martin, Azrael, Angel of Death, burst into tears. Big, sobbing, gulping, ugly tears. She was crying like he had never seen her cry before, as if her heart were breaking, and for the first time that evening—for the first time in their long and fraught and wonderful relationship—he was afraid.

Blood he could handle, and he'd had a parry for every one of her attacks. That had been the beauty of their relationship.

But tears?

Sorrow was a previously unexplored territory, at least between the two of them. Maybe he had pushed her too far. Maybe she meant it this time. "I'm leaving you," she said. "I'm done. I'm out of here."

He laughed, and it was not a mocking laugh, but a bitter one. He laughed not because he didn't believe her—part of him thought she *might* be telling the truth—but mostly he laughed because he knew Mimi was prone to be dramatic, quick to anger, and had a ferocious temper, but she never meant half of the horrible things she said. They were exactly alike, a pair of hotheads. So he just couldn't take it seriously.

They said things. They just did. It never mattered. At least, it had never mattered before.

They had been married for seven wonderful years. And it *was* wonderful to be with one's beloved. Kingsley loved her, he loved her so much, but sometimes, once you *had* your beloved, it was natural to pay attention to *other* things. After all, that was the point, wasn't it? Of a so-called happy ending? To move on to other concerns? To stop worrying about *love*? Come to think of it, what was a happy ending after all? It wasn't as if once the credits rolled and the lights came on or an author wrote, "The end," you stopped living, because there was so much more of life to live, wasn't there? Besides, there was no such thing as a happy ending for the likes of them, not the least of which because they were, ahem, *immortal*.

One could call it a happy never-ending.

Happiness was fleeting; you couldn't hold on to it, although he liked to think they had had a better run than most.

Hadn't they?

But Mimi didn't look so happy right now. Truth be told, she hadn't seemed happy in quite a while. Sure, she had been happy at first—they both were—although he had to admit, he might have been just a *teeny* bit happier than she was. He was content with their life, content with settling down, with wanting to plant a garden and to watch something grow. This land had been nothing but ashes, nothing but darkness and death. Now parts of it were green, and he'd built her a proper little home, prettier than any Hamptons cottage. Okay, so the views could use some work, and there weren't many people to talk to; most of the dead moved on from the underworld, onward to the great beyond, which was past their jurisdiction.

But they had each other, and that was enough, wasn't it? And wasn't that all you needed, at least according to the Beatles?

Love?

Obviously not.

"I can't live here. I can't live like this," she was saying, her eyes red and moist. "I want to go home."

But this is home. Our home. You are my home, he wanted to say, but didn't. Why didn't he? Pride? Anger? Because what the hell—*wink*— was this? She had promised him forever, she had promised him her undying, immortal love, and now, seven years later, just because she couldn't hack it, just because she couldn't stomach the sour taste of demon wine, missed going to Art Basel and Paris Fashion Week, had nowhere to go to buy or wear her fancy clothing, she was going to give it all up? Give *him* up? Give up on them? The idea of them? Mimi and Kingsley 4Ever? But he didn't say anything; instead he made another joke, and this one went as well as the one about the wine had.

"Who are you supposed to be now…Dorothy?" he asked and mimicked clicking his heels. "I want to go home, Toto."

Mistake.

"It's just not funny," she said in a soft, strangled voice as she mopped up the spill on the table and handed him a napkin to wipe his face. "You don't take me seriously, and I hate it."

Kingsley put the cork back into the wine bottle. Unlike Mimi, he thought it tasted all right. Nothing to write home about, but he'd certainly had much worse. The free white wine served at certain cheap Chinese restaurants in the Upper West Side during the nineties came to mind. House white. It had been good enough once. At least it had done the trick at the time.

When had everything gotten so complex?

"Fine, go then," he said nonchalantly. "Leave this place," he said, jokingly affecting a deep and portentous tone as if he were banishing her from Paradise itself.

She glanced up at him from clearing the table. "You'll let me go?"

"Darling, I can't keep you here if you don't want to be here," he said and shrugged.

"But the gates—"

"Don't worry about the gates," he said. "As far as you're concerned, I am the gates."

"Fine," she said. "I'll leave tomorrow."

"Fine."

Then he'd washed the dishes, because she had cooked and that was the deal, clean or cook—choose one—just as they always did, like a regular night, and that evening, when they went to bed, he kissed her forehead and turned to his side and went to sleep. And sometime in the middle of the night, he reached for her, and she responded, like she always did, and they made love, softly, urgently, just like they always did, and when it was over, he rolled over and went back to sleep and didn't worry about it anymore. Because fighting was part of their life together, just like the sex, and they had lived like this for years now, and because no matter what they said to each other, no matter how much they fought, he didn't believe she would ever leave him. Because hadn't she called his name in the dark, digging her nails into his back just like every other time? His wonderful sexy little wife, with her temper and her rage and her drinking and her beauty.

No, she would never leave him. Not Mimi. Not *his* Mimi. They belonged together. They would fight and love each other until the very end.

But the next day when he woke up, her bags were packed, two steamer trunks, buckled and locked, and she wasn't crying anymore; her jaw was set. His stomach began to feel a little queasy, but he ignored it. It was just a bluff, just another of her overdramatic gestures. He loved her, but he was tired of the drama as well. Why couldn't she just settle down and be happy for once? So he decided to play it out, see how far she would go, how far she would take it this time.

He motioned to her bags. "You have everything then?"

"I do," she said, without looking him in the eye. Her own were puffy but determined.

"And you're not worried about what happens when you return? You'll fare all right?"

"My trusts are airtight. I'm sure there's a way to get to my accounts. Don't worry about me." *As if I could stop you,* her look seemed to say.

"Okay, good."

"So, this is a trial separation, then?" she asked hopefully.

"Yes, exactly," he said, still unconvinced she would actually go through with it. "Let's call it our Persephone clause," he said cheerfully, thinking it was a clever line.

Clever, and hopeful. Persephone always came back.

She smiled wanly and put on her hat, because only Mimi would leave the underworld in a blousy white Western-style shirt, tight faded jeans, and a suede cowboy hat. She reached up on her tiptoes and kissed him on the cheek.

He walked her out of their house and carried her trunks. He placed them in the back of the car and looked back at their home. The Dove Cottage. The Love Nest. The Honeymoon Hideaway. The Devil's Due. They'd called it many nicknames over the years. He still didn't think she would go through with it, that when they arrived at the station, she would throw her arms around him and tell him she'd made a terrible mistake. But she only sat quietly and looked out the window at the gray, ashen desert. Mimi didn't say a word; she only looked sad, sadder than she had ever looked before, sad and tired, and then he truly felt ill. He should say something— anything—to make her stop this. *Stop this ridiculous farce where you pretend you are leaving me,* he wanted to shout. *Stop this at once. I love you. Please. Mimi. Look at me. Don't leave. Don't leave me.* But Kingsley said nothing.

The one thing that could never happen suddenly could.

He was reeling, and he was hurt, and he was silent, because he knew better than anyone that there was no way to keep Mimi from something she wanted.

So he helped her board the train that took souls back up to the surface. It was empty, because no one was ever allowed to leave the underworld, not without his permission.

Except now.

She took a seat by the window, but she didn't wave.

He watched her leave him.

The train pulled away, one empty car after another, until it was the final one, rattling on the tracks, and Kingsley cursed.

Because damn it, he wasn't about to let her go.

He couldn't live without her. He would do better, he would work harder, he would listen, he would change. She had made her point, she had shown him, by golly, that she was serious about this, and he understood now. Good God, he would change. He would do anything to get her back. Anything.

So Kingsley ran as fast as he'd ever run in his life and caught the back handle of the last train car. He jumped on the back of the train, catching his breath. He had promised her, the day they were married: *Wherever you are, I will be.* And he, for one, was not about to break a promise.

18 | TROPHY WIFE

*M*ORE THAN ANYTHING, after years as the mortal woman
behind the immortal vampire, she wanted to be more than
an appendage, more than a helpmeet. The titles the Coven bestowed
on its human kin were so...well, not degrading exactly, but they
were so inferior. *Human Conduit,* as if she were an electric current;
human familiar was even worse—as if she were a cat, a pet, something
that needed care and shelter. Finn knew Oliver did not think of her
that way, that he, more than anyone in the Coven, understood what
it was like to be her, understood what it was like to be in her place.
He had once been both Conduit and familiar to Schuyler Van Alen,
after all, so he had known what it was like to be weak, mortal, the
supporting cast, the secondary player. The Coven feared mortals
only for their greater numbers, but individually, mortals were nothing to them. And Finn didn't want to feel like nothing.

Especially now, as she stood in a place that largely resembled
nowhere. At least nowhere she wanted to be.

Finn was waiting in the lobby of a building in faraway Fort
Greene—if one could call a grimy hallway with a service elevator
a lobby. There were watermarks on what remained of beige floral
wallpaper that was well past its prime, and the ceiling was stained
with a meandering pattern of ripples and puddles the color of coffee. Sometimes she forgot this part of New York still existed, given
her life with Oliver.

Finn shivered and shifted her weight on her stacked metallic heels.

The artist she was visiting was late, and Finn had been standing and waiting for almost fifteen minutes now. She guessed she shouldn't complain, as visiting grimy buildings in sketchy neighborhoods was part of her job now.

Now that things had changed.

Wanting to prove to everyone—most of all herself—that she was more than a trophy, more than just a pretty girl on his arm, that she was not merely decorative and ornamental, Finn had lobbied for an office across from Oliver's, for a real position in the Coven leadership and meaningful work. *She was the First Lady, wasn't she? Officially or not?* If Blue Blood traditionalists didn't like the idea of a mortal entrenched in the highest levels of vampire leadership, they could go, well, suck off. A little arm-twisting from Oliver had secured her the title of cultural liaison, which gave her the responsibility of running the Overland Foundation's arts grants, among other social duties. Last year while she was poring over a few old books from the Repository, she had discovered a project where her talents could really shine and that she could take as her own little baby—to show the Coven what she could do. The Four Hundred Ball.

The one night that the world of the Blue Bloods showed itself in all its splendor and glory to the city of New York. Their night to shine.

And mine, she thought.

The community hadn't had one in years. The annual party had fallen to the wayside even before the War, and Finn had convinced Oliver that it was time for a little resurrection. It was her idea to mount the *Red Blood* exhibition as part of the festivities, and she immersed herself in the task of organizing it, choosing and meeting with the artists who would be part of the opening. Once upon a time she had dreamed of becoming an artist herself, and she had tried to express herself in pen and ink, clay and paint, but she finally had to admit that she didn't inherit her father's talent. The revelation had been a long time coming—bittersweet when it had—and at first she had refused to acknowledge it. Thankfully, though, she soon found mentoring artists and collecting their work was almost as gratifying as producing it herself. It was wonderful to be able to use her skills, her education, for something more meaningful than throwing yet another cocktail party, even if, at the moment, what she was doing for the Blue Blood community involved throwing another cocktail party.

A ball, she reminded herself. *The ball.*

The Four Hundred. This one is different.

This matters.

The artist who lived in the building was one she had discovered herself. Although *discovered* was a strong word, since Ivy Druiz had badgered Finn for a spot in the exhibit. Ivy had been a good friend from college and had wanted to be an actress back then, given that she was overdramatic, with a flair for the bombastic. She thought everything was miraculous and wonderful and exceptional, and she had a way of convincing you to agree with her, if only for the length of your conversation. Ivy's convictions had a tendency to wear off as soon as the champagne did, but usually by then she had gotten what she wanted. They had been so close in school but sadly had lost touch after graduation in that way that friendships waned when friends went their separate ways. But a few months ago, after giving an interview to one of the friendlier New York magazines that covered art and society, when Finn mentioned she was just starting to select artists for the exhibit, she had been surprised to find her old friend paying her a visit in her office one afternoon.

While Coven headquarters was located in a building that wasn't hidden in the depths of the earth anymore, it was still protected by powerful camouflaging spells that misdirected anyone who was looking at it too long, and she was surprised that Ivy had not only been able to find the building, but enter it and secure a meeting.

The girl was nothing if not determined.

Ivy told her she had read in the papers that the Overland Foundation was mounting an exhibit called *Red Blood*, and she was surprised and delighted to find her good old friend Finn was the head of it. She had a few paintings she was working on that she would love to be considered for it. Ivy left a folder containing her résumé as well as her press clips—a long gushy profile in *Artforum*, as well as several reviews from the *New York Times* and mentions in the *New Yorker*.

Ivy knew how to work a connection, that much was clear. A connection and a journalist. And maybe from the looks of it, more than one photographer. "I just had this compulsion to come and see you as soon as I heard about it," she'd said to Finn. "And I won't take no for an answer!"

That day Finn told Ivy she would think about it, secretly loving the rush of power. It would, after all, be the biggest showcase for Ivy's work yet. It could make her career. It gave Finn a lot of pleasure. After all, who was the more powerful of the two, the one who needed the favor or the one who granted it?

Now, having let Ivy sweat it out a bit, she was here to tell her the news—she would be included in the showcase. Though now that Finn had been waiting here for forty-plus minutes, she was strongly reconsidering her decision.

These artists were such flakes. A few weeks ago, Ivy had asked to see Stephen Chase's blood portraits of Allegra for inspiration, and Finn had obliged her, even though it entailed hauling them out of storage early and signing paperwork to let Ivy into the secure facility where they were kept before the exhibit. Ivy pushed for a studio visit, although Finn kept insisting she could wait until they arrived in the gallery in Manhattan, as she had no desire to go all the way to Brooklyn.

She glanced at her phone. There was no text, no call, and she had already left several messages on Ivy's voice mail. She supposed she should wait it out. For months she had been lauding Ivy's accomplishments to members of the conclave, about how while it was a last-minute addition it was an integral one, and now it would be too embarrassing to go back and report Ivy would not be participating after all.

No. She wouldn't let that happen. Finn would make it all work out if she had to paint the damn pieces herself.

Chris Jackson already looked down on her. She was sure that woman had ice in her blue veins, and Chris wasn't the worst of it. The condescension from the young ones—noovs, clerks, and new Committee members, vampires who had just come into their fangs—that was unbearable. That was the thing about vampire society: sure, human familiars were cherished by *their* vampires, but to everyone else in the Coven they were practically furniture.

Cheap, replaceable furniture from the great IKEA of humanity.

On the surface, it appeared Finn had a perfect life and had never wanted for anything, but the truth was slightly more complicated. Her father's family was rich, but she had never known her father, and she would have traded wealth for a relationship with her dad any day. Her benevolent grandmother Decca Chase was given to bestowing expensive presents and European vacations, but designer sweaters and trips to Paris only went so far. To this day, Finn couldn't look at cashmere without feeling lonely.

Her mother was a single mom, harried and overworked, and there were many things that her mother had never been able to afford and had been too proud to ask for from her former in-laws. Finn had affected a carefree air when she was younger, because it was easier to pretend she didn't care, easier to pretend she was happy with her life than otherwise. Maybe her father had been the same—that was what everyone who had known her father said when they met her: *You're just like him.*

Beautiful and doomed? she wanted to ask in return. *Will I die of a terrible disease as well, so that I never know my children?*

Will they spend their whole lives longing to know me?

It was why she had been close to her half sister after they had first discovered each other's existence. Schuyler had grown up the same way—privileged but deprived and lonely. She missed Sky and wished Sky kept in touch with her and Oliver. *The Coven is my past,* she had told Finn. *If you choose to love Oliver, it will become your future.*

Sometimes, she wished that Schuyler had not shut them out so completely. Finn understood that her sister had been fundamental in winning the War against Lucifer and was tired of vampire politics and concerns, but she found it a little selfish as well. Oliver was working so hard to keep it all together, and he couldn't do it all himself. There were several members of the conclave who were not shy about professing their doubt or dislike of him and them.

It was almost too much for one person, even if Oliver wouldn't admit it. And even if she would never let on that she knew.

Which she wouldn't.

Finn never let on about anything.

Everyone thought that Finn had nary a care in the world, that she floated along, that she had no troubles. But in fact, she loved this life Oliver had given her, because it allowed her to pretend she didn't need anything while indulging in everything. He didn't know how much more she wanted, how much more she desired, how much she wanted to be more than she was. More than just a Conduit or a familiar.

More.

19 | KILL SHOT

*L*ATE JULY IN THE CITY was always too hot and empty, Ara thought, as she stood with a watchful eye in a hot and empty alley in the Lower East Side. It was one of those rare and forgotten side streets that had escaped glamorous reinvention of the area during the early twenty-first-century boom, when the lox-and-pastrami district anchored by Katz's Deli became as polished and shiny as the rest of town, with pricey hotels and limousines lining the former Bowery. The alley was a seedy and grimy throwback, and at first glance Ara thought the pile of rags underneath a streetlamp was just that. It was a few hours after midnight, and she and her partner had swept the whole block and had found nothing so far.

The demon they had captured the other week had lied then, even in its dream. Ara had risked her immortal life, had performed that Death Walk for nothing. The Venators had kept that sucker alive long enough to try to get information out of it, but the thing was stubborn; it wouldn't tell them anything, wouldn't give up one name, or one reason why the Nephilim were back in the city. It was half-starved, weak, stark raving mad. Yet as broken and terrified as it was, it remained silent and would not surrender the hiding place of its brethren.

Stubborn, stupid beast.

Ara was sick of the stonewalling. And so one night she had invaded its dreams. Its mind was a free-floating psychotic mess of hatred and malice, but in that darkness she had seen something.

This place.

This street, this alley.

There was something here.

She was sure of it.

She couldn't tell the rest of the Venators, because she couldn't let them know she had broken the rules, and so it was just she and her partner in this empty abandoned building in the dead of night. But the only thing there was a pile of rags in a dark corner behind some trash cans.

Ara should have known better, but she kept walking, and just by luck, out of the corner of her eye, she saw the rag pile *move*; it was a blur of black and red, moving so fast, so fast toward her, a set of gleaming sharp teeth in an ash and dirt-streaked, crimson-eyed face. She had nothing to rely on but her training, her reflexes, her instinct, and as quickly as the monster leaped toward her, she had moved even faster, had drawn faster, and had fired her gun right into its head, so it dropped dead right on top of her, so close that she could smell its foul breath.

Her partner, Rowena Bailey, a hard-bodied African American Venator with the face of a movie star and the attitude of a swaggering samurai, swore loudly and creatively. "Scott, you all right?" she asked, after she had let out a string of expletives that would have made Dirty Harry blush.

"I'm fine," Ara called, grunting as she pushed off from underneath the dead body and rolled it off her. She took Rowena's outstretched hand and stood up, brushing the dirt and blood off of her shirt. "Did I get him?"

"Oh yeah," Rowena said, tentatively touching the dead thing with the edge of her boot and pushing it away from them.

"Good," Ara said, breathing heavily. Her hands were still shaking as she put away her gun.

"Yep, that's a Neph all right. If it had been a Silver Blood, you'd have needed the moon shanks." Rowena smiled, using her nickname for their crescent blades. "And you'd be lying where he is."

Ara took a deep breath and nodded, acknowledging how lucky she was to be alive. *No, not lucky,* said the voice in her head, *not lucky. Deadly. You're a Venator. You were the one to be feared in the fight, never forget that.* The demon had jumped her without warning because it was afraid of her, and the element of surprise was its only advantage.

Like its comrade whom the Venators had put to the fire soon after she had invaded its dreams, the creature was slow, almost lumbering. But maybe that was only what it looked like to her, as if everything seemed to unfold in slow motion; that was how fast she was, how quickly she had reacted to the threat.

"Check its pockets," Rowena said. "See if it has anything we can use to track down the rest."

Ara fished around the demon's clothing, trying to control her revulsion. It was one thing to kill it; it was another thing to have to touch it. She pulled out a few tiny glassine bags, the kind that jewelers used to keep loose stones, stamped with five silver triangles and the words "Chocolate Factory."

"Drug dealer?" she asked. "You know how they brand their products now? 'Ace of Hearts'? 'Government Shutdown'?"

Rowena peered at it. "Yeah, looks like some dime bags. Let's take it to the lab, see if we can catch a trace of what was in them. Maybe this was his corner."

Ara bagged the evidence to take back to the station.

"Not bad for a night's work," Rowena said, kneeling down to pour holy water on the body, making it sizzle. The human demon slowly disappeared in a cloud of black smoke.

Ara helped Rowena kick the rags back into a pile in the corner. It looked remarkably similar to how it had before. Except now it really was just a pile of rags.

She studied the plastic bags. "Five triangles. Chocolate Factory. What the hell does that mean?"

Rowena shook her head. "Who knows. Let's worry about it tomorrow. Come on, a good kill means you get the first shot," she said, slapping Ara on the back as they made their way out of the alley.

Headquarters was buzzing when they returned, and Ara was surprised and touched to find the Venators on duty cheering, hooting, and clapping at her arrival. She never got used to it and was gratified when it happened. This was her family now, her brothers and sisters in black.

"That's right, my friends, Scott put another mark on the board!" Rowena announced, slashing a big red X on the board in the hallway that was littered with bloody X's, one for each demon's death they had wrought in the last decade. "Who's up for the Holiday?"

Another round of cheers erupted from the demon hunters. They'd been working on uncovering the location of the Nephilim nest for weeks, and this was the closest they had gotten to finding them. Rowena was the tracker while Ara was the quick shot, the one who ended up pulling the fancy blades and beheading their enemy or shooting it down. It never stopped being satisfying, sending monsters back to the underworld where they belonged. But she was spooked as well, as she often was after a kill, jittery from having been seconds from death herself. She caught a glimpse of her reflection on the glass door, and her face was as pale as her short hair.

"Hey, hey! What's going on out here? What's all the hoopla?"

The Venators quieted down as their chief emerged from his office with a frown. Sam Lennox glared at the rowdy, black-clad Venators. He was beloved by his team, but it was well known that he didn't put up with a lot of nonsense.

"Scott put another *X* on the board," Rowena said. "Shot a Neph dead to rights before he could move. A beautiful thing."

"Did she now?" Lennox asked, turning to Ara with a frown. Then his broad face broke into its familiar, fatherly smile. "Well, why are all you losers still standing around here, then? First round at the Holiday's on me!"

"You think you'll take the promotion?" Ara asked, as she and Rowena took their drinks to a booth in the back. As two of the best Venators on the team, with the most kills due to Ara's quick hand, they had both been offered an opportunity to move up in the organization.

"Yeah, maybe," Rowena said. "Between you and me, I'm tired of patrol. Tired of smelling like blood and death. War's been over for a long time now, but try telling that to the underworld trash we find all over the city."

Ara sighed. She had a feeling Rowena would take the new gig. "Leaving me behind, sister."

"I know. I'm sorry," Rowena said. "Why don't you take yours? They want you, too, you know."

"Nah, I like it here. Unlike you, I like the taste of blood." Ara smiled dreamily.

"It's addictive, I'll give you that."

"Yeah, I guess. Or maybe I just know I'll ruffle some conclave member's feathers, and that'll be it for me. I'll get kicked out of the Coven for sure, pissing off the likes of Chris Jackson even more." She made a face. When she'd been a young vampire on the Committee, Chris Jackson had been the bane of her existence. Even if Ara had been known as Minty back then, the seeds of rebellion had already been planted. She remembered arguing with Chris when the Committee head had asked her to comport herself as a young lady. "I'm not a young lady, I'm a vampire," she'd shot back.

Rowena laughed. "She's not so bad. Anyway, I'm proud of you. Wonder Woman. Demon huntress."

"Thanks," Ara said, feeling both touched and sad. After her family had died in the final battle, Ara had joined the Venators to find a home again. Rowena was more than a partner to her, she was a sister. They'd fought demons together, side by side, and on the weekends they saw movies and cooked dinner. Until Rowena started dating one of the junior conclave members, of course, which was probably why she wanted to transition over to security strategy rather than continue street work; it would enable her to see her girlfriend more often. Venators were often single because no one could keep up relationships with the hours they kept.

Sam Lennox sidled up to their table. Not for the first time, Ara noticed that he wasn't as old as he tried to appear, although, of course, like all of them, he was centuries old. But to mortal eyes he looked early forties at most. "Good work today, ladies," he said, smiling. "Can I get you anything? Refills?"

Rowena winked at Ara. "I'm all right, Chief. Sully owes me one. He bet we wouldn't catch the Neph today. I'm gonna go find him and make him pay up." She slid out of the booth and Sam sidled in taking her place.

He had trained Ara and taught her how to shoot, how to kill. It was his voice she heard in her head when she was afraid. The one that reminded her how truly dangerous she was. He had crafted her into a weapon. "You know, I'm not too happy with the way you found that Neph," he said. "I know about that stunt you pulled with the Death Walk."

"You here to chew me out, Chief?"

"Maybe," he said. "What you did was dangerous—you could have let that thing into your mind. There's a reason those things are done in controlled environments. If you had traveled too deep, Rowena would never have been able to pull you out."

"But I didn't," she said with a smile.

He scratched his cheek. "All right, all right." He returned her smile to let her know he wasn't there to lecture her; tomorrow he might, but not tonight. "I heard you got him right between the eyes. Bull's-eye."

"It was him or me," she said. "And you know me, I like a clear shot."

"Isn't that the truth," he said.

She smiled at him and he smiled back. "Chief..."

"It's after hours, Ara—you can call me Sam." He winked. His face was a little pink from the lights in the bar, or maybe he'd had a lot to drink, although alcohol wasn't supposed to affect vampires that much.

"All right, then, Sam...," she said. She had known the chief for a long time, but tonight, she savored his name as if it were a brand-new present, something rare and hardly used. Samuel Lennox.

"Yes, Ara?"

She leaned forward so that she could look deep into his clear blue eyes. "You know what I heard in my head, right before I shot the fucker? What I hear every time I kill one of those mofos?"

"Tell me."

"Your voice, telling me to hold it steady. Telling me to choose my life instead of his. *Show no mercy, Scott. You're a Venator.*"

Sam slapped his hand on the table and let out a loud guffaw. "That's good advice, right there."

They grinned at each other, and Ara felt a tingle, an electric sensation pass between them. Caught up in the euphoria of the kill, at that moment, it felt like anything was possible, even that the chief might be making eyes at her. Sam was one of the Coven's heroes. The one who kept the Coven safe after the War. The one they all looked up to. And if she wasn't imagining things, he was looking at her, not as a Venator, but as if she was the most beautiful woman in the bar. Ara had never felt beautiful before. In high school, she'd run with the pretty crowd but had never felt pretty herself, just passable. And with Rowena, everyone looked at Rowena, beautiful, gorgeous, caramel hottie Rowena. Ara, with her short platinum boy's hair and lanky body, was no one's idea of a beauty. Or maybe not...

"What are you drinking? Let me guess, water?" Sam asked.

"You know me too well," she said, raising her glass. "It's sparkling."

He let out another hearty laugh. "Come on, Scott. You had a big night. Let's get you something stronger."

20 | LITTLE GIRLS

*K*INGSLEY HAD TO ADMIT IT. As she was about the wine, Mimi was right—it was good to be back in the city. It was invigorating, like a shot of cold vodka or the first hit off a morning cigarette. Speaking of... he should get a pack. His head was cloudy, and there was a persistent ringing in his ears that he couldn't shake. Nerves? A cigarette would do the trick, calm him down. Wine wasn't the only thing that was a pale facsimile of itself in the underworld. Hell's train morphed into a New York subway car when it hit aboveground, turning Mimi's trunks into two sleek wheelie suitcases. Kingsley still kept a good distance between them, but when she got out at the Times Square station he followed her, and when she caught a cab uptown he did the same.

She checked into the Lowell Hotel, a tiny, luxurious, you-had-to-be-in-the-know sort of place that Blue Bloods favored. New money and vulgar insecurity preferred to stay at the brand-name emporiums like the Four Seasons or the Mandarin, and while those colossal palaces had their name-dropping attractions, nothing beat the charm of a small, lovely, perfectly appointed, white-glove hotel. The rooms at the Lowell were just as expensive, but only the *right* sort of people stayed there, if you cared about that sort of thing, like Mimi did. Kingsley hovered in the background, and when he was satisfied that she could take care of herself and was able to secure a room, he left to get those smokes.

When he'd jumped on the train, he had been eager to get her back, but on the ride back aboveground, he had changed his mind a little. Maybe he would let her see what life was like without him for a change, maybe he would let her miss him a little. He often had to come crawling back to her; maybe it wouldn't hurt for her to feel the same pain he felt. He would watch out for her, and when it looked as if she was well and truly suffering for his presence, he would present himself—ta-da!—and they would reunite, and it would feel oh so good.

The city had changed in the ten years since he'd left it, and he found himself walking around like a tourist, gawking at the hordes of people and being overwhelmed by the noise and commotion.

Momentarily flummoxed by the new MetroCard vending machines and stunned by the fare hike, he took the train downtown to his old stomping grounds. There were so many fancy new buildings and beautiful, architect-designed hotels. The city felt more exciting, flashier, cleaner, shinier, but it was also somehow less than the city he loved. Maybe that was the truth about New Yorkers; one was full of nostalgia for the New York one had known. It was someone else's city now, all these new, eager young people rushing around attached to their gadgets. He was glad to find there were still some places that hadn't changed. That still catered to the likes of him. The Holiday. The Odeon. His old haunts. Awash with nostalgia, Kingsley decided that maybe he would touch base with his old crew; find out what was going on with the Coven; how the Regent, his old friend, was doing. Enjoy a little freedom for a change. After all, Mimi had no idea he was here yet, and he could do whatever he wanted. It wouldn't hurt to have a little fun, before he reasoned with her that she'd made her point and the two went back to their real lives.

But first, he wanted to make sure Mimi was settled. She had put some kind of cloaking spell on herself, and he had difficulty finding her again. But he soon figured out the antispell and shadowed her when she visited her bank, where the assholes at the desk told her that her identification had expired and therefore she wouldn't be able to access any of her accounts. But he took care of *that*, and they'd had to call her right after, while he held a blade to their throats, to tell her that everything was quite all right and settled and she had her money back. When she went to look at apartments the next day, he cast a spell on the couple who was about to place a bid on the one she wanted so that she had no competition. It was so satisfying. He was like her guardian angel. If only she knew that he was in the background, making her life so much easier, maybe she would think twice about leaving him.

As the days passed, Kingsley realized that he still hadn't told Mimi he was in New York. He kept meaning to tell her he was here, too, that she wasn't alone. Yet every day he remained in the shadows. He was starting to believe that she didn't seem to miss him at all and that this was a huge mistake on his part. She seemed excited about being back in the city and had even found a job. She seemed happy, and he didn't want to ruin it. Or maybe he had too much pride, and maybe he was still hurt that she had actually left.

But one evening, a little before midnight, he decided he would finally do it. He would tell her what was in his heart.

Mimi, I was wrong. You were right about our life in the underworld. I'm sorry. You are my home. Wherever you are is where I need to be.

He stood on the corner across from her building. Mimi would still be up, and while it was late, it would be nice to surprise her. He could find a nice bottle of wine, some flowers from the deli. Remind her of how much fun they used to have and how they could be like that again. Or even better. He would tell her he was sorry, that he was a fool to let her go. *Come back to me,* he would plead. He walked down the sidewalk, meaning to buy a bouquet, when he noticed a group of girls staring at him, young girls, high school girls, and they were whispering to each other and giggling and then staring at him again. "Hello, ladies," he said, smiling.

"Hey," one of them said boldly. She was blonde and looked a bit like Mimi had back when they first met, cool and confident, and she was looking at him the way Mimi used to, like he was hot and sexy and everything she wanted on a plate.

Kingsley was ageless, could appear anywhere from seventeen to seventy, a special trick of his. When Mimi had met him, he had been working undercover at the high school, had passed as a high school junior. He saw that the girl in the street saw him that way, that she didn't see him as an aging, stodgy farmer, but as a young boy, a dangerous, reckless boy, who was fun and full of life.

Not the annoying husband who wouldn't take out the trash or the long-suffering silent partner. But a kid. He could be a kid again. Seventeen. He had the rest of his life to be old, but why not be young again for a night.

Maybe it was the famous seven-year itch, or maybe it was because he hadn't been out of the underworld in so long, and breathing air again, standing in the moonlight now, made him feel a little dizzy. Maybe it was because she looked so much like his wife but without the anger and the disappointment.

The girl flashed him a blinding, inviting smile.

Kingsley thought of how he had seen Mimi earlier that day, coming back from shopping. She didn't miss him. She didn't even think about him. She was out and about, happy to be back in New York, and she didn't care that she had broken his fucking heart.

"What's your name?" the girl asked, blowing a smoke ring.

"Damien Lane," he said without thinking. He was seventeen years old. It was a name he'd used in the past, and it came to mind as easily as if he were a bachelor again. "What's yours?"

"Darcy. Come on, Damien, let's have a good time."

And before Kingsley could think too much about it, he heard a voice, his own, answer. "Sure, why not?"

21 | TATTLETALES

*I*VY FINALLY APPEARED, blowing through the lobby doors. "Finn!" she cried, enveloping her in a hug. "I'm so sorry—I didn't hear the phone and I wasn't near my computer. I was working, you know. I was lost in a daze of *creation*."

"Sounds serious," Finn said with a wry smile. "It's good to see you, Ivy."

"You, too!" Ivy said, pressing the button on the service elevator. The elevator took them to the top floor, to a large, messy studio filled with canvases that reached up to the ceiling. All of them were red, scarlet, or brown.

"This is the one I thought you would be interested in. I call it *Femme Fatale*," Ivy said, noticing Finn looking at them. "I'm fascinated by blood...women's blood...It's so deep and wounded, but it's also the source of our strength."

"Amazing," Finn said, studying them closely.

"Oh, and that's Jake, my roommate. Jake, say hi to my friend Finn. She used to be my friend in college, but she's very fancy these days."

"Hi, Jake."

Jake waved from his corner, where he had hooked up his camera to a computer and appeared to be Photoshopping his face onto a naked penis.

"Jake's work is a reaction to mine. Male rage," Ivy whispered. "Isn't it great?"

"Mmmm."

She swept clothes and shoes off a lumpy couch and motioned Finn to sit. Ivy looked the same as when they were in school, her curly hair as wild as ever, and she was dressed in a paint-splattered muumuu. She unscrewed the top of a jug of wine and poured a thin red liquid into two paper cups and handed one to Finn.

Finn accepted it and tried not to care that she had just placed her expensive handbag on a dirty, paint-splattered floor. It was amazing how one got used to living well, to drinking only the finest vintages, to sleeping on the softest sheets, to staying in only the nicest hotels. Finn's aversion to roughing it was the source of endless amusement to Oliver, yet Ivy was still drinking the same cheap swill they had drunk in college.

"Go on, drink! Go on! You'll love it! You have to try it!"

Finn took a tentative sip. It certainly tasted different. "It's interesting, what's in it?"

"That's for me to know and for you to find out." Ivy winked. "Anyway, how are you? You look wonderful. You were always gorgeous, but now you're so...elegant!" she said enthusiastically.

One of the things Finn had liked about Ivy was that she had no filter and was very enthusiastic, unlike people who hid behind ironic facades. It was one of the things that made Ivy so good at winning you over to her point of view. You ultimately had to believe in her as much as she believed in herself.

"You're so kind to say that. Of course, I'm just the girlfriend of a rich man now," Finn said, finding that the wine was going to her head a little.

"Mmm...but what a man. Remember when he came looking for you in Chicago?" Ivy asked, cradling her cup and licking her lips. "Is it my imagination or is he even hotter now than he was when we were in college? I saw him on TV the other day with the mayor, and he looked delicious. So unfair how men age better than women."

Finn smiled to think that Ivy still remembered how she and Oliver had met, when he had suddenly appeared on campus with Schuyler, the half sister she had never known even existed, the two of them intent on discovering something about her father's past. Oliver had made her laugh, and it didn't hurt that he was so cute. She had been attracted to him immediately. Even the fact that he used to be in love with Schuyler didn't bother her that much when he confessed it. "Don't think I transferred my love for her to my love for you," he'd told her once when they were first dating. "My love for you is new and pure. It has nothing to do with Schuyler." She told him she understood and had never felt jealous of his puppy dog crush on her sister.

But had she *chosen* to love Oliver? Or had she loved him from the first time she had seen him? Wasn't it Yeats who had said, "Wine comes in at the mouth, and love comes in at the eye"? Love was like that—instant, a fire that burned, a pool you drowned in. She had looked at him, and she had known. She pitied those who had never experienced a love like theirs. It was a miracle, a gift, when love happened upon you like that. It was so easy.

There really was no choice. Not when you felt like that.

Oliver had still been mortal when she first met him, but when she saw him again years later in New York, he was no longer. They dated for a few months until he told her they couldn't go on until he told her his secret, and that if she truly loved him, then she would have to make a choice whether to know him completely or not at all.

"What are you talking about?" she asked.

"I've changed," he said. But she didn't understand what the transformation had meant until he'd shown her his fangs. He explained that the Sacred Kiss would bind her to him forever. Pretty big news to drop on your girlfriend at a rooftop party at the Standard Hotel. They were sitting in a corner booth, looking over the city skyline, and in the dim light, he looked ageless and beautiful, and she felt the hairs stand on her arm.

"You will love me with every molecule, every fiber of your being. Even your blood will love me. I know what it is to be a vampire's familiar. I know the kind of love the blood bond creates. Do you want this? Do you want me?" he asked.

She had put down her drink and laughed. But when she saw he was serious, she got worried. "You're not joking?"

"No. I wish I was," he said sadly. "I understand. I won't bother you again."

But she had run after him and took him back to her apartment.

"Do it. Bite me," she had told him. "Make me yours forever." She had pulled her hair aside and offered up her neck, and she had heard the hitch in his breath, and when she put her hand on his chest, he was warm, so warm, and when he kissed her skin, his lips were soft. Then she felt his fangs, tiny needle pinpricks, and his body was over hers, and she knew instinctively what else he wanted to do, how he wanted to take her. So she had told him to wait a minute, and she took off her clothing until she was naked, and she had lain beneath him, waiting, and he was undressed so fast, it made her laugh a little. "Better," she said. "Don't you think?"

Then he had taken her, body, blood, and soul, and she couldn't remember a time when she didn't love him.

"What's he like in bed? I bet he's amazing," Ivy said, as if she had read her mind, and poured Finn another cup.

Finn blushed. "Well, he is good at everything," she had to admit with a naughty smile, accepting the cup. Ivy was right—whatever was in this *was* good.

"I'll bet," Ivy said with a droll smile. They giggled together, college girls once more.

Yet as sensitive a lover as Oliver was, as gentle as he was out of bed, as closely as they were bonded, what Finn could not admit to Ivy, and had difficulty even admitting to herself, was that Oliver didn't understand her. He loved her, but he worshipped her, too; he adored her in a way that made her feel just the slightest bit uncomfortable. She was a dream to him, a prize, a possession. She knew he didn't mean to feel that way. Maybe it was her fault, maybe she'd been too willing to go wherever he led, maybe they were too young when they'd met, even though they were well within the age of consent. The Code of the Vampires suggested that human familiars be at least eighteen years of age.

"So am I in?" Ivy asked, then launched into a spiel about how the raw red pieces would be perfect for the collection and how this would be a huge boost to her career, and she would be in debt to Finn forever.

Finn savored her desperation, her groveling. She liked this feeling, of being someone people listened to, of being treated like someone who mattered, someone who could change another person's life with a word.

"Yes, you're in," she said benevolently. That was why she had come all the way to Fort Greene that day, to change Ivy's life. She had no idea she was also changing her own.

It became a little habit. Since she first visited Ivy's studio, whenever she had a free afternoon, Finn would visit Ivy in her studio, ostensibly to look over the paintings that were to be part of the exhibit. But after taking a cursory glance at the canvases, they would talk, reminisce, and drink the potent red wine that Ivy poured from a jug, a drink that was fortified with something Ivy jokingly called "Vitamin P."

"Vitamins for painting?" Finn had asked once.

"Something like that," Ivy said mysteriously.

Finn enjoyed the company. She had forgotten what it was like to have friends of her own, someone who wasn't associated with the Coven. She realized that everyone she knew, everyone she interacted with, was part of Oliver's world, the vampire world, and that somehow, she had lost track of her own friends, her own life, along the way of being part of his.

Even furniture needed friends, as it turned out. At least that was what Finn told herself as she found herself coming and going to Fort Greene.

"Lunch?" Oliver asked, passing her office that morning. "I have a free hour for once."

"I can't," she said.

"Busy? Meeting artists?"

"Mmm." He had looked disappointed, and she improvised. "This show isn't going to run itself, Oliver."

"Be careful. Some of those neighborhoods they live in are dangerous."

"Sweetie," she scolded. "I'm a grown woman. Please don't talk to me as if I were a child."

"You always take Jerry?" Jerry was her driver and bodyguard. *And nanny*, she sometimes thought.

"Of course."

Oliver stuck his hands in his jacket pockets and looked ruffled. "You're sure you don't want Sam to send you a detail?"

She balked. "Venator bodyguards? They'll hate it. No, Jerry is more than enough for me."

"Are you sure?"

"I'm fine. I never go anywhere I'm not wanted." She smiled.

"So who were you going to visit today, Ivy again? You've seen her a lot lately."

"So? She's a friend of mine." Oliver looked a bit taken aback by her tone, so she sought to calm him. "I'm sorry I'm so defensive, darling, it's just fun to see her, that's all. And you know I'm depending on her for the exhibition."

"Of course, of course. I don't want to be in your way."

She relented as quickly as he did. He was always the first priority, and she bent like a reed to the wind.

"No—it's all right, let me call her and tell her I'll see her later this week. Where did you want to go?"

"Are you sure?"

"Of course. Shall we go to the Four Seasons?"

"Perfect."

The next day Finn was sitting on Ivy's couch, thinking she should have visited yesterday as she had planned. Or maybe she shouldn't have suggested the Four Seasons' Grill Room, because Oliver spent the entire time talking to table-hoppers when they stopped by to kiss the ring. They all ignored Finn, but that was to be expected. She was there to be ignored; how else could a great man function? She told Ivy about how tired she was of being the "wife" sometimes, and Ivy stopped, making a dramatic hand gesture.

"Hold up, hold up, you're married? And you didn't invite me? You know I love good champagne!"

"Actually no," Finn said. "We're not married. I just meant, you know, playing the part of the wife. I'm actually not his wife."

"But why hasn't he married you yet? Made a respectable woman out of you?" Ivy teased, leaning back on the lumpy couch. She had taken, in true Ivy form, only five seconds to get to the heart of the matter.

"I don't know," Finn said, taking a slow sip from her glass. The red liquid rocked in her hand.

"You've been together, what, ten years?"

"Pretty much."

"Time to make it happen, don't you think? Especially if you have to go to all these boring lunches and dinners and act like it already."

"We're practically married—it's not a big deal," Finn said. "Stop it, you sound like my mother."

"Would you say yes if he asked?"

Finn rolled her eyes. "Of course, and he knows that."

"But he's never asked?"

"No," she had to admit. "I guess it's sort of moot. I mean, the thing is…"

"What?" Ivy asked, scratching the sole of her foot.

"Nothing...forget I said anything."

"Finny, it's me. Remember?" She waggled her paint-flecked finger to remind Finn she would keep her secrets.

"The thing is, Oliver is...Oliver is different. And we're already together." *Blood bound. I am bound to him—even without the vows, I am his. Why bother with anything else?*

"Yeah, he's different all right. He's so much richer." Ivy smirked.

"I mean he's not like us," Finn said slowly. The wine had loosened her tongue, she thought. She could never tell Ivy the truth. The Coven kept its secrets by huddling together, by socializing only with their own kind. As the years went by, Finn found that it was a burden to keep her place in the Coven, her life, a secret from everyone in her life who wasn't a part of it, like her mother and grandmother, with whom she had been very close. She had never been tempted before, but she was tempted now. She wanted to tell Ivy everything, about the Coven, about Oliver, about her secret life as a human familiar to the most powerful vampire in the world.

"Tell me," Ivy said, so eager she almost tipped out of her seat. "You can tell me." She poured her more of the strangely addictive fortified wine.

The thing was, Finn couldn't, and she knew that. Of all the many things that Oliver had made clear she couldn't do, this was one of the big ones.

Maybe the biggest.

So Finn leaned back against the edge of the couch, pressing her body deep into the sagging upholstery and willing her mouth shut. She took another sip of wine.

"What is it?" Ivy asked. Her eyes never left Finn's face. *That girl should be a detective,* thought Finn. *Or maybe a shrink.*

Maybe she already is. Maybe she's mine.

"You know, I was going to be an artist." Finn smiled.

"Oh, I know." Ivy held up her glass. *Cheers.*

Finn laughed at the memories flooding back into her mind. They were especially funny, given that the two women were sitting in a studio surrounded by paint and canvases. "I was terrible, Ivy."

"I know that, too." Ivy toasted her again, and Finn raised her own glass with a nod.

"Why did you never say anything? Why did you let me take all those awful classes, week after week? Painting every piece of fruit and naked model in Chicago?" Finn sighed.

"You wanted it. Hey, man. It was your dream. Who was I to tell you what you could and couldn't have?" Ivy shook her head. "That's not my place, to steal someone's dream like that."

"But I was never going to have it. I didn't deserve it. I wasn't a real artist." *I am something else entirely, someone I don't recognize anymore.*

Ivy shrugged. "Why not?"

Finn shook her head. She had thought this through so many times that there was no harm in talking about it now. "There is such a thing as reality, Ivy."

"Are you a realist, Finny? Is that what you are?" Ivy set her glass down on the uneven stack of books supporting the plywood tray that passed for her coffee table. "Is that what this thing with Oliver is really about?"

Finn avoided Ivy's eyes. Instead, she focused on her glass. Her glass and the table. There were so many wine-red rings on the wood now that it looked like an intentional pattern, like a modernist take on grapes.

"About this thing with Oliver...," Finn said slowly, and as soon as she began talking, she couldn't stop. She didn't know if it was the wine, or her rekindled friendship with Ivy, or because it was a relief speaking out loud after keeping silent for so long. Secrets had the ability to fester and rot, and this one was beginning to itch.

"Oliver is...a vampire, he's immortal, and I am his human familiar," she said breathlessly.

Ivy stared at Finn in shocked silence. Then she laughed. Her huge, honking belly laughs, wiping her tears and clutching her sides.

"You don't believe me?" Finn whispered.

Her friend took a deep breath. "No, it's just that—It's so funny because—that's my secret, too," Ivy said. And with a dramatic gesture she was famous for, she pulled away her collar to show the two white scars at the base of her neck.

"It's why I've been so obsessed with blood lately. It's all I can think about," Ivy said dreamily. "I'm part of him and he's part of me. It's wonderful, really, isn't it?"

22 | TRUTH OR DARE

*I*T WAS DIFFICULT, if not impossible, to keep a secret from Venators. It was the most admirable and most annoying thing about her colleagues. The next evening, when Ara walked into headquarters, it was as if everyone already knew what had happened last night, and she blushed and kept her head down, feeling sheepish and self-conscious. There were way too many knowing smiles and surreptitious glances thrown her way. She tossed her bag on her desk and took a long sip from her coffee. She'd had way too little sleep last night, that was for sure, and her body ached, although it was a satisfied soreness, if one could call it that. The corner office she shared with Rowena was empty, the desk across from hers absent of her cheerful partner. Rowena must have taken the night off and was probably spending it with Jasmine.

"Hey." Deming, her superior officer, popped her head into her office. "Do you have the case file for that Neph you iced last night? I need it for my nightly report. By the way, one of the Venators thinks 'Chocolate Factory' might be a warehouse in Brooklyn. I sent some noovs this morning to three locations that match the name. We'll see what we find."

Ara nodded. "Yeah, I've got it here…somewhere," she said apologetically, rummaging through the folders on her desk.

Deming waited while Ara looked for the file. "So…you and Sam, huh?" she teased, tossing her long black hair over one shoulder.

Ara almost dropped her coffee cup. "Who told you that?" she asked, looking up from the mess on her desk.

"You just did." Deming laughed. "Oh, stop. We've seen the way the two of you look at each other. It's not a secret. There were bets on how soon it would happen."

"Oh yeah? Who won?"

"Your partner. That's why I gave her the day off."

"Sold me out," Ara complained, trying not to blush, thinking about yesterday after the Holiday closed, when she'd invited Sam up to her apartment, ostensibly for a cup of coffee. "I, um, have no coffee," she'd said when they arrived, throwing open the empty cupboards and giggling uncharacteristically. She hadn't expected to end up at home with the chief, but she'd had a little too much to drink—okay, a lot too much to drink—and she had gotten caught up in the moment and had ended up doing something she hoped she wouldn't regret. He was her boss, after all, and she should've kept her head and her distance, but she'd lost her good sense sometime around the fourth or fifth cocktail. Alcohol didn't affect vampires, or so she'd been told.

They had fallen asleep in each other's arms, and when the alarm rang at midnight, she hit the snooze button. But when she woke up with a start an hour later, she realized she'd made a mistake, that wasn't the snooze she'd hit. Sam had laughed and made a joke about finally discovering why she was late all the time. Then he'd kissed her again.

"You're going to make me late for work," she whispered.

"That's okay, I know your boss," he'd said.

She blushed at the memory, found the file, and handed it to Deming.

Deming took it, crossed her arms, and appraised Ara from head to toe, as if judging her. "Sam's great," she said. "A real good guy. You're lucky." Her face changed a little, a little sadder, a little wistful, and Ara wondered what that was about. Deming was dating one of the senior conclave members, and they were all over each other at parties. It wasn't jealousy, Ara thought, but sadness that she saw in Deming. Why did Sam make her sad? she wondered.

"Thank you," Ara said finally, since she had no idea what else to say. She was a little intimidated by Deming Chen. Sam was lying, anyway, when he said she and Rowena were the Coven's best Venators. It was a sweet lie, but Deming Chen was far more formidable. Even Ara was a little scared of her.

"Be good to him, okay?" Deming asked. "He's more fragile than he looks."

Ara went back to her work. The demon she'd killed last night and the one they had caught the other week confirmed there was a nest somewhere in town, as Nephilim tended to travel in groups for protection. Lucifer's half-demon kin were drawn to New York, since the Coven was here, but it certainly felt as if there were more of them lately than usual. Was it because of the upcoming Four Hundred Ball, as other Venators whispered? Was the prospect of the vampire celebration causing agitation among their enemies? Or was there another reason—something they didn't see? Rowena was sure they were running a drug operation of some sort.

Ara pored over the secret underground maps of New York, circling spots in the city where they'd tracked the Nephilim. Her shift was long, tedious, and lonely without Rowena making jokes. Before she clocked out, she stopped by the chief's office, where Sam was sitting at his desk, frowning at his computer, looking as red-eyed and sleep deprived as she was. When he saw her, he smiled, and his blue eyes crinkled. He motioned her in.

"Hey," she said. "When'd you get in? I didn't see you do the walk of pride."

"There's a back entrance around the side. Keeps the noovs from gossiping too much." He motioned for her to shut the door, and he stood up to close the blinds so they could have a little privacy. Which only served to make the Venators all the more curious, she thought. "You all right?" he asked worriedly.

"Should I not be?" she asked, shrugging.

"You seem...anxious," he said.

She took a seat across from his desk and bit her thumb. There was something else that was bothering her. "It's like everyone knows. About us, I mean. About last night." It felt vulnerable and exposing.

"They're truth tellers," he said. "Of course they know."

"Deming flat out congratulated me."

"Nice to know I've got her approval." He was wearing a clean pressed shirt, not the same one from the night before, but she knew he went straight to work from her apartment. He must keep them in a drawer in his desk, she guessed. For conclave meetings or when the Regent visited. Or for when he had a late-night booty call with one of the young Venators? No. Deming had said so herself. Sam wasn't a player. He was loyal and steadfast, not just a good Venator, but a good guy.

"Do you care? That people know about us?" she asked hesitantly. There weren't any rules about dating superiors, like in the mortal world. There wasn't as much gender bias in the Coven, as their strongest leaders had been female. But she still felt self-conscious about it, thinking of Chris Jackson and her frosty smile.

"I couldn't give a fuck." He laughed. "Come over here."

So she laughed, too, and sat on his lap and kissed him. She made him happy, and she liked that. She'd never done that before. She'd never had any ability to put a smile on anyone's face. It felt good, he felt good, his lips against her neck felt good.

"Why do you think the Nephilim are back?" she asked, when they'd taken a break from kissing. Sam was one of the first Venators to discover their existence during the War, that Lucifer was breeding demons with human mothers since the fifteenth century. "Do you think they're running drugs, like Rowena does?"

"Who knows what the hell those fuckers are up to? Lucifer bred them to spread evil in the world; that's all there is to it," he said, looking uncomfortable. Ara knew the Nephilim brought him a lot of bad memories.

"Yeah, you're right," she agreed. Her job was to kill the demons, not ask questions.

"You know that stunt you did with the Death Walk was pretty ballsy," he murmured between kisses. "But don't do it again. I'm serious, Ara—that demon could've taken you hostage in its mind."

"I had to," she said. "Rowena's a good tracker, but it seemed like every time we were closing in on the Neph, he would move—like he knew what we were going to do before we did it. It was the only way to get ahead." She was still feeling a little defiant and defensive—it had worked, after all.

"Yeah, well, I'll let it slide for now," Sam said with a yawn. "But next time, cute as you are, you're going to have to answer to me."

She looked him in the eye and smiled. "I think I can handle that."

23 | MYSTERY GANG

*I*VY WASN'T AT HER STUDIO the next time Finn came to visit. Granted, it was not at her usual time but after midnight. Oliver was working late as usual, and Finn had been up all night until finally she gave in to what she wanted to do and set out to see Ivy immediately.

A sleepy Jake let her in, nonplussed at having a late-night visitor. Artists kept vampire hours, she thought. He presumed she was there about Ivy's work and pointed out that it was all ready. Indeed, the eight large canvases scattered around the loft on various easels looked stunning. The gallery was picking up the works later that day, and they would then send it over to the museum for the exhibition. But that wasn't why Finn was there.

"She's not here?" she asked. After learning Ivy shared her secret, she felt even more bonded to her than before. "When did she leave? I just saw her yesterday."

"I don't know, she's hard to keep track of. I don't even try," Jake said, sounding bored and a little annoyed that she was still in his space.

Finn nodded. Ivy was impulsive and careless. She thought back to their conversation the other day and her utter shock. *Ivy was with a vampire?* It seemed utterly improbable, and Finn never heard her name come up at the Coven. She tried to press her for details about this mystery man, but Ivy was tight-lipped. "Oh, I could never tell..."

"Well, at least tell me where you met him?" Finn had asked.

"The craziest thing," Ivy said. "He was looking for me," she said triumphantly. "He said he'd heard I was an artist, and he wanted to meet me."

"So he's a fan."

Ivy had giggled. "Something like that, I guess."

"Where did she go?" Finn asked Jake.

"Like I said, I really have no idea. The desert? Paris? Washington Heights...who knows?" he said, turning back to his computer. "I'm sure she'll post a photo online or check into Foursquare."

Jake began typing, and it was clear that the conversation was over.

Finn walked around the studio, toward the kitchen, and found the jug of the cheap red wine. To be honest, this was what she had come for in the first place. She wanted to see Ivy, sure, but Finn had started to crave the taste of this cheap wine mixed with whatever her friend put in it. "Do you know where she gets the secret stuff she puts in the wine?"

Jake swirled around in his chair and grinned at her as if she was finally speaking his language. "Vitamin P?"

She blushed. "Yeah, that's what Ivy calls it."

"Some guy up the block by the warehouse district. They call him Scooby. He's got crazy spiky red hair, you won't miss him. By the way, it's a club drug. You should be careful with that. It's dangerous," he said in a serious tone.

"Club drug?"

"The kids take it. Enhances their senses, loosens their inhibitions. You know why they call it Vitamin P?"

"Why?"

"'Cause it takes you to Paradise. Oh, that's what you have to say when you find Scooby, by the way. Otherwise he won't sell it to you." Jake saluted her, then went back to his computer.

When Finn was in college in Chicago, getting your hands on drugs was laughably easy. There was always a guy who lived in the hall in a hemp sweatshirt, or dreadlocks, or Birkenstocks, who had a connection. If you wanted some, you would stop by his room—which reeked of pot—and he would open the door and give you a glassy, red-eyed smile. It was always a guy, never a girl, Finn thought, wondering about that. Why was it that she had never known any girl drug dealers? Girls with connections?

Finn had been a good girl. She had never knocked on the door, she tended to shake her head when the peace pipe was offered, and she never went to the bathroom with a tiny amber bottle and a miniature spoon, never grew the nail on her pinkie finger too long. So she was surprised to find herself giving the new driver instructions on how to find this Scooby person. Jerry had called in sick—and she knew she would never attempt this if he was on duty that night. She wasn't even sure why she was doing it; she just needed to get more of it—whatever it was.

They drove up the block, the doors locked, the windows tinted, but Finn felt so exposed as the car made its way slowly down the empty street. In the afternoons, this place was busy with peddlers selling designer knockoffs, peanut vendors, office clerks in suits and sneakers heading home. But tonight it was empty, abandoned, and eerie. What was she doing? She knew she should turn the car around and go back to Manhattan immediately. Whatever was in the wine was not worth this, she thought. She'd never been any sort of addict, and she sure wasn't about to start now. But just as she was about to give the driver directions to turn around, Finn spotted a kid with bright red hair wearing a Mystery Gang T-shirt. He was underage— he couldn't have been older than sixteen.

Finn hated herself for what she was about to do, but she couldn't help it. She lowered the backseat window. "Scooby?"

He nodded. He was a stringy, pimply, gangly fellow, and for a hysterical moment Finn wondered why his nickname was Scooby instead of Shaggy. "Wass up?" he asked.

Was she really going to do this? She felt uncertain and a little frightened at the prospect, even if her heart was beating rapidly and her mouth was starting to salivate. She had never done anything like this before, and she worried that the driver would say something to Oliver. Maybe she could bribe him to stay quiet, hand him one of the hundred-dollar bills in her purse. That might do it.

"What's your poison? We got it all, Molly, crystal, bennies, Acapulco gold, candy, Ivory, dollies, downers, horse. What's your ride, pretty lady?"

"Take me to Paradise," she whispered.

"Vitamin P?" He squinted. "Mmm. Gonna cost you."

Finn looked through her wallet and held out five one-hundred-dollar bills. "That enough?"

"Double," he said, making a *come on, come on* gesture with his hand.

She handed him ten.

"Pills or powder?"

"Oh, um...powder." Ivy put it in wine. She would do the same. He handed her a small foil-wrapped package and slapped the car door to indicate they had to get out of there.

"Thanks."

The car rolled forward. She put the drugs away in her handbag, her heart beating. She noticed someone at the corner, someone she recognized, one of those new Venators—a young one and cute. Ben Denham, she thought his name was. Then she realized there were more of them, more Venators, coming out of the woodwork, fast, their guns drawn and their blades glinting, swarming into the warehouse building at the corner where she had just scored.

It was a Venator raid.

And she was right in the middle of it.

"Let's get out of here," she told her driver.

But as she watched the Venators swarm the building, she saw a figure run out of it. Someone who ran right in front of her car, and who stumbled across the hood, and their eyes met hers through the windshield. Her blood ran cold. She was caught red-handed.

There was no getting out of this. Except...

He was running *out* of the building, not running into it like the other Venators.

What the Hell?

24 | LOSS

THE NEXT DAY Ara was working late when there was a rap on her office door. "You still here, Scott? I thought they'd have buried you in paperwork by now," Sam asked.

"Venators never sleep. Where've you been all night?" she asked.

"Meeting with the Regent. Wanted an update on that Nephilim raid."

Last night the Venators had finally caught a break and uncovered the location of the hive—the largest nest yet—five Nephilim huddled together in a Brooklyn warehouse. In the melee, the Venators had shot them dead. It was a shame they hadn't been able to take one alive to answer questions. Ara hadn't been on duty, but she knew Rowena had led the investigation, her first in her new position. They found a few more of the same plastic bags marked with the five silver triangles that Ara had found on the Neph downtown. It looked like they were selling crystal; there were traces of methamphetamine in the bags this time. Rowena grumbled that since the Venators had burned down the place, they'd never find out exactly what the Nephilim were doing there, but orders were orders.

She'd told Ara in confidence that the conclave was beginning to think that someone in the Coven was tipping off the Nephs, and she had been asked to head up the internal investigation. She'd been promoted to head spook; basically, her task was to spy on her fellow Venators. Rowena and her team were running deeper background checks on Venators, from noovs to commanding officers, as well as comparing notes to see if anyone could possibly have tampered with files or evidence.

Ara hoped the conclave was wrong about that. She didn't like doubting or distrusting her colleagues. She was happy, though, for her partner's new responsibilities and the trust she obviously had with the conclave, but she missed Rowena in the trenches. Ara stared at her partner's empty chair and wondered who would fill it. She would be getting a new partner soon, but she liked working on her own.

"You know, I think I've found a way to link the pentagrams around the city to the Nephilim," she said to Sam.

"Yeah, how so?"

"The five triangles on the dime bags."

"Yeah?"

"I started playing around with it, and look, when you draw the outline—look what it makes." She showed him the paper she was working on.

"A pentagram," he said, impressed.

"Right? It can't be a coincidence."

"Nothing ever is," he agreed. "Good work. But I mean it. Knock it off. It's way past noon. Go on home." He stopped by the door and turned. "I'll see you there?" he asked with a wink.

"You bet." She smiled.

A few hours later, after dinner, he was helping her with the dishes when he pushed her against her sink, kissing and smelling her neck. "You stink," he said.

"You like it." She laughed against his mouth, let him kiss her.

"I do," Sam said, helping her out of her tank top.

"You smell good, too," she said. "Aftershave?" It was a comfortable, manly smell, and it made her feel protected.

"You like that," he murmured, lifting her easily so that she wrapped her legs around his waist as he carried her to the bedroom.

They made love quickly and furiously. When they were done, they lay in an exhausted heap, his arms still wrapped around her. "Sex and blood, that's all there is to life," he whispered.

She started to laugh softly. "You're a philosopher now?"

"Maybe. You ever taken a human familiar?"

"Not yet."

"I noticed—you haven't registered one. You should. Blood's all we have left. That's all there is to this life."

"Pretty bleak way to look at it," she said.

"Just being realistic. This is no way to live." The bitterness in his tone surprised her.

"Considering what we just did, I have to take that as an insult," she said lightly.

"Sorry," Sam said, kissing her forehead. "I didn't mean it that way. I just meant—"

"Forget it, Chief," she said. "I understand." Even though she really didn't and wasn't sure what had brought on that sudden darkness in him.

They went to bed. When the alarm rang, she turned it off and slowly moved from underneath his bulk, feeling guilty and awkward. She began to dress quietly and had just sheathed her blades when he woke up.

"Midnight already?" He yawned.

"Yeah, I thought I'd make it in on time for once," she said. "I have a hunch about those pentagrams. I think they're using it as some kind of marker."

"Who?"

"The Nephilim."

"Okay," he said, rubbing his eyes and reaching for his clothes. "You might have something there. Keep working on it."

"Sam," she said hesitantly, while he got dressed and put on his shoes.

"Yeah?" he asked, immediately concerned when he saw the look on her face.

It had been on her mind and she had to say it now or she never would. She took a deep breath. "I don't think this is a good idea... us... what we're doing."

He looked surprised. "Oh?"

"I mean, you're my boss, you know?"

Sam crossed his arms and nodded. "Yeah, I'm aware."

"I just—"

He took a sharp breath. "Don't worry about it. We had fun, right?" he asked lightly, even though she could sense the trace of bitterness in his voice.

Blood's all we have left, he said. *That's all there is to this life.* It was as if he had nothing to live for. He was a good guy, but there was a bleakness in him that she hadn't expected to find. It creeped her out a little.

"Well, I guess I should be going," he said, turning around.

"I hope we can be friends?" she said faintly.

He nodded. "Don't worry, Scott. We'll be friends. You still work for me. And I'll still look out for you. I promise."

"Thanks, Chief."

She closed the door behind him and exhaled. She felt as if she were free again, unfettered, unburdened. Alone. It was a good feeling.

The next evening, she ran into Deming Chen, who deliberately pushed her into the wall with her shoulder and muttered "bitch" under her breath.

"Excuse me? Do you have a problem?" Ara asked, confronting her.

"He wasn't good enough for you?" Deming asked, wheeling around. "Why lead him on, then?"

"I didn't do anything of the sort," Ara hissed. "He was the one who picked *me* up. And explain to me how this is any of your business?"

"It is my business."

"Why? Who's he to you anyway?"

Deming leaned in so that she could see her ivory teeth and her poreless, perfect skin. "He's the twin brother of my lost bondmate."

Twins who had married twins. Sam and Ted Lennox. Deming and Dehua Chen. Ara remembered the story now. But she had never put it together that Sam and Deming had been the surviving twins, that they each had suffered two great losses.

"I'm sorry." Ara felt the fight go out of her. "I didn't know."

"You should be," Deming said. "You don't know what it's like to lose somebody."

No, I guess not, Ara thought bitterly. *The War only took my parents, my friends, and everyone I ever loved.*

When she went home that night, she decided not to do the dishes from the dinner she and Sam had shared the night before. She was exhausted from work and feeling low about the awkwardness that had crept into her formerly healthy relationship with the chief. The next day she couldn't make the effort, either, and soon the garbage overflowed and the dust balls resembled gray fungus, like the darkness she was worried was growing around her heart.

Was Sam right? Was there nothing to this life but sex and blood? Not that she was having either at the moment.

Sam remained a friend, just like he'd promised, even though Deming hated her and turned the whole team against her. After a week or two, Ara began to feel better and vowed one day soon she would clean her apartment.

25 | WOLF IN THE DESERT

*F*UCKING DUST HOLE. You want to see the Sahara Desert? It's right in the middle of this goddamned city." Edon shook his head. There weren't a lot of places in the world that were pleasant in August, and Morocco sure wasn't one of them. Marrakech's famed marketplace was supposedly full of the treasures of an ancient world, except everything was covered in the same red-brown layer of fine dirt.

Edon took a swipe at a pile of elaborately hooked rugs on a bazaar table next to him. A cloud of dust rose at the touch of his hand. "You want a rug? Here's one. Brown, just like all the rest." He nodded at the rug salesman, pushing him aside with one hand when he got in Edon's face to cuss him out in a singsong Arabic.

The man walking next to Edon laughed. "I don't want a rug, asshole." Rodriguez was a suit, regular brass, right off the plane from the States. Edon didn't know what he was doing here, but he didn't like it. Excepting his own kind, it didn't make a difference which asshole he worked for, which asshole he took his orders from. They were all the same.

Not his kind.

Creatures of Heaven and he was a wolf bred in Hell.

Edon grinned because that was what you did when you were handling a snake. "See that hookah? You can have it in brown. Brown, brown, or brown." He pointed into the nearest stall, where a table was piled high with intricate brass figurines, baskets of pipes, rows of hookahs and lanterns.

He held up a lantern with one hand and blew on it. Dust flew into Rodriguez's face, and he started to splutter and cough. "Christ, Marrok."

"Wait, I got something for that cough." Edon grabbed an orange off a nearby fruit stand. "You want an orange? I got one for you. Only it's brown. Seriously. That orange is fucking brown."

"And your point?"

"Orange is a color. Oranges are supposed to be orange, brother." Rodriguez took the orange out of Edon's hand, shaking his head. He sniffed it. "What's wrong with you, *brother*?" The ancient woman hovering over the fruit stand started to howl, and Edon flicked a coin at her.

"Get me out of here before I lose what's left of my shit, that's what's wrong. Brother." Edon glared at Rodriguez. *Cut to the chase, man. I hate this dance.*

"Yeah? You really want to get out of here? Because the way I see it, you seem pretty happy. Look at yourself. You're wearing a scarf on your head."

"It's a djellaba. You want to get knifed in the back while you walk down the goddamned street? Don't wear one. I've been undercover for almost a year, man. Don't fuck around."

Rodriguez raised one hand. Half an apology.

Edon snorted. "You got something to say to me?"

"Me? What makes you say that?" The suit tossed the orange up and down in his hand, looking like he was savoring the moment. *Like he wants me to beg for it,* Edon thought.

"You're a long way from the city for a boy with no djellaba. Must have a hell of a message, if you couldn't just spit it out over the phone," said Edon.

"Or maybe I was just in the mood for a brown fucking orange." Rodriguez smiled, sort of. Then he finally shrugged.

Here it comes, Edon thought. *Say it. Please. Get me the hell out.*

"You been good out here. That's what I heard, anyways."

"Damn right I have." Edon nodded.

"You took down that Neph cell. Rounded up a fucking harem's worth of pros and hos. That got some notice back home." Rodriguez tossed the orange, up and down.

Edon looked away. "It was all part of that Neph gambling ring. They weren't just betting on camel races. Tough little shits."

"So I heard. Impressive. And the drug-trafficking thing, that was a nice catch." He didn't sound so impressed. He was trying to keep it together, but you could hear the jealousy in his voice.

Interesting.

Edon shrugged. "You mean an easy catch. Warehouse full of silk pillows and shit, and not one of them was brown." He winked, then ducked to avoid getting clipped by the front of a spluttering truck as it careened through the narrow street.

Rodriguez watched the truck disappear around the corner. "You got somewhere we can really talk?" The streets were safe, but not completely.

Edon nodded. "This way."

The room was dark and the coffee was even darker. Rugs piled on rugs beneath their feet. Brass lanterns—the same ones that had been hanging in the marketplace—hung over their heads, filling the room with soft flecks of light. Not enough to illuminate a face. Not enough to give away the kind of detail that could get someone identified by the local authorities.

Rodriguez replaced a little brass cup on the painted, carved table between them. He shifted uncomfortably on the hard wooden seat. "Nephilim activity in New York."

"No shit." Edon was unfazed.

"Pentagrams are turning up everywhere. Across the city."

"Whatever. So some psychopath tagger gets a little wild with his spray paint. Mortals think pentas are cool, you know."

Rodriguez shook his head. "It's the real deal."

"So?"

"So some brass wants you taking one of their Venators under your wing."

It wasn't what he was expecting, and Edon grimaced before he could check himself. "I don't babysit."

Rodriguez shrugged. "I know. It's an asshole job. I'm not here to sell it. Thing is, I don't know what a guy like you did to end up on the shit end of this stick. As far as I can tell, you've been tearing it up out here." It was as close as he could come to trying to be sympathetic.

Edon didn't buy it. "Thanks. You're a prince." Of course he could go back to his people, back to the timekeepers, but ever since the War, Edon hadn't wanted to get in the way. He had never been top dog with his guys. His younger brother, Lawson, had won that spot, and while he didn't begrudge it, it never ceased to sting a little. And so he had found a place with the vampires, with the Fallen. They resented his help, but they couldn't live without it, either. Cracking that Neph cell was hard work, but he'd gotten them all, except for that one little slipup that had almost caused the death of innocent mortals. It was a close call, and no one had been harmed, but the brass saw red. He was being punished for that mistake, he could tell. *Thanks for hunting them demons, dog, but you're off the team.*

Rodriguez looked genuinely sorry for a minute. "Chief says she's a real wild card, that she needs handling."

Edon looked at him blankly. What kind of shit assignment was this? He was a demon hunter, not a babysitter.

Rodriguez sighed, examining the contents of his cup. "Buck up, asshole. At least it gets you out of this place."

"She's a *wild card?*" Edon raised an eyebrow. "What does that mean back in New York City? She rides the subway? She runs in the park at night?"

Rodriguez looked at him now. "She's been taking Death Walks."

Death Walks. That was some dark gig. Edon couldn't help but be a little impressed. "No shit."

"Oh yeah."

"Jesus. Why me?"

Rodriguez shrugged. "Maybe your little bullshit new sheriff-in-town stunts out here aren't really all that important, buddy." He smiled, showing his teeth. Any attempts at solidarity over the uniform were fading.

Edon bristled. "Ah. Okay. I'll remember that next time a Neph attacks you on my watch. He's not all that important. You got it."

Politics. Bullshit. The usual.

New York meant the old-school Blue Bloods. The fancy-pants group who looked down on the wolves, no matter that they couldn't have won the War without them. Old prejudices still held, and a wolf who chose to work with vampires didn't exactly inspire trust, not in anyone he worked for or worked against.

So why did he do it?

Edon only wished he knew.

He lay in bed the rest of that night wondering the same thing, and by the time he found his shitty middle seat on his shitty three-way connecting flight, he still had no clue.

New York. Oh, well. At the very least, it wouldn't be covered in brown dust. He was starting to hate the taste of grit in his teeth. Yeah, he could work it. Go see the old sights. Reacquaint. He hadn't been there since during the War. Maybe catch up with Deming or something. Who was this Venator he was supposed to babysit anyway? Why'd she need a hound to hold her leash?

Dark Night

THE PRESENT

FRIDAY TO SUNDAY

O guiding dark of night!
O dark of night more darling than the dawn!

—Saint John of the Cross

26 | LOYALTIES

Chief hadn't been at his desk the night before, and so Ara got to work early Friday morning, for once, and was waiting in his office when he arrived.

"Did you know?" she demanded, holding the two photographs up together, not even giving him a chance to take off his coat. "Did you know Kingsley was back in town?"

"Sit down," Sam growled. He motioned for Edon, who arrived after hearing the commotion from down the hall, to take a seat as well. "Calm down, Ara."

He shut the door and glared at his Venators. "Now what the fuck is this about? What did you find?"

She showed him the two photographs. The one of Kingsley Martin during his time as Venator chief, with his old crew, along with Sam and Ted Lennox and Mimi Force, taken in the city of Rio, the Jesus statue in the background. The next one was a screenshot from one of Darcy McGinty's parties that had been posted online. The grin was identical, the hair a bit shaggier in the older photo, slicked back in the new, but it was unmistakably the same person.

Sam squinted at the two pictures. He looked up at them and drew a heavy sigh. "No," he said, massaging his temples. "I didn't know he was here."

"Bullshit," she spat. "He's your former commander. Your best friend. You're telling me Kingsley Martin came back from the underworld, and you didn't know a thing?"

"I swear, Ara, I didn't know he was back in town. I didn't."

Edon kept silent, looking from one to the other. "To be honest, Scott, I fought with Kingsley during the War and I didn't make the connection. It's been ten years, you know."

"What's ten years to an immortal? It's like you saw him yesterday," she said, her voice filled with accusation.

"Well, I didn't recognize him," Edon muttered.

"Wolves," she said under her breath.

"I heard that," Edon said.

She turned her attention back to Sam. "The security breaches at headquarters, the missing time stamps—yeah, don't look so surprised; I read the reports, too; they're available to the whole team— it *has* to be him. He's the only one who knows enough about our system to be able to break into this place. He was here, Sam. Kingsley Martin was *here*."

Sam shook his head. "You don't know that for sure. You're just guessing."

"And you're defending a friend," she accused. "I pulled his file. He's an unregistered vampire with a list of priors as long as my arm and a liking for young girls. He met his wife, Mimi Force, when she was in high school. And by the way? Georgina Curry looks exactly like Mimi did at the same age." Ara placed two more photographs on the table. One of Mimi Force from the Duchesne School yearbook and one of Georgina from Holy Heart.

"Look, he didn't kill her," Sam said. "How many times do I have to tell you? Kingsley Martin did not kill Georgina Curry."

"No? How can you be so sure?"

"Because I know Kingsley. He's an honorable man, a good man."

"You haven't seen him in ten years. He's lived in the underworld. People change. And maybe, being down there...maybe he went back to his *original* nature."

"What are you getting at?" Edon asked, while Sam looked horrified.

"I'll say it. Kingsley Martin is a demon. He's not a Nephilim, and he's not one of us, either. He's a Silver Blood. Lucifer's own. Araquiel, Duke of Hell."

"Kingsley has proven himself many times over to be faithful

to our cause," Sam said sternly. "You can't keep throwing his past against him. He was the Venator chief before me, for God's sake, and he proved he was doing the Coven's work all along as a double agent for the Regis during the War. He's a hero."

"He knew Georgina. He was with her on Saturday night when she disappeared. He's a demon, he's out of Hell, and he's out for blood. You need to put out a VPB." A Venator Point Bulletin would go out to the entire squad. She could see she wasn't convincing him, and she did something she didn't have the nerve to do before. She read his mind; she broke down through his defenses and caught a glimpse of his subconscious. In and out without the chief even noticing. She was a Death Walker. She was good at this.

"Why are you protecting him?" she asked. "What's he got on you?" She glared at the chief. "He's got a cloak on him—otherwise he would have shown up in our radar. A good one, too, good enough to keep us from knowing he was here all along. Get me the warrant so I can arrest him. Come on, Sam. Please, you have to trust me. I deserve that."

Edon shot Ara a curious look and raised his eyebrows.

Sam sighed. "I do trust you."

They stared at each other until Sam looked away. "Fine. I'll get your warrant. My gut tells me he'll show up at the ball tonight."

"Yeah?"

"Yeah, I know Kingsley. And if he's here, he won't keep away from the Four Hundred Ball. God knows Kingsley loves a party."

"Fine."

Sam's face sagged. "I can't believe it. But maybe you're right. He's been in the underworld for a long time, and I've seen him give into temptation way too many times to count. All right. Bring him in. Let's get to the bottom of this."

"So you and the chief, huh?" Edon asked, elbowing her as they made their way back to their desks and trying to make light of the situation after the chief's blistering lecture. "I should have known."

"Was it that obvious?" Ara snorted.

"Not really. I've got a good nose for these sorts of things." He shrugged. "So what happened, Chief dump you?"

She swirled toward him. "Why would you say that?" she snarled in the middle of the hallway, causing a few Venators in the area to cast disapproving glances their way.

"I dunno. Because you're off your chain right now? Calm down, will you?" Edon said, putting two hands on her shoulders, which she shook off. He opened the door to their office, let her in, and closed it behind her.

Ara sighed. "No. I broke it off," she said, falling onto her chair and kicking at her desk.

"Ouch," he said, taking the seat opposite her, where Rowena used to sit.

"It's why Deming hates me," she said. "You asked what she had against me—that's it. Sam. She's mad at me because I hooked up with Sam and told him we had to stop."

"Why would she care—Oh, right—because he's practically her brother." Edon nodded his head sagely and put his feet on his desk. "Why didn't they just date each other, do you think? I mean, you know...they're exactly alike. I mean, how hard would it be to make the switch with twins?"

"You're awful," she said, making a face.

Ara seethed, but held in her temper. "Well, what do you think? Do you think the chief is right? That Kingsley's innocent?"

"I don't know. But what I do know is that lots of people said terrible things about the wolves forever, called us Hellhounds, all sorts of trash. And we're not all bad." He grinned. "And anyway, what I heard, Mimi Force turned him into a one-woman man." He made a whipping sound and gesture.

"It's been ten years. Once a ladies' man, always a ladies' man," she said bitterly.

"Yikes, remind me never to get on your bad side."

"Who says you're on my good side?" she said. "A wise man once said, 'Show me a beautiful woman and I'll show you a guy who's tired of boning her.' What if he was here for variety—and Georgina looks a lot like Mimi, you have to admit, just younger," she said.

There was a rap on the door. Ben Denham stood there with a new file.

"What's up, noov?" Edon drawled.

"That other body—the one we found in Fort Greene?" he asked.

"Yeah, what about it?" Ara asked.

"The ID just came back. It was that artist who's part of the exhibit. Ivy Druiz."

"No shit," Ara said.

"Yeah, Chief wants you guys to start knocking on doors. Trace her steps. You know the deal."

"I thought Chen and Acker were leads on this case," Ara said.

"Not anymore."

Ara stood up, grabbing her gun and her blades, looking as if she were armoring up for battle. "Come on, let's go."

"Right this second?" Edon asked, twirling in his chair. "Can you let me read the docs first? Where are we going?"

She consulted the file. "We've got a bunch of people here we need to talk to, and when we're done, we're getting you a tux," she said. "God knows you can't go to the ball looking like that."

27 | DIVINE DETAILS

*A*T LONG LAST, her vision for the Four Hundred Ball was almost complete. On Friday morning Finn was at the museum bright and early, taking care of a hundred little details, from picking out the silverware they would use to making sure the stage was set where the investiture would take place to what time to have the orchestra stop playing music so that the DJ could take over for the after-party. It was going to be perfect, and it was all because of her.

She felt a heady rush of excitement and dread as she saw the palm trees being planted in the courtyard. It was yet another expense, but she knew it was just the perfect thing that the party needed. Her assistants, the museum staff, and event staff were buzzing with a million questions about the timing, seating, and setup.

Finn walked around the courtyard watching as they set up the billowing white tents for the party. There was so much activity all around that she hardly paid attention to the two Venators making their way toward her.

"Yes?" she asked, when the museum assistant whispered in her ear that they wanted to talk to her. "Can I help you?" She recognized one of them as the angry girl with the short hair—her name was Ara something—and the other had to be the wolf that had joined the force, the one who had been called in from Morocco. He looked like he crawled in from the desert all right.

"Miss Chase, I'm Venator Scott and this is Venator Marrok," the girl said, motioning to her partner.

"I know who you are," she said coldly. "What is this about? Does Oliver know you're here?"

"We haven't spoken to the Regent, but we're here on orders from the chief."

"Sam? He sent you?"

"Yes, ma'am."

"Let's talk in the office," she said, feeling a bit nervous that two of the Coven's hard-boiled Venators had been sent to see her. She took them inside the museum and asked the curator if she could borrow his room for a while.

She bade them have a seat.

The wolf never said a word, just looked at her with those topaz-colored eyes of his. Finn tried not to shiver. "Now what is this about?" she asked.

"Can we ask you a few questions about Ivy Druiz?"

"Ivy? What's wrong? What's happened?" she asked.

"She's an artist with this exhibit?" Ara asked, consulting her notes.

"Yes," Finn said. "I chose her especially for this exhibition."

"And was she ... how would you say she felt about being part of it?"

"Oh, she loved it. She was so excited."

"And yet she failed to attend an important dinner last night, and she has not returned the museum's calls about her work?" Ara asked.

"Yes, she has been hard to get ahold of. Is there something wrong? Why are you asking me these questions?"

Ara decided it was time to tell her the truth. "The body they found last night. The ID finally came in. It's Ivy. She was bled to death, and her hand hacked off. A pentagram was painted over the body."

"Oh my God. That's terrible," she said, turning pale. "Poor Ivy. What happened? Who did this to her?"

The wolf looked at her sternly. "We've been talking to a lot of people, and the thing is, Miss Chase, you were the last person to see her alive."

"Her blood isn't on file with the records. She wasn't registered as a human familiar," Ara said somewhat apologetically. "It looks like we're dealing with the same renegade. Did she say anything to you? Did she mention anyone in the Coven?"

Finn thought about those two bites on Ivy's neck and how happy Ivy had been the day they had confided their secrets to each other. She glared at the Venators, as she could feel them tentatively reaching through toward her subconscious. But Oliver had taught her how to keep her mind protected from outsiders. "No, she didn't," she said, the lie falling smoothly from her lips.

"Do you remember anything? Anything at all that can help us? Her body was found not far from the Nephilim hive we torched the other week. We think her death might be related. Have you ever seen one of these?" asked Ara, pushing over a dime bag with the five triangles on it.

Finn stared at it. The bags that contained Vitamin P. "No," she said. "I've never seen that before." She hoped they didn't notice the beads of sweat beginning to form on her forehead.

"No?" Ara asked. "Take a close look at it. The corner not far from her studio was a big drug freeway. Was she addicted to anything?"

Finn shook her head. "I'm so sorry. But we didn't know each other very well. We only ever talked about her art. If you knew Ivy, you'd know she didn't find many other topics very interesting."

The Venators got up to leave.

"Looks like it's going to be a great party," Ara said as they left the museum.

"I hope so." Finn smiled. "We'll see you both tomorrow night?"

"Count on it." The wolf nodded with his deadpan stare.

When they left, Finn went to the bathroom and tossed the last of the drugs she had in the toilet and flushed them down. She shivered, feeling cold all of a sudden, as if the hand of the dead reached out and touched her for a moment. There was no way she could tell them what she knew without implicating herself, and she couldn't let anything spoil Oliver's big night.

Their night.

28 | THE DEVIL YOU KNOW

*I*T WAS FRIDAY NIGHT. Kingsley had been gone for two days, and Mimi was starting to get really irritated that she had just let him walk out of her life without even asking him when he planned to come back. If he was in terrible danger, she could never live with herself. Donovan invited her out that evening, saying he was tired of seeing her pout around the office. "Get that scowl off your face, we're going to have some fun!" he said. "There's a new club I've been meaning to check out, let's go. What are you doing except waiting for your husband to call? Let him worry about where you are!"

"Okay, fine," she said, making to grab her coat.

"Not now!" He laughed. "It doesn't get hot until after midnight. Maybe two in the morning."

"Two in the morning? But we have to be at work at the gallery at nine!" Saturday was their big day, as they had all the weekend shoppers.

"Exactly." Donovan smiled wickedly, and Mimi suddenly understood why Donovan couldn't as much as staple an invoice and why he made mistakes like rolling art into FedEx tubes. The poor boy wasn't stupid; he was sleep deprived.

Fine. She would go out after midnight. She would see what the young people were up to. Donovan insisted they meet there, so at the appointed hour Mimi got out of a taxi and walked to a rather nondescript-looking warehouse building where clumps of people were standing on the sidewalk, smoking. She walked up to the entrance, fully expecting to face the door patrol and the velvet rope, but to her surprise, there was only a sleepy bouncer and no face control.

What happened to the desperate crowds dying to get inside an exclusive nightclub? What happened to being picked? Being special?

She asked Donovan as much when she saw him. Unlike his usual gallery attire of white shirt and black pants, he was wearing a fishnet shirt, heavy eye makeup, and what looked like a tartan kilt.

"Velvet ropes and champagne tables are so nineties," he explained when she asked about the lax door policy. "We don't need someone to tell us we're cool—we know we're cool."

Mimi nodded. At least one thing remained the same: the cocktails were still as watered-down as ever. She took a look around the large dark room, where groups of people danced together or were sprawled on each other on the couches. She had been expecting something extraordinary but the music was the same techno she had danced to when she was a teenager.

Donovan didn't seem to need to dance or drink too much; he just sort of stood there with a zoned-out smile. "Cool, huh?" he asked.

She shrugged. She supposed it was fun to be out, especially after being at home for almost a decade. "Let's dance," she said, pulling him to the dance floor.

Mimi danced and swayed, letting the music move through her body. She closed her eyes, enjoying the sensation and remembering a night at a club not too different from this one, when she and Kingsley had danced together. Kingsley was so handsome, and he was such a good dancer; look how he moved with that girl...

She stopped short and pushed Donovan out of the way.

Yes. That *was* her husband dancing with that girl. That girl who had her hands all over his chest and who was laughing as she pressed something into his hand.

Kingsley smiled his lazy smile and took it and murmured something in her ear.

Then he looked up and saw her.

Mimi just stared at him, and then she turned around and walked out of the club, out into the cold, her tears already freezing on her face. It had been warm lately, until now, the weather changing on a dime.

"MIMI!"

He was running after her.

She didn't know where she was going or what she wanted; she just wanted to get out, and the girl—she looked so much like the girl she had seen in his mind the other day—when she had peeked into his memories (a young girl so much like her that for a moment she had thought it *was* her), and Mimi felt her heart not break exactly, but frost over with a cold rage; she had been faithful to him—but, of course, he had not. There he was, running around with girls again, and this one was so young and so pretty. Mimi felt the spike of jealousy and envy and hatred, and it fueled her as she raced to the corner, desperate to find a cab and be anywhere but here.

"Mimi." Kingsley was standing in front of her now, panting.

"Don't say a word! I don't want to talk to you! So this is what you've been up to!"

"It's not what it looks like," he said.

"Really? She's practically a child! I think it looks exactly like what I think it looks like." She spat the words.

"Mimi," Kingsley said. "I'll explain everything, darling, please. Hear me out."

"You have nothing to say to me that I want to hear," she said. It all made sense now. His mysterious disappearances, his guilt, his secrecy. This was what he was doing in New York.

He was back to his old tricks, back to running around—she didn't believe he had run around on her before, but there was always a first time, wasn't there? There's always a first time for everything, he always said.

She remembered the way he'd looked in there, dancing with that young girl, and it made her feel old, and useless, and unattractive, and she'd never felt like that before. She was Mimi Force! The most beautiful girl in the history of New York City. But the truth was, there were so many beautiful girls, and so many younger girls, everywhere you looked. They were a dime a dozen, really—there was nothing special about her, not anymore.

God she hated him, because Kingsley had made her feel special, had made her feel chosen, had made her feel that she was more than her looks, that he loved her for her soul. But the truth was, she was no longer the girl she had been, no longer at the height of her glory. He was just like all the rest, just like a man, eager for a new toy, tired of his old one. Perhaps she should move to France, where they appreciated women like her. Of course anyone else would have slapped her on the head to hear such talk, as she had barely turned thirty.

He kept calling her name, but as she did back in Hell, she kept walking away.

When she got home, she still felt awful. She couldn't believe it. She knew he was keeping something from her—but she didn't really believe that it was this. So stupid. She was so very stupid. Mimi stood in her walk-in closet, removing her shoes, when she was suddenly grabbed from behind.

"Don't move. Don't turn around," a dark and menacing voice commanded. "Don't make a sound." Soon she was blindfolded, and before she could reach for her sword, hidden as a needle in her bra, her hands were tied behind her back with silver handcuffs that kept her from moving.

"Kingsley, this isn't funny," she growled. Because of course it was *him*—coming to apologize in the only way he knew how. "If you think you can make love to me now, you're wrong. Let me go!"

"But you're so hot like this," said the voice in her ear. "And I don't want to. I should've done this the minute I got back to the city. I don't know why it didn't occur to me until now."

She wanted to curse him, but she could already feel her body respond to his, could feel how hot and hard he was, and despite her anger, she started to feel very aroused.

"Kingsley, if you don't let me go, I'll—"

"You'll what?" And Kingsley only laughed softly, and with one slash of his knife tore her dress in two, and did the same quick work with the rest of her garments.

"I swear...," she said, breathing heavily, her heart pounding. But she could feel her defenses weakening with every moment, every thrill.

He pushed her to the floor facedown, and she could hear him unbuckling his belt.

"Isn't this what you wanted? To have a little fun?" he whispered. "To celebrate our anniversary?"

"I hate you," Mimi said. "I hate you so much."

"I hate you, too," he said and kissed her neck.

She was shaking. What was going on with him? They had never

done this before—never played this way—and it was turning her on, her stomach sick with anticipation. Dear Lord, he was right. She wanted this—wanted *him*—so badly. "Don't!" she breathed.

"Don't what?" he panted.

"Don't stop," she whispered, hating herself for loving him still.

He grinned and nipped her with his fangs. Vampires weren't supposed to drink each other's blood, but Kingsley often broke the rules. She felt his blood mingle with hers.

Then he was inside her, and she was arching her back against him and riding wave after wave of exquisite pleasure until she thought she might actually pass out. In seven years, they had never had hotter sex.

They lay together entwined for a few moments; then Kingsley gently unwound the blindfold, and when she turned around, he was looking at her with so much love and tenderness she almost forgave him. Almost.

She wrestled out of his embrace. "Don't think this means anything," she said. "Look what you did! You ruined another Chanel!"

He raised an eyebrow. "You said you wanted to have a little fun, and that's what we had."

"What are you doing here, anyway?" she asked as she reached for her robe and tugged it around her waist.

"I wanted to explain. About everything. But you wouldn't listen, so I thought—"

Why not have sex, because sex was the way they connected. Wasn't that the truth—he had shown her, with his body, that he was still in love with her, that no one could replace her, and that no one had. She knew that now; she had seen it in their blood bond, had read the truth in it. But she was still angry at him.

"So if you weren't sleeping with that girl, then why were you with her? What have you really been doing in the city?" she asked. His blood only told her he had been faithful, but not the rest of the story.

So Kingsley told her.

"We have to tell Oliver what's going on," Mimi said when he was done. She fingered the small plastic bag stamped with five silver triangles that Kingsley had shown her, and she shuddered to think what it had contained. This was what the girl had pressed into his hand when they were dancing. She couldn't believe it quite yet. But if what Kingsley had discovered was true, then this was malice of the most insidious kind. "You can't keep this from him, not anymore. That pentagram on his building means he's a target as well. The Nephilim—and whoever is leading them—is out for him. Out for mortal blood, and since Oliver was once mortal—he's vulnerable in a way the rest of us aren't."

"Well, what are we waiting for? Let's go see him," he said. "No time like the present to foil the demons."

"No—it will be too suspicious if we show up at his office unannounced. We don't want to alert whoever's behind this." She told him about Chris Jackson and the serpent she wore around her throat, the one with the stones from Lucifer's Bane. The White Worm.

"Do you really think it's her?" Kingsley asked. "Somehow I don't see it. Although she is the head of the Committee."

"I don't know. Maybe. Remember, her brother...," Mimi said. She realized she was doing the same thing that others had done to Kingsley, holding his past against him. "Maybe not. Oliver will find out. It's his Coven. He should deal with it."

"So if we can't meet with him at headquarters, then what?"

"We'll catch him at the Four Hundred Ball. There will be a huge crowd; we can blend in, there will be tons of strange vampires there," she said. "We'll tell him what's been happening inside his own Coven."

He nodded. "What you said earlier—about you and me—are we done?" Kingsley asked. He looked tired and sad, and every year of his age showed on his face for a moment, and her heart ached for him, but she wasn't ready to let him off just yet.

"Say something, darling," he said.

"I don't know," she said, unwilling to give in just yet.

"I'll wait," he said. "I'll wait till you make your decision. In the meantime, I guess we should get ready for this party."

29 | PROM NIGHT

*Y*OU GONNA MAKE ME WAIT out here all night? 'Cause I think the old lady in 9B has a thing for me."

Ara peered through the keyhole to find Edon waiting at her door, wearing the new tuxedo he'd rented from the shop. He stood there stiffly, like the sleek suit jacket might as well have been a bulletproof vest.

He probably wishes it was, Ara thought, unchaining the door with a smile.

At least he was freshly shaved, clean and handsome. His golden-brown eyes glinted and his grin was genuine. She opened the door and he struck a playful pose. "Come on, tell me you can't resist; no one can resist a wolf in a penguin suit."

"Wow," she said. "You really clean up nice. For a penguin."

He stared at her, forgetting about the pose. Ara smiled. She'd seen herself in the mirror just before the buzzer had rung. She knew where this was going.

"Yeah, yeah, yeah," he said, suddenly shy and dismissive. He tried not to look at her. "You ever really smell a penguin? All them birds shitting on one giant ice cube? Those bad boys'll curl your toes. I got myself posted in South America once—"

She shot him a look and he shut himself up. Still, she couldn't help but smile. *I look so good I made a penguin babble.*

"Right. Yeah. You don't look too bad yourself, Scott." He looked her up and down in the black tuxedo suit *she* was wearing. It was from the latest spring collection, designer, with a cropped jacket, skintight pants, and a silk shirt she left daringly unbuttoned. His eyes lingered on the very last button. "But don't worry, you're still not my type."

"You know, I think the boy protests too much," she said, pushing her way past him, holding the beaded clutch where she kept her gun and her blades.

He followed her down the stairs. "Yeah? Then you don't know much." She could almost hear him smiling as he said it, even if she couldn't see his face.

"I know you're staring at my ass right now," she said with a smile of her own. She stopped just inside the front door.

He barked a laugh and pushed the door open.

"You could do worse. At least a penguin mates for life, angel," he said, reddening unexpectedly as he held the door for her.

She ignored the angel dig. Truthfully, she was almost starting to like it. At least it didn't offend her, the way he said it. Teasingly, like they were friends. And she realized something: they *were* friends.

The night was cool and clear, the whole street lit by the front headlights of the sleek, black car in front of them.

Ara looked confused. "You got a car service? For me?"

"Nah. I got it for the vintage hottie in 9B." Edon shrugged, pulling open the limo door. "But now that you're here, you might as well get that sweet ass inside."

She smiled, shaking her head—but all the same, she slid onto the black upholstered leather seat. "This isn't a date, you know."

"It's the Four Hundred Ball. We need to live a little," he said, scooting in after her. "And besides, I didn't think you wanted to go on the back of my bike. What with all the, you know, hair situation you got going on there. Is that what they call a 'do'?"

Ara punched him in the arm and glared. She had styled her hair differently that night, making sure her long platinum bangs swept over one eye. He was right, but she wasn't going to let him know that. "My hair would have been fine. We're not going to prom together, asshole."

Edon scoffed. "Yeah, you wish."

She made a face. "I don't wish."

"Sure you do. You and all the lovely ladies. It's all right. You don't have to be embarrassed about it, angel."

Ara just rolled her eyes.

Edon winked at her. "But I'll let you in on a little secret. Hounds like me, we don't go to proms."

She raised an eyebrow. "Yeah? And what is it hounds like you do, Marrok?"

He leaned closer. She could feel his breathy whisper in her ear as he spoke, his tone as low and solemn as if he were telling a pack secret. "We spike the punch bowl and eat all the penguins."

She shoved him as hard as she could, and he went flying against the inside of his door. "Oww. All right. Jesus. No wonder it's just you and 9B up there all alone. You're a couple of thugs."

"But we're your thugs," she said with a smile.

They sat in comfortable silence as the car moved at a crawl with all the traffic. Ara decided to finally ask Edon a question that she'd been wondering about ever since they met. She glanced at Edon, taking in his long, lean form and his glittering golden eyes. Edon Marrok, the golden wolf. Back in his glory. "What happened to you?" she asked.

"What do you mean?"

"I mean, from what I hear, you used to look like this all the time."

"Ouch, Scott—you saying I look like shit the rest of the time?" he asked, side eyeing her.

"You know what I mean. Stop acting all sensitive."

Edon fiddled with his cuff links. "Yeah, well. You're not the first girl to notice, if that's what you're thinking." He grinned.

She shook her head. "Yeah, yeah. All the lovely ladies." But they both knew that wasn't what she was talking about.

And Edon didn't have a comeback this time.

"Who was she?" Ara put her hand on his arm, softly. A new kind of gesture. One that they'd never tried out before, not between the two of them. He looked down at her hand.

"Her name is Ahramin. She was my mate," he said, his voice soft and sad.

"What happened to her?" she asked, sympathetic. "Did you lose her in the War?"

"Yeah, I did." Then he looked up, and seeing her face, he quickly corrected, "No, not like that. I didn't lose her *in* the War. I lost her *because* of the War."

"What are you talking about?"

"She's alive. She's fine. She's out there guarding the timeline like a good wolf." He shook his head. "We had— Well, that was some fucked-up shit."

"What happened?"

"It's a long story, but when the wolves escaped from Hell, Ahramin got left behind, and she never really forgave me."

"Yikes. Sorry, man."

Edon ran his fingers through his thick, honey-colored hair. "Yeah, well, can't have everything."

"But what about you and Deming?" she asked.

"Oh, that was after the battle. After she lost her...you know," he said. "She was sort of crazed—I guess I was, too—after Ari said she didn't want me anymore. We...ah...consoled each other." He suddenly looked as awkward as she felt, and she pulled her hand away from his arm.

"Right," she said, shifting in her seat and feeling inexplicably annoyed.

"Yeah, well, blood sex, battle fatigue. Anyway...," he said moodily. "Let's not dwell on the past." His eyes flickered back to her face, and he tried to muster a smile. "We only get one prom night."

Ara nodded, reaching into the cheesy limo minibar, pulling out a bottle of drugstore champagne. She yanked open the screw top and handed it to Edon.

"To fucking prom."

He swigged at the bottle, wiping his now-grinning mouth with the back of his hand. "To fucking penguins."

She drank from the bottle and let the city sights flash past them, noticing the Empire State Building bathed in a bright blue light for the Coven. Nice touch, she thought, impressed by the Regent's reach and connections.

They were in Manhattan now, making their way to Midtown, toward the museum. As the limo moved up the street, it also moved toward the light. A beacon shot light directly into the sky from what had to be the museum, as if the entire city of New York was just a decoration on the perimeter of what was destined to be the event of the season.

"Such bullshit." Edon shook his head.

"It's the scope of the thing. That's what's so impressive. One word from the Regent and the whole city shuts down." She was as amazed as he was, now that she was seeing it for herself.

"All for a fucking party." He sounded disgusted, and she smiled. At least you knew where you stood with the wolf.

He called bullshit on everything, every time, and there was something to be said for that. It was refreshing that he said what he was thinking, which was a rare quality even among the truth tellers. She thought about how they had questioned Finn Chase yesterday. Ara had sworn that the Regent's girlfriend was hiding something, but her words had the ring of truth. As a Venator, Ara hadn't given it a second thought; after all, no mortal could lie to her and get away with it. Maybe Ara was just seeing shadows everywhere.

The car swooped into a long line of limos fronting the block. The streets were roped off, and the museum was lit up with half a dozen spotlights, shining on the facade and up into the sky.

The time for jokes had passed, and Edon and Ara were silent as they climbed out of the limousine. They made their way up the long red carpet, pausing for the crowd of photographers behind the stanchions, who were taking photographs of all the people coming into the party. Lightbulbs flashed like strobes, freezing the couple's every motion, letting every gesture and look hang in the air for just a moment longer than it should.

It was all so disorienting, Ara thought. Old Minty would have been much better at this. It was harder than it looked.

Ara stumbled in her high black stilettos, and Edon put his hand on her back. "Steady, now." He smiled down at her and they let the photos flash.

She scoped out the scene while they posed. "Jesus. Talk about a public event. Every Blue Blood in the city will be known by the time this is over. I hope the Regent knows what he's doing."

Edon snorted. "Yeah, right. You know what they say. *Brass* rhymes with *ass* for a reason."

She tried not to smile. "Nobody says that."

"Sure they do."

She looked at him.

He shrugged. "I say that."

They reached the end of the carpet and checked into the tables, pricking their fingers onto the blood identifiers that analyzed and matched their blood to the ones on record.

A moment later, immense glass doors slid open and they were in.

Edon kept a light hand on her back, and they walked through the party, nodding to acquaintances. No expense had been spared. The gala was the most decadent and lavish one she—or even the old Minty—had ever seen.

As if the architecture of the museum wasn't stunning enough—intersecting concrete panels and steel beams, all sleek lines and stark planes—two enormous white silk tents filled the courtyard between the wings of the museum, their hand-embroidered panels fluttering in the soft, damp wind of the early evening. Tiny lights twinkled in the upper eaves of the tents, which were themselves hung with thick clusters of night jasmine and hydrangea and lily. The white-linen-draped tables sparkled with delicately cut geometric crystals that reflected candlelight in every facet. Clearly, even the most minute details of the gala had been executed to perfection—every scent, every angle, every texture.

Someone has an even shittier job than we do, thought Ara, determined to remain unimpressed. This was the side of the Coven—the swanky, snobby side—that had never appealed to her. The Venators worked in the darkness, but these angels were bathing in the light, as if it cast no shadows.

"See him anywhere?" Edon asked.

"No." Ara bit her lip as she scanned the room, looking for the dark head of Kingsley Martin. She had seen something in the chief's mind yesterday. She had thought he was protecting Kingsley, but Ara realized right then that it wasn't that at all. Sam was anxious about Kingsley, and Ara thought she might have sensed something else along with the anxiety. A feeling she couldn't decode. Dread? Whatever it was, the chief had mixed feelings about his friend.

"You said you don't think Kingsley did it," she said. "That's what you said yesterday. That you don't think it's him."

"I guess I don't. No."

"The chief didn't, either. But when I kept pressing him, he finally relented—almost like he was relieved that I was pressing my point."

"So?"

Ara didn't respond, as she was too busy studying the vampires and their dates, their human familiars, the small scars on their necks.

She felt absently at her own, long and smooth, with no scars—and she blushed as she felt Edon's eyes on her.

"Don't stop on my account," he said with a wink.

"Shut up. It's just—"

He looked at her more closely. "What?" he asked as a waiter came by with a tray of champagne flutes and another arrived with a tasty-looking selection of hors d'oeuvres.

"Those dead girls weren't in our files—which meant the vampire who killed them wasn't in our Coven. At least that's what we assumed."

"Uh-huh," Edon said, grabbing a bacon-wrapped date off of one waiter's tray and two glasses of champagne from the other.

"But what if their killer was someone who had access to the blood records and was able to change them?" she asked as Edon handed her one of the glasses. She took a sip.

"You've got a point there."

"Hold on, my phone's ringing," she said and answered it. She listened and nodded, growing pale. "That was the chief. Something's up. The dead girls. Georgina and Ivy. They're missing from the morgue."

"Missing? What the hell does that mean?"

"They don't know. Nobody saw anything and cameras didn't catch anything, as usual. But they're gone."

"Where'd they go?"

"No one knows."

"Corpses don't just get up and walk away," Edon said. "At least not unless a witch has resurrected it."

But Ara had clocked their prey; the hunter in her smelled a new kill. "Forget it for now. Look who's here."

Edon turned. It was Kingsley Martin all right.

"Let's go," she said, reaching for her blades.

"Damn it, we haven't even taken prom pictures yet," Edon said, sucking on a sticky finger.

Together they made their way across the party, intent on getting their man.

30 | GOLDEN COUPLE

*T*HE RING WAS THE MOST pure diamond he had ever seen. It sparkled like ice, water captured in stone. Of course, it was no mere diamond, but a sacred firestone, forged in the white fires of Heaven to mark the eternal bond between Regis and Coven. The ring the former Regis, the archangel Michael himself, had worn. The Repository vault held many such treasures, but this was one of the Coven's greatest heirlooms. And now it was his to bestow on his beloved as a sign of *his* devotion.

Oliver put the ring back into its velvet box and put it in his pocket. "Ready, darling?" he called out.

Finn walked out of her dressing room, and he had to take a step back. She was blindingly, heart-stoppingly beautiful, more beautiful than he had ever seen her. He was looking at her in awe, as if he had never seen her before.

She was wearing a red dress, which plunged down to the navel and was slit up to the thigh. Her hair was pulled up, leaving her neck and shoulders bare, the expanse of her décolletage and her delicate collarbone almost too painful to bear.

"How do I look?" she asked, giving a little spin. But her eyes were shining, and Oliver thought she might have been crying.

"Ravishing beyond words," he said, kissing her forehead. "You are the most precious thing in the world to me." Seeing the look on her face, he frowned. "I know what you're thinking, and there's nothing we can do now," he said. "But we'll find her killer, I promise you." He had heard the news about Ivy the other night, and while he was annoyed that Sam had sent his Venators to question Finn on her involvement, he understood the necessity.

"It seems awful to celebrate when Ivy is dead," she said.

Oliver nodded. The fact that the second dead girl was so close to the Coven was unsettling. He had come close to calling off the party, but it was simply too late. *The show must go on, as they say.* And yet, he was on high alert tonight. A bundle of nerves, if he was honest. Because it was clearer and clearer by the moment—there was a killer in their Coven. And it was targeting mortals.

Mortals like Finn.

She flashed him a blinding smile, one that didn't quite meet her eyes, and he paused for a moment. "What's wrong?" he asked. He had caught her looking at him strangely, and it worried him.

"Nothing, darling, I'm just a little scared, that's all," she said with a laugh that somehow sounded a little hollow to him.

"Really?" he asked. "Don't worry, I'll keep you safe," he said, flashing his fangs.

The party was everything they wanted, everything they had planned. The Coven had turned out in its glory, and any doubts, any darkness, was hidden in the sound of the orchestra playing a jazzy tune, in the sound of laughter. The exhibit was a smash, the portraits of Allegra Van Alen were beautiful artifacts, and many in the Coven came up to him, to thank Oliver personally for commemorating their past. But even as wonderful as the party was, Oliver couldn't help but feel that it was all a precursor to a gathering darkness. He wanted it over as soon as possible. To perform the ceremony and then leave for the comfort and safety of their home. Somehow, he had a feeling that the sooner it was over, the sooner it would end.

"A toast to the happy couple," Sam said, approaching with two champagne glasses.

"This is good," Finn said, after taking a sip.

"You picked it," Oliver reminded her.

"No, actually this is a special bottle I've been saving for this occasion." Sam smiled. "Congratulations. To new beginnings!"

She nodded to Sam and gulped down the entire glass in one shot.

"Easy there, pardner." Oliver smiled. He sensed how anxious Finn was.

"It's the Four Hundred. Let's celebrate!" Finn said with resolve. She spun away to talk to her guests, leaving Sam and Oliver together.

"About that break-in," said Sam. "We found out what's missing." His forehead crunched.

"Tell me."

"I didn't want to ruin this night but— We checked the vault and... Lucifer..."

"His remains are gone," Oliver said, guessing immediately. "Fuck me."

"A bunch of ashes. What can they do with it?" Sam shrugged. "We'll get the Nephs."

Oliver nodded, keeping down the bile in his stomach. He just had to get through this night alive, and then he would deal with what Sam had told him.

At midnight, the Coven gathered in the lobby of the museum for the investiture ceremony. Oliver walked to the altar that had been set up on the dais. It was a beautiful marble table, and there was a golden cup, the Holy Grail, another of the Repository's treasures.

Inside the cup was the blood of each vampire in the Coven. They had given their blood when they pricked their fingers on the security locks. The Venators had kept each and every drop, and it was now in the cup in front of him.

The Sangre Azul.

The living blood.

The immortal blood.

Oliver lifted the cup to his mouth and drank. In an instant, he was multitudes. He held the lives and the consciousness of every vampire in the world—he saw the face of the Almighty in the blood (the past, the present, the future); it was dizzying—heady—an overwhelming rush of power and strength—

And then it was part of him.

The Coven's heart beat with his heart.

"Your blood is my blood. My heart is your heart. My soul is your soul," Oliver said, saying the words of the blood investiture.

"I am the Regis.

"I am the One and the Only. The Coven and the King. We are one and the same."

There were cheers, tears, roaring applause from the crowd. The Coven had survived the War, had survived Lucifer's revenge, and now there was a new Regis to take them to the next century and beyond.

Then the lights came back on.

And it was time to party.

Oliver politely ignored the swarms of people who wanted to congratulate him. He had one goal on his mind now. He made a beeline for Finn and, smiling, took her hand and led her back to the cozy greenroom where they had gotten ready.

"Oliver, we need to get back to our guests," she protested. "Let's go, they're waiting." Her face was even paler than earlier, and he noticed the dark circles under her eyes. Something was wrong with her, but he was sure it was just exhaustion from the stress of the event. After the ball, he would make sure she got the rest she needed, and he was confident that this would cheer her up.

"I just need a moment alone with you, Finn. Come in." He drew her into the room and closed the door behind them.

He fumbled with the box in his pocket, and even though he knew what her answer would be, he was still nervous. She made him nervous still. He didn't deserve her. He would do anything to let her know how much he loved her for all the days of his life.

"I have something for you," he said and showed her the ring. He took a deep breath, more scared than he had been at the blood ceremony. This mattered most to him; it didn't mean anything without Finn by his side. Without her support, her love, he would have nothing to live for. He had taken leadership of the Coven as part of an ingrained duty toward the vampires, a responsibility he carried as a loyal human Conduit. Only in Finn did he find an escape from the crushing burden and pressure of his position. Only in her did he find happiness and meaning to his life. As Sam noted, Oliver was lucky. Not everyone had what he had. He had Finn, and so he had everything.

"Oh, Oliver," she breathed, her hands fluttering.

"I love you. Will you take me as your own?"

"I already have." She said softly. "But are you sure you want to do this?"

Later, he would realize it was almost a warning. But for now, he touched her neck gently with the tips of his fingers, caressing her smooth alabaster skin; then he leaned down and kissed his favorite spot, his other hand curling into her hair. She pressed her body against his, and when he could not wait any longer, he plunged his fangs deep into her neck and drank her blood. She swooned against him, and he was delirious with love for her. Drinking her in, it was as if he had never tasted her blood before—it was sweeter, addictive, crazy making. He had noticed a difference about a month before... Her blood was different...It was even better...

He was drinking so much of her, more than he ever had, and she murmured, "Hey now...leave some for me."

"I love you," he said again. "I love you."

I am you. You are me.

We are one. As I am now one with the Coven.

Her blood...

Her blood...

Rich and pure and lovely...

He drank her soul...

Finn's soul—a butterfly, a songbird, a flower—it was his; it was golden and beautiful and light, and he drank all of it...until he came to the very end...

And in that end...

In her soul...

Right at the edge of its consciousness...

Was a silver darkness...

A darkness that laughed out loud when he finally stumbled upon it. A darkness that mocked his love and his joy. A darkness that reared up its head and grabbed him by the throat and sank *its* fangs into *his* skin, into *his* blood. And drank *him* instead.

But no, it was Oliver who was still drinking, who held Finn's neck in his fangs, and he was drinking poison and he couldn't stop.

Silver Poison.

That was the last thing he remembered.

After that, everything went black.

31 | FRIENDS IN NEED

*H*ER FOUR HUNDRED BALL was so much better, Mimi wanted to tell Kingsley, except he wasn't next to her. He was somewhere in the shadows, hiding. They decided it was better for Kingsley to remain hidden for now, as no one in the Coven knew he was back from the underworld yet, and it was better to keep it that way. She walked alone through the crowd, letting the murmurs flutter around her.

That's right, take a good long look. The bitch is back.

Mimi had decided to go the classic route and was delighted to find the dress she had worn to her first Four Hundred Ball was still in her storage closet. She'd had it aired out, dry-cleaned, and readied. The white dress made of the thinnest white silk satin fit as well as it had back then, and the keyhole opening at the hip was as sexy as ever. The white dress showed every curve of her body; when the light hit her, her form was shown in the blackened silhouette. She was covered but exposed, clothed but bare.

Kingsley's eyes had almost fallen out of their sockets when he saw her in it. "Jesus, is that what you're wearing? Where has *that* dress been in ten years?"

She smirked and pinched his cheek. "Let's go, put your tongue back in your mouth."

When they arrived she couldn't help but notice that while the party was in full swing, there was a sense of anxiety running through the crowd. What were they all waiting for? The Regent, she supposed. They were nervous about the investiture. This was a big moment for the Coven. A new leader, a new king. But where was Oliver? She didn't see him anywhere. He would probably be angry that Kingsley had kept this information from the Coven, but they would make him understand soon enough.

Mimi took a glass of champagne from a passing tray. Just because they were working didn't mean they didn't get to have fun. They had arrived right in time to catch the blood ceremony, it seemed, as the crowd began to gather around the stage in the middle of the room.

"I was wrong," Chris Jackson said, noticing Mimi. "I thought for certain that something would happen at the ball, but it looks like I was wrong." She looked relieved. "Long live the King."

Mimi nodded. "Nice brooch," she said. "A gift from your brother?"

Chris Jackson's eyes watered and her face flushed. "As a matter of fact, yes. I know I should be ashamed of him, and I am. I'm more ashamed of what Forsyth did than you can imagine. But he was my brother. He was kind to me. And I miss him."

"I understand," she said. "But I'm still glad he's dead."

But at least it cleared up one suspicion. Chris Jackson was not the enemy.

Oliver walked up to the altar, slipping out from a hidden room. He looked somber and grave, but powerful. Different. He was a vampire now, immortal like her. His hazel eyes glinted in the darkness, and Mimi approved of his new haircut. There was nothing boyish about him anymore. He had grown up; he was a man now, a vampire.

He raised the cup to his lips.

Drank the Coven's blood.

And it was done.

The lights came back on and Mimi exhaled. Chris was right. She, too, had been holding her breath and was glad that the investiture had gone off without a hitch. She startled as someone touched her arm, but it was only Kingsley, who had stepped out of the shadows to whisper in her ear. "Oliver's in the greenroom, behind the stage. Let's go."

"Roger that." She nodded.

He smiled. "Roger that?"

"I thought you'd like it. For old times' sake."

He took a good long look at her and smiled. "You look beautiful, darling."

She cocked a hip and winked. "You don't look so bad yourself." Even though she was still a little mad at him, she couldn't help flirting with him. He was her husband after all, and Kingsley looked deadly handsome in a tuxedo.

He leaned down, and she allowed him to brush the hair off her face and kiss her cheek. He was murmuring something in her ear when she saw them.

Two Venators looking right at them, and they were drawing their guns and heading their way.

"They've made us," she told Kingsley, pushing him back and snapping his spellcloak into place. "Hide!"

Kingsley shrugged. "They won't catch me. I'll see you there."

They separated and Mimi saw the Venators run after her husband. He was fast, though, and already cloaked. They wouldn't find him. Mimi cloaked herself and ran through the party toward the room on the first floor that had been reserved for the Regent. The ceremony had been held in the middle of the vast lobby, and there was a hallway of doors behind a hidden wall just as Kingsley had told her, where Oliver had disappeared to.

Mimi was the first to see the blood seeping out from underneath the doorway. Goddamnit.

She looked up to see Kingsley arrive, breathless. They exchanged a stricken glance. Kingsley broke down the door. Inside the room they found Oliver slumped over the body of Finn, both of them covered in blood. They had come to warn Oliver about the danger and it was too late.

Mimi knelt to take Finn's pulse. There was nothing. "She's dead," she told Kingsley, her eyes widening with shock. "And it looks like he killed her. What the fuck is going on?"

Oliver wasn't a killer. He would never do this. He loved Finn; they knew he loved her.

Then she realized.

Some way, somehow, this was Lucifer's doing. It had to be. Lucifer had made this happen.

"It wasn't Ollie," Mimi said. "Or if it was, he didn't know what he was doing."

"No, of course not," Kingsley agreed. "She's gone, and now he's a dead man. If the Venators see this, they'll come after him. He won't be safe anywhere in the Coven."

Mimi cursed. "What do we do?"

"Get him out of here before they find him like this, or they'll burn him for sure," Kingsley said. He knelt down and shook Oliver awake. "Oliver, get up. Oliver."

Oliver blinked his eyes open and stared at them. "Kingsley? What are you doing here? What's happened?"

In answer, Kingsley helped him up and let Mimi shoulder the weight. "You got him?"

She nodded.

"I'll follow."

Oliver looked at them bleary-eyed. Blood was dripping from his fangs onto his white tuxedo shirt. He certainly looked like a killer.

They heard footsteps, shouting in the hallway. The Venators. They had tracked them.

"GO!" Kingsley said. "I'll deal with them."

"But what about you?" she asked. Suddenly, she didn't want to leave him. She was scared for him. Scared to leave him alone, without her protection. No matter how much he'd hurt her, he was still hers.

"Don't worry about me," Kingsley said. "You know I can take care of myself." He pushed her away. "Hurry!"

Mimi half held, half pulled Oliver into the back corridor, thinking she would take him through the kitchens and out the back way, out of the party and out of the Coven before anyone could find out what had just happened.

"Mimi?" Oliver asked, finally opening his eyes. They strove to focus and make sense of the situation. "Mimi, is that really you? What are you doing here? In New York? And where's Kingsley? Didn't I see him just now?"

"Oliver, please, can you stand? Can you walk?" she asked, pulling him. "I can do it, but it would be easier if you could. Come on. We need to go."

"Go? Where are we going? Where am I?" He looked around. "Wait—why are we in the kitchen?"

"I'm trying to get you out the back entrance, so that no one will see you."

"Why?"

"Because they're going to be looking for you in a second," she said, hurriedly casting ignorance spells on the kitchen staff.

"Looking for me? But why?" He threw her off him, his face red, blood seeping from his fangs. "What's happened? Where am I?"

"Oliver, calm down. We don't have much time, and you're in terrible danger, my friend."

"Why? Where's Finn?" he said, looking around. His shirt was covered in blood, her blood. Dark red blood all over his white shirt, except there was more of it than he had ever seen, so much more; he was sticky and wet with it. Her blood.

"MIMI, WHERE IS FINN?" he yelled.

Mimi looked stricken. She didn't know what to say, but it was better to be blunt and let him have the truth rather than talk around it. Maybe if she told him the truth, he would hurry up and help her get him out of here. "Oliver, I'm sorry, but Finn is dead and the Venators are coming after you."

He just stared at her. "What are you talking about? What— Why?"

"Because it looks like you killed her, you drank too much blood," she said. "I'm so sorry, Oliver. I'm so sorry, but I've got to get you out of here. I'll explain later, but if you don't come with me now and the Venators find you, they'll kill you on sight. On your orders."

32 | TO CATCH A KILLER

$\mathcal{H}$IS MISTAKE WAS THAT he had left the shadows to say hello to his wife. The minute Kingsley Martin had taken off his spellcloak to say hello to his beautiful wife, Ara had spotted him. "There," she said. "There he is."

He was smiling and laughing as he kissed Mimi on the cheek. Ara was surprised to find she was even more striking than she had heard. The famous Mimi Force, now Mimi Martin. One would think marriage or the underworld would have aged her, changed her, but she was as glorious and beautiful as ever, if not more so.

Ara felt a little jealousy at the affection between them. You could tell from across the room he was mad for her. For a moment she thought that maybe Edon was right—there was no way Kingsley Martin would take a little mortal girl over Mimi Force. Anyone could see he loved her. But there was only one way to find out—detain and question him.

"Let's go get him," she told Edon.

The investiture ceremony had cleared the tents; everyone was gathered in the main hall now, to watch Oliver take the blood of the Coven into his immortal spirit. It was harder to cut their way through. Ara kept an eye on the couple, but Kingsley disappeared again.

"Where is he?" she whispered to Edon.

"Lost him. He's cloaked again."

"Keep an eye on her."

"No! It's him we want. Let's go."

They separated and Ara scanned the party. Onstage, the Regent was taking the cup in his hands and drinking the blood of the Coven. The audience was silent, attentive, as Ara and Edon snaked their way through.

Your blood is my blood. My heart is your heart. My soul is your soul.

When it was over, the newly crowned Regis smiled and disappeared with his human familiar. They walked toward the back rooms, toward the shadows.

Then she saw him, a flash of his dark head. Kingsley was following them, hot on their heels. He looked intent and focused.

"There he is," she said.

What did he want with the Regis?

What was Kingsley up to?

But the crowd was packed tightly, and they couldn't fight their way through without giving away their position. They couldn't let him know they'd spotted him, couldn't risk him getting away. But by the time they'd found the hidden door that led to the hallway, there was a blood trail and footprints leading out to the kitchens.

Blood. So much blood... but whose?

Ara drew her gun. Edon was at her elbow. "I'll go after them, you check out the room," he said and left, following the trail of blood.

Ara burst through the door.

"Hands up!" she cried, horrified at the sight in front of her.

Finn Chase, the Regent's human familiar, was lying in a pool of her own blood, bleeding from the wounds on her neck, and Kingsley Martin was looming over her, blood on his shirt and jacket.

"You're making a terrible mistake. This isn't what it looks like."

"DON'T MOVE!"

"I'm merely trying to help," Kingsley said.

Ara wavered. Her training, her orders were to kill an enemy on sight. Shoot to kill. She had done it to the Nephilim and she would do it to Kingsley. *Shoot,* she told herself, *shoot.*

He stood up and faced her. "Now if we can discuss this as civilized adults—"

She shot him.

Kingsley fell to the ground.

But not a moment later, before she'd had time to understand

what she'd done, he got up again. Kingsley picked the bullet out of his dinner jacket and flicked it to the ground, leaving a hole in the coat. "I liked this tuxedo. My wife is going to be very annoyed with you," he said, wagging his finger.

"But I shot you," Ara said, still holding her gun.

"So?" Kingsley shrugged.

"These are demon-killers."

"Well, there's your problem. I'm not a demon." He smiled, just as she realized her mistake. He was no demon, but a Dark Angel. A Silver Blood. She should have used the crescents. What did Rowena say? *Use the shanks if you want to be standing after meeting a Silver Blood.*

"I was telling you the truth," Kingsley said. "Use your training to figure out if I'm telling the truth. Listen to me. I didn't kill her. Oliver did."

She did. He was right. He wasn't lying. "The Regis—did this?"

"It appears so," Kingsley said. "But like I said, things are never quite what they seem."

Edon thundered into the room. He shook his head. "I followed the blood trail—it was Mimi and Oliver, but they're gone. I let the chief know, though, and Venator teams have been sent out. They'll find them."

"I can explain everything," Kingsley said.

"You can tell your story at headquarters," Ara said, slapping silver cuffs on him. "I need it on record for the chief."

33 | A CERTAIN SATURDAY NIGHT IN AUGUST

*D*O ANY OF YOU HAVE A LIGHT?" Kingsley asked. "Nobody smokes anymore? That's a shame." He snapped his fingers and a small flame appeared. He lit his cigarette and took a deep inhale.

"Start at the beginning. When did you come back from the underworld and what have you been doing here?" Ara demanded.

"Everything?" Kingsley asked. "Then I suppose I'll have to start with Darcy."

He propped his foot up on the table and unreeled his tale.

Come on, Damien, let's have a good time.

Her name was Darcy McGinty, and Kingsley knew the minute he set foot inside the taxicab that he had made a mistake. He should get the fuck out of there. What was he doing with these kids? He was too old for this; he had been out of his mind to think he wanted this. He wanted to get out of the car, get back to Mimi, and clear his head. Stop that ringing in his ears, which was starting to drive him insane. He thought he might know what caused it, but he wasn't sure. Although he knew for certain that it was irritating.

"Listen, I've got to go," he said, reaching for the door latch.

"What? Why? Stay," Darcy said, annoyed.

"No, I should go." He told the cabdriver to pull over.

"Stay, this party is going to be something else," she said, uncurling her fist and showing him a white pill.

"Thanks, but no thanks, darling. I don't do drugs. I'm high on life," he said with a smile, thinking of his friend Oliver, who used to say that.

"It's not a drug. It's from angels," she said. "Right, Georgie?" She turned to her friend, who looked just like her. Blonde, too much makeup, too little clothing. The girl in the front seat turned around with an avid smile. "It's awesome, you should try it."

"Angel dust?" Kingsley asked. "That all?" He shrugged. Big deal.

"No, not that sad, old seventies thing. Angel *blood*. *Sangre Azul*. Blue Blood. Holy blood. Because angels are real."

Kingsley stopped and turned around to look at her. "They are? How do you know?"

Darcy giggled. "I've seen one. I'm looking at one right now," she said and pretended to shoot him.

She was pretending, of course. She had no clue, he saw soon enough. It appeared she was already a little high on something. But what was this talk about angel blood, the *Sangre Azul*, and angels being real? Where did she hear *that*? Kingsley leaned back into his seat. "All right, then, give it to me." A drug made from angel blood. Was it a joke? It had to be. Were the Venators aware of this? Weren't they supposed to keep the Coven's secrets safe? What was going on if kids could get their hands on this stuff?

"How does it make you feel exactly?" he asked.

"It's awesome. You feel so good, and all your senses are, like, alive; you hear better, you see better, everything you touch feels good," she said dreamily, as the cab stopped in front of a dark warehouse building. "All right, here we are. Time to fly with the angels."

The room was pitch-black, and the music was more than loud; the stereo system pumped the rhythm so violently it beat in your heart, throbbed in your chest, you drowned in the music, it washed over your soul, became part of your body, until you were just a vehicle for the beat. *Thump, thump, thump.* Kingsley squinted. He was used to nightclubs, to dance floors, to weeklong music festivals in the rain, but this was different. It was like the music was more sinister, more intimidating, or maybe he'd just gotten old.

"Feeling good?" Darcy laughed, and ran her hands up and down his chest.

He smiled and took her hands off him, shaking his head. She was way too young, and besides, he was married. Maybe he was with her at this party because old habits died hard, but he had stayed because he was working a job now. He fingered the pill he'd hidden in his pocket. So far, it didn't seem to do much to the kids except what you would expect, a lot of floppy dancing, a lot of glazed eyeballs, a lot of sweaty foreheads. Maybe the pill was nothing but a placebo. Maybe the Conspiracy was behind it, although those mythmongers usually stuck to creating pop fantasies, not influencing underground drug culture. He was starting to have a bad feeling about this.

Kingsley danced for a few more songs, then went into the men's room. He removed the pill. There was a quick test that would let him know whether Darcy was telling him the truth. He was sure the girls were being ridiculous, but out of overabundance of caution, he decided it wouldn't hurt to test the product.

He pulled out his blade and cut his thumb, and let his blood drip on the little white pill.

It hissed and smoked.

There was Fallen matter in it all right.

The blood of the angels, she had called it.

Fuck.

Kingsley shuddered. This was the stuff of nightmares. He'd been in the underworld for a decade and everything was off the rails. He had to get to the bottom of this.

He wandered around the party, talking to people, and heard other names for the drug. They called it Angel Wings, or Vitamin P, or Type A, or Sang Blue (some kind of mishmash of *Sangre Azul* and Blue Blood). Others called it something even more insidious— *Allegra's Sacrifice.* How did these mortal teenagers know about Allegra? How did they know so much about the Coven?

They were all popping or snorting it. But no one would tell him anything about the drug or where to get it. Whenever he asked, they only said, "Darcy." And when he asked Darcy, all she did was give him a seductive little smile. He tried reading her mind, sifting through her memories, but he found little that could offer a concrete answer.

Maybe she was too out of it to remember where she got this from, or maybe she didn't care.

He motioned to Darcy that he was going out for a smoke and made his way through the sweaty tangle of bodies toward the door.

"Hey, can I have a light?" a girl asked, walking out with him. She was one of the girls from the taxicab with Darcy. The one who looked just like her, blonde and pretty, but somehow outside, alone, Kingsley saw he was wrong. She wasn't like Darcy at all. Her pink dress had looked more scandalous in the dark, but the cut was actually conservative. She didn't look like the type to hang out at some rave on the outskirts of Brooklyn. "You're too young to smoke," he told the girl. "And you should never start." He was immortal, after all, but she was not.

"Fine." She sighed.

"What's your name again?"

"Georgie," she said, hugging herself tightly.

"What's wrong, Georgie?" he asked because he sensed she was feeling low, and he felt bad for her. She looked too young to be at a place like this.

"I'm tired. I have school tomorrow. I don't know why I'm here."

"Come on," he said, tossing the cigarette. "I'll take you home."

"What about Darcy?" she asked fearfully.

"What about Darcy?" He shrugged.

Georgina was a nice kid. He called for a car and dropped her off at her apartment building in Midtown. She was different from Darcy, he could tell right away. He liked Georgina. He and Mimi should have a kid, he thought. Why didn't they? Oh, right, she didn't want to raise a kid in Hell. *This is no place for a baby,* she'd said many times.

"Call me," he said, plugging his digits—he'd picked up a burner the other week—into her phone. "We'll hang." He needed an informant, he thought, someone who could tell him where Darcy was getting this stuff and who was making it.

For the next week or so, Kingsley worked on Georgina, spending time with her, befriending her. Darcy told everyone Georgina had "stolen" him, and they let her think that. There was nothing inappropriate between them. Kingsley could see that mostly what Georgina needed was a friend. School had started, and she was working too hard; her parents put a lot of pressure on her to do well, and it was getting to her. Plus, there were the usual teenage crises like not having enough money and friends being more like enemies, like Darcy for one.

She liked to come to his place and study there. It was a nice house, he had to agree; a little dusty and the air was a little stale, but once the windows were open it was all right. He'd told her his parents were in Bermuda and he was homeschooled.

"Do you know where Darcy gets those pills? Angel blood?" he asked casually one afternoon after they'd met. He was smoking by the windows.

Georgina tapped a pencil against her cheek. "I don't know. She mentioned some friends from some kind of committee were passing them out."

"Committee?" He raised an eyebrow. There were many committees in New York, but there was only one that mattered to the Coven.

"Yeah, I think it's some kind of social group, etiquette classes, that sort of thing."

"And it's a drug front?"

"I don't know, okay?" She laughed. "I mean, I just heard her talking about getting more of it during a 'committee meeting.'"

"Can you find out more?"

"Sure, why? I thought you didn't take that crap. What are you, some kind of cop?" she asked.

"Maybe." He smiled.

"Damien, you are so lame. Okay. Whatever. I'll find out. See you later. My mom's here," she said. She walked out the door of Schuyler's old house. It was the safest house in the Coven, and his old friend wouldn't mind. It wasn't as if she was using it right now. Kingsley had put up wards around the place and made sure he wouldn't be disturbed.

"I found out where the Committee's getting it," Georgina said on his voice mail, sounding terrified the next Saturday evening. "Darcy's having a party tonight. Meet me there. I'll text you the address. By the way, if you are a cop, I want some kind of award or citation or something. I don't know what this is, but I'm scared, Damien. I don't want any part of it. I think someone's been following me around since I've been asking questions about the pills. But you'll make it okay, right, Damien? Right?"

Kingsley called her back, but she didn't pick up the phone. He had been working on his own on this, and his first instinct was to contact his old friends in the Coven. But when he heard the Committee was involved and that Georgina was scared, he changed his mind.

Someone from the Coven was distributing angel blood. Possibly even Allegra's blood.

But who?

Georgina wasn't at Darcy's party, and no one seemed to know where she had gone. There was another text on his phone. He'd asked her to try to ask the kids she knew in the Committee to let them know she was buying and would pay a pretty price for it. It looked like they hooked the big fish.

DARCY'S SUPPLIER SAID TO MEET HIM AT CANAL AND MOTT. I TOLD HIM WHAT YOU SAID THAT YOU WOULD PAY TRIPLE WHAT SHE DOES.

Good girl, Kingsley thought. She could work undercover one day. Maybe he would get her a job as a human Conduit for the Venators.

It was a busy Saturday night in Soho, and the crowds were thick on the sidewalk—NYU students roaming in packs, girls in high heels tottering down the cobblestones to the cocktail bars, couples on dates, arm in arm, headed to the little restaurants. The stores were shuttered, but their window displays were illuminated. He stood at the corner, waiting for Georgina, and decided to grab a double latte. Coffee was a weakness of his.

Kingsley sat on a bench and waited. Fifteen minutes. Thirty. There was no Georgina. No one at all. He called her cell phone again. No answer. Forty-five minutes passed. Even with New York traffic that was a long time. An hour stretched into two, and he was worried now. He wandered off to get another coffee, and when he came back, he saw that the intersection of Canal and Mott had a small hidden door in the ground. One that had a pentagram etched on its surface.

Kingsley suddenly had a terrible feeling that he was too slow. Too slow. He dashed into the hole and fell into the dark cavern. "GEORGINA!" he yelled. "WHERE ARE YOU?"

But already he knew it was too late. Why had he given her the job? Why had he asked her to do something so dangerous? Had he really been in the underworld that long to have made such a tragic mistake? To give a schoolgirl a Venator's job? What was he thinking?

When he found her, she was dead.

She was lying in a puddle, bleeding from the wounds on her neck. She had found out who was distributing those angel pills and it had gotten her murdered. She had struggled and fought, but she was no match for her enemy, for her killer. Her killer had taken her left hand and had drawn a bloody pentagram on the wall.

He carried her away from the pentagram's dark influence and hid her body in a safe place in the tunnels, where the Venators would find her, because they always did.

"So that's my story. After that happened, I realized I needed help, so I went to see my wife. She's the only one I can trust. I was, ah— Reluctant to tell her what I was up to—I didn't think she would take kindly to finding out I was clubbing with teenagers—but I decided I had to risk it. Then I went back to hang out with Darcy to see if she would tell me anything more about where she got it. But she didn't know. She said the pills would just appear in her locker one day. In this bag."

He showed them the plastic bag he had shown Mimi, the one with the five silver triangles. The one that Ara had found on the Nephilim and in the burned-out hive.

"You've seen this before, I take it?" Kingsley asked.

Ara nodded. "We found their hive. So I was right—they were using the pentagrams to mark their territory and identify their targets. That's why they were all over New York. Because they were everywhere."

"They knew I was here. They marked my hiding place as a warning," Kingsley said.

"Yeah, we saw the pentagram on the Van Alen safe house," said Edon. "Nephilim selling angel blood. Allegra's Sacrifice. Who'd have thought?"

"In death is life," Kingsley muttered.

"What did you say?" asked Ara.

"It's something I read in the *Book of Hell*, below a pentagram. In death is life. Why?"

"That's interesting, isn't it? Because those two dead girls—the ones who were bitten—their bodies are missing, and the Venators said it was as if they had just walked out of the morgue," Ara said.

Kingsley snapped his fingers. "Because that's exactly what they did. In death is life, the Little King will rise again. Somehow, whoever has done this has made the Conspiracy real. It's a joke on us, on the Blue Bloods," Kingsley said. "A cosmic joke."

"Because of course there's no such thing as vampires. A vampire bite can't turn you into one. That's only a fairy tale," Edon said.

Kingsley sighed. "Except now it isn't. Lucifer's made a mockery of us. He's made our lies true. Mortals take the angel drug, and when humans are bitten to death, they rise up again as vampires."

*A*RA JUMPED DOWN from the table in excitement. "We need to stop it— Find out who's gotten it— Get every human familiar tested before their vampires bite them..."

"We will," Kingsley said. "So far, it looks as if it's just a few club kids. It can't have gotten far."

"But where were they getting it? The blood, I mean?" Edon asked. "Allegra has left the building, so to speak."

"The paintings," Kingsley said. "They have to be from the paintings. Stephen's paintings of Allegra. He used his blood in the paint."

"His blood—but not hers."

"But when a vampire takes a human familiar their blood mixes— so even if it was his blood, it was hers as well. They are one and the same. That is the essence of the blood bond," Kingsley said. "When Mimi reminded me of that last night, I knew where it came from." He should have confided in her earlier, he thought. His wife had always been so clever.

"The paintings had been in storage until a few months ago. We can check the records, see who had access to it," Ara said.

"But here's the thing," Kingsley said. "This is the same pill from a few weeks ago. The one Darcy gave me. Look." He removed an envelope from his pocket.

He showed them the pill—it was coal black now, shiny, like a black diamond. "This isn't just angel blood. If it was, it would remain white. Allegra was pure-blooded. And if what we think is true, if those dead girls are walking around, alive, it's not just her blood that made them so. An angel's blood is not enough to wake the dead. You need a demon for that."

"Demon's blood?"

"Or a demon's remains," Kingsley said. *"The chimes of Helheim signal the beginning of the eternal darkness brought by the Morningstar's White Worm to poison the gift of the Heavens."* He quoted from the *Book of Hell.* "White Worm...like a snake...A snake sheds its skin...its skin remains...Lucifer's remains. His ashes," Kingsley said. He turned to Ara. "Do you know where they are?"

"Blood-locked in the Repository, in the safest safe in the world. Guarded by Venators." Ara looked at them. "Oh my God, the missing time stamps...this is what was stolen that night."

"Lucifer's remains are in these pills," Kingsley said, his voice hoarse. "It's the only explanation. An angel and a demon together. Lucifer stole the gift of procreation from the mortal world to create the Nephilim, but his blood would be too potent; it would be enough to raise the dead, but not turn them into—"

"—vampires," Edon said. "At least the popular conception of such. Whoever did this needed Allegra's blood for that. Together they turn mortals into monsters."

"The Nephilim mean to infect the populace but let the Blue Bloods do the dirty work for them," said Ara.

"We need to find those dead girls before they bite anyone else. Limit the contagion. Shut it down before it gets too far," Kingsley said.

"But first—we need to stop the distribution at the source. Darcy said she got it from the Committee, right?" Ara asked.

"That's all she would tell me. I kept trying to get her to tell me more. I even used the mind lock on her, but someone had tampered with her memories," Kingsley said.

"You broke the rules."

"I decided it was time. Georgina was dead. There were no more rules. But the supplier had gotten to her first. Someone knew I was looking around and started covering their tracks."

Ara told them of the suspicion she'd had earlier, that they had assumed because the blood signature on file wasn't in the records that the vampire who had killed Georgina and Ivy was a renegade.

But what if the records had been scrubbed? What if they were able to find it that way?

"So whoever did this had access to the Committee, access to the Repository, access to the blood records...someone who can manipulate the time stamps...Other than Oliver...who has this kind of access?" Kingsley asked.

"There's only one other person in the Coven," Edon said. "You know who it is."

Kingsley nodded.

"No," Ara said. "No, you're wrong."

"Ara," Edon said. "He sent for me to muzzle you. He thought I would be a fuckup and that I would distract you from your work. You and Rowena were getting too close to the truth."

She closed her eyes and felt ill. She had been close to solving the mystery of the pentagrams, and after she had killed that Nephilim downtown, he had taken her home, had made love to her, so she couldn't see what he really was.

Sam Lennox.

Venator chief.

Murderer.

35 | KING WITHOUT A CROWN

*T*HE APARTMENT WAS ALL WHITE, and when Oliver woke up, his first thought was that maybe he had died and gone to Heaven. Only he was never going there. He was immortal now, a vampire; he had chosen to live on earth forever. Maybe it was all a bad dream, and when he got out of bed, Finn would be alive and well, and everything would be just the same as ever.

Except the girl who walked through the doorway was not his love but his friend. Mimi smiled at him sadly. "How are you feeling?"

"Like I'm living in a nightmare. Wake me up, will you?"

"You're safe with me. Kingsley cloaked my apartment, they won't find you here," she said. She placed a glass of water on the side table. "Look at us, nothing ever changes; we're still here, still fighting Lucifer."

"Lucifer is dead."

"Yeah, that's what I kept telling Kingsley, too," she said. "Buck up, Oliver, we'll figure it out."

"Mimi, how you've changed," he said with a smile.

"Have I?"

"You were never this optimistic before."

"Well, we did get him last time," she said.

Oliver brooded on that. They hadn't seen each other in ten years, and they should have been catching up on their lives, sharing stories. Instead, only the heavy weight of grief hung between them. He had been so proud of all he had done, so proud of his work, what he had built, and now he had lost everything.

"What happens now?" he asked aloud.

"Rest," Mimi said. "Rest. When Kingsley gets back, we'll figure out what to do."

She left him alone again.

Oliver slumped back into the pillows. What happened back there? Had he really killed her? How had he lost control? He had stopped—he knew he had to—he would never deliberately kill her. Oh, God—did he kill her?

Finn.

Where are you?

This can't be real.

She was killed by her vampire and she was blood bound to him. He held the blood of the Coven in his blood, he was their Regis but now his own Venators were after him, they were hunting him; he was a criminal.

Mimi told him that there was something going on, about some drug Kingsley had discovered that was being distributed by the Committee to the mortal populace. It was contained with club kids for now, but who knows where it would end. Angel blood, it was called. There was a traitor in the Coven, just like before. His Coven. His peaceful, wonderful Coven. The community he had brought back from the ashes. The community that was now falling apart, right when they were to celebrate its return. What was his mistake? What had he done wrong?

There was something in Finn's blood, he remembered...

Angel blood. Infection.

How had he not seen it before?

Poison.

It was why he had lost his sense of taste, his sense of smell, why the sun had started to hurt his eyes. Whatever had poisoned her had also poisoned him. The darkness was inside him as well, but he had to be certain.

He put on a robe over the pajamas Mimi had loaned him and walked out to the living room where she was on the phone.

"I need to see her," he said. "I need to see Finn. I need to see her body."

"Yes, we do," Mimi said, putting down the phone. "Oliver—I don't want you to freak out, but it might be too late."

"What do you mean?"

"That was Kingsley. The two dead girls are gone, and he just found out that Finn's body disappeared from the morgue a few hours ago," she said, her face ashen.

"What do you mean, it just disappeared? Dead bodies don't just walk out the door!" Oliver yelled. Then he knew.

He stared at Mimi.

She stared back at him.

Oliver suddenly remembered everything. Everything that happened when he drank Finn's blood last night.

The taste of the silver poison.

It spread throughout his entire being, and as he drank from her, he realized the poison was not meant just for him or his blood, but the blood of the entire Coven—which he had just taken into his soul during the investiture ceremony. If he let the poison run its course, it would infect every vampire in the Coven, turning them into their enemies—

Silver Bloods—

Vampires who hunted vampires—

Lucifer's army—

A new demon army would rise from the Coven's ashes, and he would be in the middle of it, as their dark and fearless leader. The darkness would be alive within him.

If he let it.

He had to fight it.

Fight the ghost, fight the shadow, fight the creature that was starting to gain control...

Oliver fought. He struggled against his hold on Finn's neck, attempting to extricate himself, to remove his fangs, but he could not—and so the only way to fight was to drink harder, to suck out every molecule, to cleanse the poison of Lucifer's soul with his own blood, to let it wash through his own spirit, a soul that had been blessed by the Almighty, and he would hold it in his heart; and he would not let the blood of the Coven, that bright, shining star in the center of his universe go dim; he would accept the darkness first— he would take all of the darkness *into* himself...

He took the darkness. *I accept your anger and your rage and your hate, and I meet it with love. I take it all. I wrap my soul around your anger and your fury.* He drank from her blood, filled himself with the poison, and took it all—

—and in the end, he won.

The darkness was defeated in a blazing light of his surrender, and when it was over, the poison was gone.

Defeated.

He told Mimi what he just remembered. "I was able to stop the worst from happening, to stop the Silver Bloods from taking the Coven. But in order to do so, Finn died."

"But she's *not* dead, Oliver," Mimi said. "That's the worst part about all this." She picked up her ringing phone. "Kingsley says to meet him at Coven headquarters. He knows who's behind it, and he wants you there when they arrest him."

36 | A GOOD MAN

OLIVER WAS WAITING FOR THEM at headquarters, and together they went to the security floor. The chief was in his office, almost waiting for them, when they arrived. Ara burst open the door, her blades in her hands, and death on her face.

Sam was putting away his files. He looked up at them, disinterested, unafraid. "I wondered when you would get here," he said.

"Why, Sam?" she asked. "Why did you do it? You fought so hard to defeat Lucifer—how could you do this?"

"I fought, and fought, and fought. All I did was fight," he said wearily. "I was a Venator for longer than any one of you can know. Kingsley," he said, spotting his old friend in the doorway.

"Sam," Kingsley said, and there were tears in his eyes. "Sam... you should have told someone you needed help."

"I told them it wasn't you. I told them, but they wouldn't listen." Sam shrugged. "I told them you were a good man."

"*You* were a good man."

"I was. But the War broke me." He brought out a frame and showed Ara. "You didn't know her. Her name was Dehua Chen. Deming's sister. My bondmate. She died in the War. I lost her."

"We lost a lot of good people," she said.

"You didn't," Sam said, looking at Kingsley and Mimi accusingly. "You got your happy ending. But when she died, all I got...was nothing. Just this fucking job..."

"I thought we were friends, too, Sam," Oliver said. Everyone turned to look at the beleaguered Regis who had just arrived.

"Friends?" Sam snarled. "You had everything—the Coven—her. Your little human familiar. You were happy. I blamed you for her death. Dehua died saving your ass."

Oliver twitched. He had been mortal in the battle; it was before his transformation. Sam was right—Dehua had saved him, had died saving him.

"She gave her life for yours. I never forgave you. Never."

"She would hate you," Mimi said. "Dehua fought Lucifer; she gave her life fighting him. She would hate you for what you've done here."

"Don't you think I know that? Don't you think I think of that every day of my life?" he spat. "Peace. Fuck your peace. I don't have peace. Now you'll never have peace. Suck on their blood, and see what monster you create." He laughed. "See how Lucifer is in all their hearts, all their minds."

"What did the Nephilim promise you, Sam?" Oliver asked quietly. "Did they promise that you could have Dehua back? Is that what they promised?"

Sam smiled a deathly smile. "How did you know?"

"I know the way they work. They feed into your desires, and they twist them. They give you what you want, but what they meant to do was for you to join her—in death."

"You killed Georgina," Kingsley said.

"Had to be done. She was asking too many questions, nosing around. She saw me do a drop-off at the corner, and she asked me point-blank if I was Darcy's supplier. I told her I was, and that if she met me later that night I would tell her where I got it."

"Ivy—she was the one who got the blood for you, wasn't she? She scraped them off the paintings. You targeted her, you needed Allegra's blood as well as Lucifer's, and you needed an artist to get it."

He smiled. "Then she goes and tells Finn that she's my human familiar. Little tattletale. But that's the best part of this story. Finn."

"What about Finn?" asked Oliver, seething. He hated to hear her name on this traitor's evil lips.

"I didn't do anything to Finn," he said with a smile. "She volunteered. Your little perfect trophy. I found her trolling for drugs on the streets."

Oliver was shocked into silence.

"When she found out what I was doing, she wanted to be part of it. She was the one who put the pentagram in your office, and on your building, to mark you as one of our victims."

"No," Oliver said softly. "No. Not Finn."

"I didn't see it. Edon and I questioned her and I didn't see it," said Ara, appalled. "She was mortal—I didn't think she had the ability to lie to me."

"We bumped into each other, right before the raid on the Nephilim nest," Sam said. "She asked me what I was doing there and I told her. Poisoning the kids would be the first step; if it worked, the infection would spread. I thought I'd kill her like the rest, but she said she had a better idea. She thinks big, I'll give that to her."

"No," Oliver said. "No, you're lying."

"She begged me not to kill her; she said she would take the rest of the remains in one pill the night of the ball. I had only been using a tiny bit of it in the drugs, but she said she wanted me to make her one with every last ash in it. She would take it right before the investiture. Afterward she would offer herself up to you. She knew you wouldn't be able to help yourself, that you would want to suck on her right there." His eyes gleamed with a terrible madness. "So that you would take her—kill her—and then she could come back. As something else. Reborn, shall we say. She wanted another life. Eternal life. She wanted you to give it to her. To be the one to kill her; it would be her last gift to you and the Coven." He smiled an evil, empty grin. "What did you do to her, Oliver, to make her hate you so much?"

Oliver lunged at Sam, but Kingsley held him back. "Easy, man... don't be like him. Don't give in to revenge."

Sam laughed.

Edon moved to handcuff him, and Mimi was there with her sword, but before they could stop her, Ara had her blades out. The crescent blades, her moon shanks. A Venator's deadliest weapon able to kill the most dangerous of enemies. Lucifer's men.

She ran toward Sam and with an agonized, angry scream cut his head off his body with her weapons.

No trial, no courtrooms. Justice was meted out by the Venator's blades.

No mercy, because she was a Venator, and she had found the

monster lurking in the shadows. Just as she had vowed, she had uncovered the secrets of the darkness and brought the truth to light.

Ara dropped the blades to the ground and fell on her knees, sobbing. "I'm so sorry, I'm so sorry." She didn't know to whom she was apologizing, but she knew she had to ask for forgiveness.

Edon looked askance and pulled her up to stand, held her while she cried. "Don't blame yourself, Ara. It's not your fault. You did what you had to," he said. His voice was the kindest she had ever heard.

"Hey," Edon growled. "Look at me. You're not a killer. You're a good person."

She nodded and gulped her tears and sobbed some more. Because Sam Lennox was a good man, but things had been taken from him—hope, love, life—and so he had done this. He needed salvation just as much as she had.

"Ara." Edon sighed.

"I can't...I can't...," she said.

Edon embraced her. The Regis was standing there, looking lost, and Kingsley and Mimi were standing behind him; Mimi was patting his shoulder.

The door burst open again and Deming Chen entered with a group of Venators, blades and guns at the ready. She saw Sam's body on the floor. "What the fuck is going on?"

"Go," Kingsley said to Edon. "We'll take care of this. But you take her out of here. Take care of her."

37 | NEVER SAY GOOD-BYE

I SUPPOSE THIS IS GOOD-BYE?" Kingsley asked, when they were alone in her apartment again. After Ara had killed Sam, he and Mimi had explained everything to the Venators and had gotten everything set to rights, or as much as they could. The angel drug, the Silver Poison, everything that Sam had done was now out in the open, and the only thing unresolved was their relationship.

"Is it?" Mimi asked. "Does it have to be?" She sighed and turned her back to him, and a few minutes later, his breath was in her ear and his hands circled her waist. "Is that what you want? Or do you want to have a little fun?" he asked.

"What do you have in mind?" she asked.

"Why don't you put on that dress you were wearing the other night and I'll show you?" He grinned.

"This doesn't mean anything," she said, pulling him closer.

"Of course it doesn't." Then his mouth was on hers, and he was kissing her, and she was kissing him back, urgently, passionately, just like the first time, just like before.

"I'm still mad at you," she said, and now his hands were all around her body, and one of them was pulling down the zipper of her dress.

"Of course you are, darling." He hooked her leg around his knee, and he let her dress fall to the floor, while she tore at his shirt, ripping it off his body. His laughter was dark and rich and knowing.

But this time, she caught his hands and chained them to the bedpost. "My turn." She smiled.

Then she rode him, and he was helpless, watching her, loving her, his eternal, immortal love, and they cried out together, and she put her head on his chest and wept, because she hated him for what he could do to her. And because she loved him so much.

Kingsley finally told her what he had meant to say before she left. "You are my home. Wherever you are, I will be. Don't leave me, ever. Don't ever do that again. You almost destroyed me," he said tenderly.

She wiped his tears and her own. "I'm sorry," she said. "The minute I left the house, I knew I'd made a mistake, but I couldn't stop myself."

"I want to be where you are," he said.

"I'll never leave you. Never," she promised.

"Well, even if you do," he said, "I'll follow you."

"What are we going to do?" she asked. "We're terrible at this."

"What we always do," he said. "What we can. We'll stay together because that's the only thing I know how to do. You can never get rid of me. Never."

She smiled happily, tracing a lazy finger on his chest and downward, feeling him spark back to life for more. "Are you ever going to take these off?" he asked, pulling against the chains.

"I don't know." She smiled. "I sort of like you like this," she said, leaning over his body, teasing him with her tongue, and taking all of him in her mouth.

His eyes rolled to the back of his head and he groaned happily.

There was no such thing as a happy ending, only a happy present. Mimi knew they would fight again, and they would scream at each other again, but they would never break apart. Whatever happened, they would be together, always.

After the third time they made love that night, Mimi decided she had tortured the poor boy enough and unlocked the chains.

"What about those bells?" she asked suddenly. "Hell's Bells, you said—something had escaped from Hell."

"Yes. Something had," he said sheepishly, rubbing his wrists, his eyes glazed and content after their lovemaking. "Can you guess?"

"You never unlocked the gates for me, did you? You bastard," she said. "You *wanted* to set off the alarm."

"No, I didn't. But when it first rang, I was convinced something had escaped from Hell. I only realized later that I had made a huge mistake. That I had forgotten to unlock the gates for you, and that's why the alarm went off. But it was a wake-up call, wasn't it? A dangerous creature had escaped from the underworld, escaped from my notice. You." He smiled sheepishly.

She rattled the chains threateningly.

"Enough," he laughed, taking her in his arms and kissing her once more. "I turned them off a long time ago. Don't you notice? You can't hear them anymore."

"What are we going to do?" she asked. "Will you take the position?" The one the conclave had offered him after they had processed all the information.

He sighed. "I don't think I have a choice. What about you?"

"I'll do it if you do," she said.

Oliver had left the Coven. He was no longer Regis, as it turned out that the purification he had performed on the poison had also washed out the blood of the Coven from his soul. He had left to find Finn. She was out there—alive, alone, lost, corrupted—and he had to find her; he had to save her.

Before they had left headquarters, Chris Jackson, who was the acting head of the Coven since Oliver relinquished the title, had asked them to return and serve, with Kingsley as Venator chief and Mimi as Regent, and while it was not something they wanted or had aspired to, they decided it was the best for now.

At the very least, it meant they could stay in New York. Together.

38 | WOLF AND ANGEL

*T*HE MISSING DEAD GIRLS had been found right inside the Coven headquarters. They had managed to stagger out of the morgue and to the basement, but that was as far as they had been able to go. Both of them were dead; they would not rise again. The angel and demon blood had resurrected them for a time, but it had not turned them into vampires. The Nephilim's plan hadn't worked as well as they had hoped. Vampires could not turn mortals into vampires, at least not yet. That was still a fairy story distributed by the Conspiracy.

Sometimes everything went as it was supposed to. Sometimes the bad guys didn't get away. At least, not all of them. And not often enough, thought Ara.

But sometimes.

Sometimes the world got saved. Parts of it, at least. Partly saved.

This was one of those times, and Ara didn't question it.

The investigation concluded swiftly. She was cleared on every count, and the death of Sam Lennox, former boss and former lover, was deemed justified. Ara was found to have delivered justice, as was her calling, and she had been reinstated on the Venator team by the following week.

One long week.

She entered her office, promptly (for once) at midnight, and found Edon at their desk. He motioned to the cup of coffee waiting on her side, next to her empty chair. "Three sugars," he said. "And I tipped the barista this time."

Ara smiled, sinking into her hard, wooden chair. "Miracles never cease," she said.

"Welcome back, boss," he said, leaning back in his chair with a grin. Edon kicked his feet up on the desk. "I knew you couldn't keep away."

Ara shoved them back off. "What, you missed me, Marrok? You going soft?"

He scoffed. "No. But your neighbor in 9B keeps calling me up for dates and, you know, I could use an extra set of hands around to answer the phone. Just to keep track of all my lady friends."

"Is that all I am to you? A pair of... hands?" She smiled teasingly.

"You really want me to answer that?" He flicked a coffee stirrer across the desk, in her direction. "I'm just sayin'. I saw how you looked at me, back there in my penguin suit."

"I don't know what you're talking about, wolf."

"I know. You're not all that bright. I don't know why nobody listens to me about that." He sighed dramatically.

She smiled. "What about you? Are you leaving? Going back to keeping time?"

Edon shrugged. "I dunno. I think I might kick back here awhile. Or go visit my brother Mac in Vienna. But who knows, I find I'm quite fond of the Big Apple."

"You know, no one who's from New York ever calls it that, right? It's like calling San Francisco 'Frisco.'" She shuddered.

"Aiiight," he drawled. "Calm down now."

She stiffened. She didn't want to think about splitting up with another partner. Not so soon. Not even after all they'd been through together.

So she did what she always did, which was say the opposite of what she meant or even felt. "You should probably go."

"Go?"

"See your brother. Vienna. It's full of pastry and shit like that."

"Yeah?" He looked her in the eye. "That's what you think?"

She shrugged. "Why not? This city is a shithole. This department is screwed. The whole community is on edge. Why not get out while you still can? Even the Regis is gone, right? Why should anyone stay?"

He thought about it, tapping the desk. "You're right. Everything about this job blows. And you know what else?"

"What?"

He sat up. "We never even got one fucking slow dance. I mean, forget about the picture, angel. Not one dance. Can you believe that shit?"

"Seriously."

He stood up and held out his hand.

She shook her head, laughing. "Shut the fuck up."

"Come on."

"Go away."

"No."

"I am not dancing with you in the middle of the fucking office, Marrock."

"Why not, angel?" His eyes twinkled. "We only have one prom." He leaned closer, and she could feel the warmth of his face as it neared hers.

"We only have one anything," he said softly.

And that was when he kissed her, kissed her on the lips, swiftly, tenderly, and she kissed him back, and they were kissing right there in the middle of their office. And it felt good to kiss Edon after what had happened, almost as if he were reminding her of her better nature.

Something about it worked. Something about him worked.

She pulled away from him, not in a bad way, but because he had already made it better.

He nodded to let her know he understood.

Ara looked around, but no one had noticed as far as she could tell. She cleared her throat. "Turns out that kid who was distributing the pills, that guy who calls himself Scooby, is one of us. Sam recruited him. He disappeared once everything went down," she said and tossed him the file.

He caught it. "Where do we start?"

"Don't scare the kids this time. We need them to talk," she warned.

"Whatever you say, boss."

Ara followed him out of the office. Edon Marrok. Her partner, her friend. She wasn't alone in the world anymore, and if there was this thing between them, she had no way of knowing how real it was.

But she had a feeling they had all the time in the world to find out.

39 | VAMPIRE BRIDE

OLIVER WAS PACKING HIS BAGS, getting ready to leave. After a week at Mimi's, he was finally ready to face home. *Their home.* He had given the staff the night off, had wanted to be alone on his last night in New York. He knew where he was going first, but that was all. He was tired, so tired, and he missed her. And that was when he realized he wasn't alone. He knew she wasn't dead. Whatever she had in her, it was much more potent, much stronger, than the dose the two girls had taken. He had killed her and she had risen from death into eternal life.

He walked to the French windows and saw her. Finn was standing on the balcony of their home at 13 Central Park West. Their favorite place, the terrace from which they surveyed their kingdom—the city of New York, the city of vampires.

Oliver opened the doors and joined her.

"I was waiting for you," she said, without turning around. "I wondered when you'd come home."

She was still wearing the dress from the night of the ball, and her creamy skin was translucent against the red. She looked like a vampire bride, Oliver thought. *That's what I made her into. I did this to her.*

"I know it's my fault," he said. "I knew something had changed—I saw it in your blood, I felt it in my own, but I ignored it. I ignored your sadness, your disappointment in this life. I'm so sorry." He ignored every warning, every doubt, because he was so afraid of knowing the truth about her. He hadn't known her, not really, and he would regret it forever.

"You couldn't change it. You couldn't change what you did to me," she said. "What I asked you to do to me. You didn't know and neither did I."

"Finn... I know I killed you. I know it was my fault that you died. And I'm not talking about last night; I'm talking about ten years ago, when I made you my human familiar. I turned you into this, into what you are now. But we can fix it. I can fix it. We can leech out the poison in your blood. I did it to the Coven, I can do it to you."

"No," she said. "It was my idea to take the darkness into my soul. I thought I was biding time; at first I thought I was just saying it so that Sam wouldn't kill me. But then I realized what he was offering and I wanted it. I wanted it badly. I wanted it more than I wanted anything in my life."

"You don't know what you want," he said, agonized. "Please Finn, don't say this."

"I'm beyond help, Oliver. When I started taking the drug, I knew there was something in it that was terrible, and I *welcomed* it. I'm one of his now. I am one with Lucifer. I carry pieces of his soul inside me."

"There has to be a way to save you."

"But I don't need saving," she said. "This is exactly what I wanted. To be more than I was. To have more than you could ever give me."

He walked toward her but she held up her hand. "Stop, don't come any closer. I wanted to say good-bye, Oliver. I wanted to see you again before—"

"What are you saying?"

"You never understood me. You loved me, you wanted me, but I was a thing to you. The most precious jewel in your empire. But I'm not a possession, Oliver; I'm not a prize. I'm not a spoil of War."

"I never thought you were," he said. "Did you really think that?"

"You didn't know what I wanted. I wanted to be you. I wanted power. To be able to change lives. To have the power over life and death." Her voice was hers, but the words were not her own. They were the words of their enemy, the silver poison that had seeped into her soul, corrupting her, that had turned her into one of them. A demon.

"That's Lucifer speaking—not you," he said. "That's not you. I know you. You're a good person, you're good. You're my angel."

"Maybe I was once. But I'm not anymore, and if you come after me, I will destroy you," she said.

She was beautiful and terrible, and he loved her still.

"Good-bye, Oliver," she said, and she burst into white flame and disappeared into the night.

I will fix this, he thought, standing alone on the rooftop of their former home. *I will fix you.* He would clear his name and take back the Coven. He could do this. Once upon a time, he was the most powerful vampire in the world. He had been blessed with the gift of the Coven and the responsibility of the remaining souls in his care.

He could do it.

He just needed a little help from his friends.

EPILOGUE

*T*HEY SAW HIM BEFORE he made it to their door, and when he did, they had dinner laid out and candles lit, and a warm fire and a glass of wine ready.

Jack nodded to Schuyler as she held up the bottle for his approval. She smiled at him, and he smiled back, although his smile was touched by worry. They had lived so happily here, so peacefully. From outside their window they could see the lights of the valley and the black car inching its way up toward their hill.

He took the bottle from her hands and appraised it. His life's work so far, the best one, a fantastic year; the rains had been good, the grapes fat with flavor, the soil itself blessed by the gods. They had been saving this for a special occasion. He had hoped to open it on a different kind of night.

"Are you sure you want to do this?" she asked. "We can still say no."

"We've been away long enough. They need us. He needs us."

"Then we are agreed," she said. She was older now, no longer the young girl who had led the Coven safely to Paradise. But what was salvation? There was no ending, not for them. There was only vigilance and effort.

She put her hand in his and squeezed. "Thank you."

Jack nodded, but he wasn't doing it for her, although she might believe that. He wanted a world that was safe for his family, and if

Oliver was here, then it meant that the world was not safe, not for them, not for their children.

Schuyler had known almost as soon as it happened—she had seen the pentagrams in her dreams. She could feel the darkness spreading. They were about to leave for New York when Edon came to visit on his way there, and he told them to stay where they were, he would take care of it. Schuyler had given enough, and it was time for the wolves to answer the call this time. And so they had stayed put.

But they had made plans. They had begun slowly, letting the staff go first, then shutting down the little store they kept in the village. They would not sell the vineyard, not yet; they would just hand it over to a caretaker for the time being. They had kept the twins with them for as long as they could. The twins. It had been so difficult to say good-bye to them. Schuyler did not speak for a few days, and Jack was just as wrapped up in his own misery, but they were kind to each other, and they did not blame each other for what they had to do. They knew the children would be in good hands, and that would be enough to sustain them through the dark days. They were only seven years old. Too young to fight, but he would teach them, Jack thought; he would teach them everything he knew, not just about wine, but about the darkness that was in them, that was part of them, the darkness and the light.

"I'm ready," Schuyler said. She looked not like a mother in her thirties, but like the girl he had fallen in love with, and he loved her still. She would always be that girl to him, no matter what happened. That was love, after all, the ability to see one's youthful beloved in the aging stranger with her face. He would always love her, he thought. He was made to love her.

He smiled, and Schuyler smiled, because he was still Jack Force, Abbadon, the Angel of Destruction. They had kept their true natures hidden in this quiet life, but it was time to wake up again. "Let's do it."

The doorbell rang.

Schuyler opened the door and smiled. "Ollie. It's been too long," she said. She hugged him tightly and let her friend inside her house. She showed him the fire, handed him a glass of wine, bid him take a seat at their table.

"Jack. Sky," he said. "I'm sorry to do this. But I didn't know where else to go."

"It's all right," she said. "We're here. Tell us what happened. From the beginning."

And so he did.

TO BE CONTINUED...

ACKNOWLEDGMENTS

Thank you to my family, especially Mike and Mattie, who put up with having wife/mama on deadline all the time. Thank you to my work family, Richard Abate and Melissa Kahn, for catching me when I fall. Thank you to my wonderful editor Christine Pride and the team at Hachette—Betsy Hulsebosch, Martha Levin, and Mauro DiPreta—for their patience, support, and willingness to bring the Blue Blood vampires into a new decade.

Thank you to "the gang" and for that wonderful night in the power tower: Andy Goffe, Tristan Ashby, Tyler Rollins, and Peter Edmonston.

Thank you to the Blue Bloods readers who have followed my characters for more than a decade. Your enthusiasm makes it all worthwhile. It's been an honor sharing their stories with you.

New York Times bestselling author Melissa de la Cruz's novels are "a bubbling cauldron of mystery and romance."

—*People* magazine

Meet the Beauchamp women—Joanne, Freya, and Ingrid—who live seemingly quiet lives in Northampton on the tip of Long Island while harboring a centuries-old secret: they are powerful witches forbidden to practice magic. But a devastating murder makes it clear that it is time to dust off those wands and spell trouble for a mysterious enemy.

The Beauchamp women could use a little time off—now that the prohibition on practicing magic has been lifted. No such luck…a long-lost relative returns; a lover betrays; and the spirit of someone dead is determined to get Joanna's attention, whether for fair or foul purposes. No wonder this second Witches of East End novel is praised as "just a little bit wicked!"*

Freya is trapped in time in 1692 Salem—not a good place for witches! Back in twenty-first century Northampton, the family searches for a totem that could allow them to open the passages of time and rescue Freya, while challenges ancient and new appear with alarming frequency. *Winds of Salem* is, in a word, bewitching!

Read on at www.melissa-delacruz.com

* Deborah Harkness, author of *A Discovery of Witches*